Brother Cadfael's Penance

D0280120

Ellis Peters

Brother Cadfael's Penance

THE CADFAEL CHRONICLES XX

WARNER BOOKS

A *Warner* Book

First published in Great Britain by Headline in 1994
This edition published by Warner Books in 1995
Reprinted 2000

A CIP catalogue record for this book
is available from the British Library.

ISBN 0 7515 1370 9

Printed and bound in Great Britain by
Clays Ltd, St Ives plc

Warner Books
A Division of
Little, Brown and Company (UK)
Brettenham House
Lancaster Place
London WC2E 7EN

Brother Cadfael's Penance

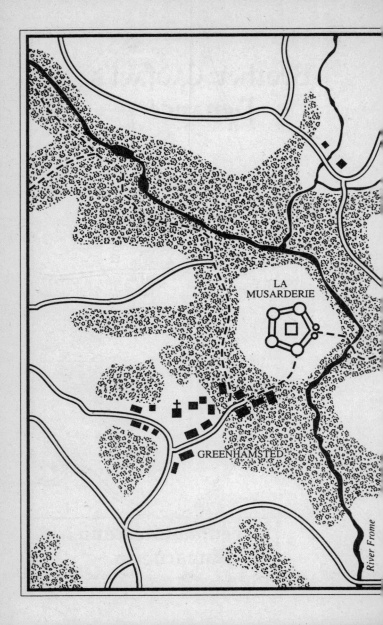

LA
MUSARDERIE

GREENHAMSTED

River Frome

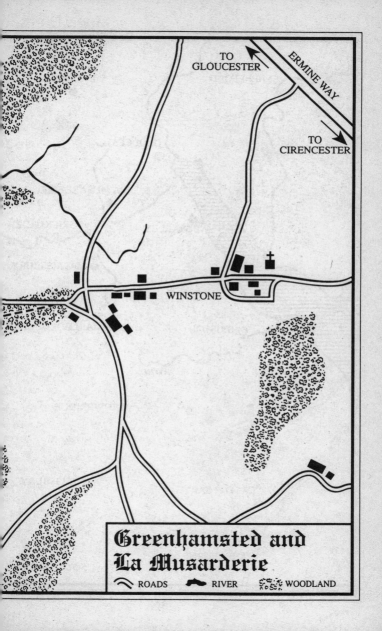

TO
GLOUCESTER

ERMINE WAY

TO
CIRENCESTER

WINSTONE

Greenhamsted and La Musarderie

🌲 ROADS   〰️ RIVER   🌳 WOODLAND

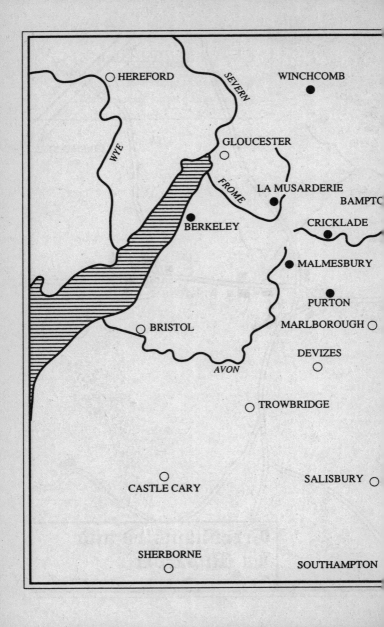

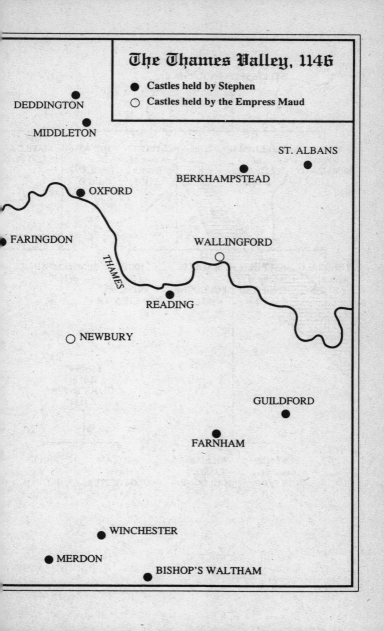

The Thames Valley, 1146

- ● Castles held by Stephen
- ○ Castles held by the Empress Maud

DEDDINGTON

MIDDLETON

ST. ALBANS

BERKHAMPSTEAD

OXFORD

FARINGDON

WALLINGFORD

THAMES

READING

NEWBURY

GUILDFORD

FARNHAM

WINCHESTER

MERDON

BISHOP'S WALTHAM

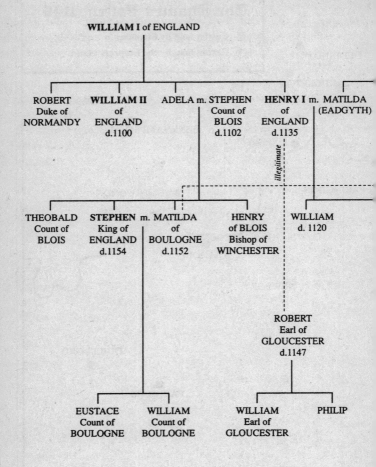

WILLIAM I of ENGLAND

ROBERT
Duke of
NORMANDY

WILLIAM II
of
ENGLAND
d.1100

ADELA m. STEPHEN
Count of
BLOIS
d.1102

HENRY I m. MATILDA
of
ENGLAND
d.1135

(EADGYTH)

illegitimate

THEOBALD
Count of
BLOIS

STEPHEN m. MATILDA
King of
ENGLAND
d.1154

of
BOULOGNE
d.1152

HENRY
of BLOIS
Bishop of
WINCHESTER

WILLIAM
d. 1120

ROBERT
Earl of
GLOUCESTER
d.1147

EUSTACE
Count of
BOULOGNE

WILLIAM
Count of
BOULOGNE

WILLIAM
Earl of
GLOUCESTER

PHILIP

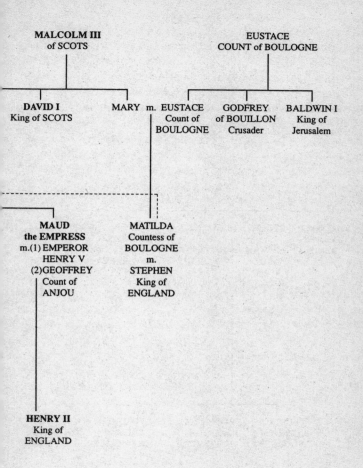

Chapter One

HE EARL of Leicester's courier came riding over the bridge that spanned the Severn, and into the town of Shrewsbury, somewhat past noon on a day at the beginning of November, with three months' news in his saddle-roll.

Much of it would already be known, at least in general outline, but Robert Beaumont's despatch service from London was better provided than anything the sheriff of Shropshire could command, and in a single meeting with that young officer the earl had marked him as one of the relatively sane in this mad world of civil war that had crippled England for so many years, and run both factions, king and empress alike, into exhaustion, without, unfortunately, bringing either sharply up against reality. Such able young men as Hugh Beringar, Earl Robert considered, were well worth supplying with information, against the day when reason would finally break through and put an end to such wasteful warfare. And in this year of the Lord, 1145, now drawing towards its close, chaotic events had

1

seemed to be offering promise, however faint as yet, that even the two cousins battling wearily for the throne must despair of force and look round for another way of settling disputes.

The boy who carried the earl's despatches had made this journey once before, and knew his way across the bridge and up the curve of the Wyle, and round from the High Cross to the castle gates. The earl's badge opened the way before him without hindrance. Hugh came out from the armoury in the inner ward, dusting his hands, his dark hair tangled by the funnelled wind through the archway, to draw the messenger within, and hear his news.

'There's a small breeze rising,' said the boy, unloading the contents of his satchel upon the table in the anteroom of the gatehouse, 'that has my lord snuffing the air. But warily, it's the first time he's detected any such stirring, and it could as easily blow itself out. And it has as much to do with what's happening in the East as with all this ceding of castles in the Thames valley. Ever since Edessa fell to the paynims of Mosul, last year at Christmas, all Christendom has been uneasy about the kingdom of Jerusalem. They're beginning to talk of a new Crusade, and there are lords on either side, here at home, who are none too happy about things done, and might welcome the Cross as sanctuary for their souls. I've brought you his official letters,' he said briskly, mustering them neatly at Hugh's hand, 'but I'll give you the gist of it before I go, and you can study them at leisure, for there's no date yet settled. I must return this same day, I have an errand to Coventry on my way back.'

'Then you'd best take food and drink now, while we talk,' said Hugh, and sent out for what was needed. They settled together confidentially to the tangled affairs of England, which had shifted in some disconcerting directions during

2

the summer months, and now, with the shutter of the coming winter about to close down against further action, might at least be disentangled, and open a course that could be pursued with some hope of progress. 'You'll not tell me Robert Beaumont is thinking of taking the Cross? There are some powerful sermons coming out of Clairvaux, I'm told, that will be hard to resist.'

'No,' said the young man, briefly grinning, 'my lord's concerns are all here at home. But this same unease for Christendom is making the bishops turn their thoughts to enforcing some order here, before they make off to settle the affairs of Outremer. They're talking of one more attempt to bring king and empress together to talk sense, and find a means of breaking out of this deadlock. You'll have heard that the earl of Chester has sought and got a meeting with King Stephen, and pledged his allegiance? Late in the day, and no easy passage, but the king jumped at it. We knew about it before they ever met at Stamford, a week or so back, for Earl Ranulf has been preparing the ground for some time, making sweet approaches to some of Stephen's barons who hold grudges for old wrongs, trying to buy acceptance into the fold. There's land near his castle of Mountsorrel has been in dispute with my lord some years. Chester has made concessions now over that. A man must soften not only the king but all those who hold with the king if he's to change sides. So Stamford was no surprise, and Chester is reconciled and accepted. And you know all that business of Faringdon and Cricklade, and Philip FitzRobert coming over to Stephen, in despite of father and empress and all, and with a strong castle in either hand.'

'That,' said Hugh flatly, 'I shall never understand. He, of all people! Gloucester's own son, and Gloucester has been the empress's prop and stay as good as singlehanded

3

throughout, and now his son turns against him and joins the king! And no half-measures, either. By all accounts, he's fighting for Stephen as fiercely as he ever fought for Maud.'

'And bear in mind, Philip's sister is wife to Ranulf of Chester,' the courier pointed out, 'and these two changes of heart chime together. Which of them swept the other away with him, or what else lies behind it, God he knows, not I. But there's the plain fact of it. The king is the fatter by two new allies and a very respectable handful of castles.'

'And I'd have said, in no mood to make any concessions, even for the bishops,' observed Hugh shrewdly. 'Much more likely to be encouraged, all over again, to believe he can win absolute victory. I doubt if they'll ever get him to the council table.'

'Never underestimate Roger de Clinton,' said Leicester's squire, and grinned. 'He has offered Coventry as the meeting-place, and Stephen has as good as agreed to come and listen. They're issuing safe conducts already, on both sides. Coventry is a good centre for all, Chester can make use of Mountsorrel to offer hospitality and worm his way into friendships, and the priory has housing enough for all. Oh, there'll be a meeting! Whether much will come of it is another matter. It won't please everyone, and there'll be those who'll do their worst to wreck it. Philip FitzRobert for one. Oh, he'll come, if only to confront his father and show that he regrets nothing, but he'll come to destroy, not to placate. Well, my lord wants your voice there, speaking for your shire. Shall he have it? He knows your mind,' said the young man airily, 'or thinks he does. You rank some-where in the list of his hopes. What do you say?'

'Let him send me word of the day,' said Hugh heartily, 'and I'll be there.'

'Good, I'll tell him so. And for the rest, you'll know

4

already that it was only the handful of captains, with Brien de Soulis at their head, who sold out Faringdon to the king, and made prisoner all the knights of the garrison who refused to change sides. The king handed them out like prizes to some of his own followers, to profit by their ransom. My lord has got hold from somewhere of a list of those doled out, those among them who have been offered for ransom, and those already bought free. Here he sends you a copy, in case any names among them concern you closely, captors or captives. If anything comes of the meeting at Coventry their case will come up for consideration, and it's not certain who holds the last of them.'

'I doubt there'll be any there known to me,' said Hugh, taking up the sealed roll thoughtfully. 'All those garrisons along the Thames might as well be a thousand miles from us. We do not even hear when they fall or change sides until a month after the event. But thank Earl Robert for his courtesy, and tell him I'll trust to see him in the priory of Coventry when the day comes.'

He did not break the seal of Robert Beaumont's letter until the courier had departed, to make for Coventry and Bishop Roger de Clinton's presence on his way back to Leicester. In the last few years the bishop had made Coventry the main seat of his diocese, though Lichfield retained its cathedral status, and the see was referred to impartially by either name. The bishop was also titular abbot of the Benedictine monastery in the town, and the head of the household of monks bore the title of prior, but was mitred like an abbot. Only two years previously the peace of the priory had been sadly disturbed, and the monks temporarily turned out of their quarters, but they had been firmly reinstalled before the year ended, and were unlikely to be dispossessed again.

Never underestimate Roger de Clinton, Robert Beaumont's squire had said, no doubt echoing his formidable patron. Hugh already had a healthy respect for his bishop; and if a prelate of this stature, with the peril of Christendom on his mind, could draw to him a magnate like the Earl of Leicester, and others of similar quality and sense, from either faction or both, then surely in the end some good must come of it. Hugh unrolled the earl's despatches with a cautiously hopeful mind, and began to read the brief summary within, and the list of resounding names.

The sudden and violent breach between Robert, earl of Gloucester, the Empress Maud's half-brother and loyal champion, and his younger son Philip, in the heat of mid-summer, had startled the whole of England, and still remained inadequately explained or understood. In the desultory but dangerous and explosive battlefield of the Thames valley Philip, the empress's castellan of Cricklade, had been plagued by damaging raids by the king's men garrisoned in Oxford and Malmesbury, and to ease the load had begged his father to come and choose a site for another castle, to try and disrupt communications between the two royal strongholds, and put them, in turn, on the defensive. And Earl Robert had duly selected his site at Faringdon, built his castle and garrisoned it. But as soon as the king heard of it he came with a strong army and laid siege to the place. Philip in Cricklade had sent plea after plea to his father to send reinforcements at all costs, not to lose this asset barely yet enjoyed, and potentially so valuable to the hard-pressed garrison of his son's command. But Gloucester had paid no heed, and sent no aid. And suddenly it was the talk of the south that the castellan of Faringdon, Brien de Soulis, and his closest aides within the castle, had made secret compact with the besiegers, unknown to the rest of the garrison, let in the king's men

6

by night, and delivered over Faringdon to them, with all its fighting men. Those who accepted the fiat joined Stephen's forces, as most of the ranks did, seeing their leaders had committed them; those who held true to the empress's salt were disarmed and made prisoner. The victims had been distributed among the king's followers, to be held to ransom. And no sooner was this completed than Philip FitzRobert, the great earl's son, in despite of his allegiance and his blood, had handed over Cricklade also to the king, and this time whole, with all its armoury and all its manpower intact. As many considered, it was his will, if not his hand, which had surrendered the keys of Faringdon, for Brien de Soulis was known to be as close to Philip as twin to twin, at all times in his councils. And thereafter Philip had turned too, and fought as ferociously against his father as once he had fought for him.

But as for why, that was hard to understand. He loved his sister, who was married to Earl Ranulf of Chester, and Ranulf was seeking to inveigle himself back into the king's favour, and would be glad to take another powerful kinsman with him, to assure his welcome. But was that enough? And Philip had asked for Faringdon, and looked forward to the relief it would give his own forces, only to see it left to its fate in spite of his repeated appeals for help. But was even that enough? It takes an appalling load of bitterness, surely, to cause a man, after years of loyalty and devotion, to turn and rend his own flesh and blood.

But he had done it. And here in Hugh's hand was the tale of his first victims, some thirty young men of quality, knights and squires, parcelled out among the king's supporters, to pay dearly for their freedom at best, or to rot in captivity unredeemed if they had fallen into the wrong hands, and were sufficiently hated.

Robert Beaumont's clerk had noted, where it was known,

the name of the captor against that of the captive, and
marked off those who had already been bought free by their
kin. No one else was likely to raise an exorbitant sum for
the purchase of a young gentleman in arms, as yet of no
particular distinction. One or two of the ambitious young
partisans of the empress might be left languishing
unfathered and without patron in obscure dungeons, unless
this projected conference at Coventry produced some sensible agreement that must, among its details, spare a
thought to insist on their liberation.

At the end of the scroll, after many names that were
strange to him, Hugh came to one that he knew.

'Known to have been among those overpowered and
disarmed, not known who holds him, or where. Has
not been offered for ransom. Laurence d'Angers has
been enquiring for him without result: Olivier de
Bretagne.'

Hugh went down through the town with his news, to
confer with Abbot Radulfus over this suddenly presented
opportunity to put an end to eight years of civil strife.
Whether the bishops would allow an equal voice to the
monastic clergy only time would tell; relations between
the two arms of the Church were not invariably cordial,
though Roger de Clinton certainly valued the abbot of
Shrewsbury. But whether invited to the conference or not,
when the time came, Radulfus would need to be prepared
for either success or failure, and ready to act accordingly.
And there was also another person at the abbey of Saint
Peter and Saint Paul who had every right to be told the
content of Robert Beaumont's letter.

Brother Cadfael was standing in the middle of his walled
herb-garden, looking pensively about him at the autumnal

visage of his pleasance, where all things grew gaunt, wiry and sombre. Most of the leaves were fallen, the stems dark and clenched like fleshless fingers holding fast to the remnant of the summer, all the fragrances gathered into one scent of age and decline, still sweet, but with the damp, rotting sweetness of harvest over and decay setting in. It was not yet very cold, the mild melancholy of November still had lingering gold in it, in falling leaves and slanting amber light. All the apples were in the loft, all the corn milled, the hay long stacked, the sheep turned into the stubble fields. A time to pause, to look round, to make sure nothing had been neglected, no fence unrepaired, against the winter.

He had never before been quite so acutely aware of the particular quality and function of November, its ripeness and its hushed sadness. The year proceeds not in a straight line through the seasons, but in a circle that brings the world and man back to the dimness and mystery in which both began, and out of which a new seed-time and a new generation are about to begin. Old men, thought Cadfael, believe in that new beginning, but experience only the ending. It may be that God is reminding me that I am approaching my November. Well, why regret it? November has beauty, has seen the harvest into the barns, even laid by next year's seed. No need to fret about not being allowed to stay and sow it, someone else will do that. So go contentedly into the earth with the moist, gentle, skeletal leaves, worn to cobweb fragility, like the skins of very old men, that bruise and stain at the mere brushing of the breeze, and flower into brown blotches as the leaves into rotting gold. The colours of late autumn are the colours of the sunset: the farewell of the year and the farewell of the day. And of the life of man? Well, if it ends in a flourish of gold, that is no bad ending.

Hugh, coming from the abbot's lodging, between haste to impart what he knew, and reluctance to deliver what could only be disturbing news, found his friend standing thus motionless in the middle of his small, beloved kingdom, staring rather within his own mind than at the straggling, autumnal growth about him. He started back to the outer world only when Hugh laid a hand on his shoulder, and visibly surfaced slowly from some secret place, fathoms deep in the centre of his being.

'God bless the work,' said Hugh, and took him by the arms, 'if any's been done here this afternoon. I thought you had taken root.'

'I was pondering the circular nature of human life,' said Cadfael, almost apologetically, 'and the seasons of the year and the hours of the day. I never heard you come. I was not expecting to see you today.'

'Nor would you have seen me, if Robert Bossu's intelligencers had been a little less busy. Come within,' said Hugh, 'and I'll tell you what's brewing. There's matter concerning all good churchmen, and I've just come from informing Radulfus. But there's also an item that will come close home to you. As indeed,' he owned, thrusting the door of Cadfael's workshop open with a gusty sigh, 'it does to me.'

'You've heard from Leicester?' Cadfael eyed him thoughtfully from the threshold. 'Earl Robert Bossu keeps in touch? He views you as one of his hopefuls, Hugh, if he's keeping that road open. What's he about now?'

'Not he, so much, though he'll be in it to the throat, whether he quite believes in it or not. No, it's certain of the bishops have made the first move, but there'll be some voices on either side, like Leicester's, to back their efforts.'

Hugh sat down with him under the dangling bunches of drying herbs, stirring fragrantly along the beams in the draught from the open door, and told him of the proposed meeting at Coventry, of the safe conducts already being issued on either part, and of such prospects as existed of at any rate partial success.

'God he knows if either of them will so much as shift a foot. Stephen is exalted at having got Chester on his side, and Gloucester's own son into the bargain, but Maud knows her menfolk have made very sure of Normandy, and that will sway some of our barons who have lands over there to safeguard, as well as here. I can see more and more of the wiser sort paying mouth allegiance still, but making as little move in the martial kind as they can contrive. But by all means let's make the attempt. Roger de Clinton can be a powerful persuader when he's in good earnest, and he's in good earnest now, for his real quarry is the Atabeg Zenghi in Mosul, and his aim the recovery of Edessa. And Henry of Winchester will surely add his weight to the scale. Who knows? I've primed the abbot,' said Hugh dubiously, 'but I doubt if the bishops will call on the monastic arm, they'd rather keep the reins in their own hands.'

'And how does this, however welcome and however dubious, concern me closely?' Cadfael wondered.

'Wait, there's more.' He was carrying it carefully, for such news is brittle. He watched Cadfael's face anxiously as he asked: 'You'll recall what happened in the summer at Robert of Gloucester's newly built castle of Faringdon? When Gloucester's younger son turned his coat, and his castellan gave over the castle to the king?'

'I remember,' said Cadfael. 'The men-at-arms had no choice but to change sides with him, their captains having sealed the surrender. And Cricklade went over with Philip, intact to a man.'

'But many of the knights in Faringdon,' said Hugh with deliberation, 'refused the treason, and were overpowered

11

and disarmed. Stephen handed them out to various of his allies, new and old, but I suspect the new did best out of it, and got the fattest prizes, to fix them gratefully in their new loyalty. Well, Leicester has been employing his agents round Oxford and Malmesbury to good effect, to ferret out the list of those made prisoner, and discover to whom they were given. Some have been bought out already, briskly enough. Some are on offer, and for prices high enough to sell very profitably. But there's one name, known to have been there, listed with no word of who holds him, and has not been seen or heard of since Faringdon fell. I doubt if the name means anything to Robert Bossu, more than the rest. But it does to me, Cadfael.' He had his friend's full and wary attention; the tone of his voice, carefully moderate, was a warning rather than a reassurance. 'And will to you.'

'Not offered for ransom,' said Cadfael, reckoning the odds with careful moderation in return, 'and held very privately. It argues a more than ordinary animosity. That will be a price that comes high. Even if he will take a price.'

'And in order to pay what may be asked,' said Hugh ruefully, 'Laurence d'Angers, so Leicester's agent says, has been enquiring for him everywhere without result. That name would be known to the earl, though not the names of the young men of his following. I am sorry to bring such news. Olivier de Bretagne was in Faringdon. And now Olivier de Bretagne is prisoner, and God knows where.'

After the silence, a shared pause for breath and thought, and the mutual rearrangement of the immediate concerns that troubled them both, Cadfael said simply: 'He is a young man like other young men. He knows the risks. He takes them with open eyes. What is there to be said for one more than the rest?'

12

'But this was a risk, I fancy, that he could not foresee. That Gloucester's own son should turn against him! And a risk Olivier was least armed to deal with, having so little conception of treachery. I don't know, Cadfael, how long he had been among the garrison, or what the feeling was among the young knights there. It seems many of them were with Olivier. The castle was barely completed, Philip filled it and wanted it defended well, and when it lay under siege Robert failed to lift a finger to save it. There's bitterness there. But Leicester will go on trying to find them all, to the last man. And if we're all to meet soon at Coventry, at least there may be agreement on a release of prisoners on both sides. We shall all be pressing for it, men of goodwill from both factions.'

'Olivier ploughs his own furrow, and cuts his own swathe,' said Cadfael, staring eastward through the timber wall before him, far eastward into drought and sand and sun, and the glittering sea along the shores of the Frankish kingdom of Jerusalem, now menaced and in arms. The fabled world of Outremer, once familiar to him, where Olivier de Bretagne had grown up to choose, in young manhood, the faith of his unknown father. 'I doubt,' said Cadfael slowly, 'any prison can hold him long. I am glad you have told me, Hugh. Bring me word if you get any further news.'

But the voice, Hugh thought when he left his friend, was not that of a man fully confident of a good ending, nor the set of the face indicative of one absolute in faith and prepared to sit back and leave all either to Olivier or to God.

When Hugh was gone, with his own cares to keep him fully occupied, and his errand in friendship faithfully discharged, Cadfael damped down his brazier with turves, closed his workshop, and went away to the church. There was an hour yet to Vespers. Brother Winfrid was still methodically digging over a bed cleared of beans, to leave it to the frosts of the coming winter to crumble and refine. A thin veil of yellowed leaves still clung to the trees, and the roses were grown tall and leggy, small, cold buds forming at the tips, buds that would never open.

In the vast, dim quiet of the church Cadfael made amicable obeisance to the altar of Saint Winifred, as to an intimate but revered friend, but for once hesitated to burden her with a charge for another man, and one even she might find hard to understand. True, Olivier was half Welsh, but that, hand in hand with all that was passionately Syrian in his looks and thoughts and principles, might prove even more confusing to her. So the only prayer he made to her was made without words, in the heart, offering affection in a gush of tenderness like the smoke of incense. She had forgiven him so much, and never shut him out. And this same year she had suffered flood and peril and contention, and come back safely to a deserved rest. Why disturb its sweetness with a trouble which belonged all to himself?

So he took his problem rather to the high altar, directly to the source of all strength, all power, all faithfulness, and for once he was not content to kneel, but prostrated himself in a cross on the cold flags, like an offender presenting his propitiatory body at the end of penance, though the offence he contemplated was not yet committed, and with great mercy and understanding on his superior's part might not be necessary. Nevertheless, he professed his intent now, in stark honesty, and besought rather comprehension than forgiveness. With his forehead chill against the stone he discarded words to present his compulsion, and let thoughts express the need that found him lucid but inarticulate. This I must do, whether with a blessing or a ban. For whether I am blessed or banned is of no consequence, provided what I have to do is done well.

At the end of Vespers he asked audience of Abbot Radulfus, and was admitted. In the private parlour they sat down together.

'Father, I believe Hugh Beringar has acquainted you with all that he has learned in letters from the Earl of Leicester. Has he also told you of the fate of the knights of Faringdon who refused to desert the empress?'

'He has,' said Radulfus. 'I have seen the list of names, and I know how they were disposed of. I trust that at this proposed meeting in Coventry some agreement may be reached for a general release of prisoners, even if nothing better can be achieved.'

'Father, I wish I shared your trust, but I fear they are neither of them in any mind to give way. Howbeit, you will have noted the name of Olivier de Bretagne, who has not been located, and of whom nothing is known since Faringdon fell. His lord is willing and anxious to ransom him, but he has not been offered the opportunity. Father, I must tell you certain things concerning this young man, things I know Hugh will not have told you.'

'I have some knowledge of the man myself,' Radulfus reminded him, smiling, 'when he came here four years ago at the time of Saint Winifred's translation, in search of a certain squire missing from his place after the conference in Winchester. I have not forgotten him.'

'But this one thing,' said Cadfael, 'is still unknown to you, though it may be that I should have told you long since, when first he touched my life. I had not thought that there was any need, for I did not expect that in any way my commitment to this place could be changed. Nor did I suppose that I should ever meet him again, nor he ever have need of me. But now it seems meet and right that all should be made plain. Father,' said Cadfael simply, 'Olivier de Bretagne is my son.'

There was a silence that fell with surprising serenity and gentleness. Men within the pale as without are still men, vulnerable and fallible. Radulfus had the wise man's distant respect for perfection, but no great expectation of meeting it in the way.

'When first I came to Palestine,' said Cadfael, looking back without regret, 'an eighteen-year-old boy, I met with a young widow in Antioch, and loved her. Long years afterwards, when I returned to sail from Saint Symeon on my way home, I met with her again, and lingered with her in kindness until the ship was ready to sail. I left her a son, of whom I knew nothing, until he came looking for two lost children, after the sack of Worcester. And I was glad and proud of him, and with good reason. For a short while, when he came the second time, you knew him. Judge if I was glad of him, or no.'

'You had good reason,' said Radulfus readily. 'However he was got, he did honour to his getting. I dare make no reproach. You had taken no vows, you were young and far from home, and humanity is frail. No doubt this was confessed and repented long since.'

'Confessed,' said Cadfael bluntly, 'yes, when I knew I had left her with child and unfriended, but that is not long ago. And repented? No, I doubt if ever I repented of loving her, for she was well worth any man's love. And bear in mind, Father, that I am Welsh, and in Wales there are no bastards but those whose fathers deny their paternity. Judge if I would ever deny my right to that bright, brave creature. The best thing ever I did was to cause him to be brought forth into a world where very few can match him.'

'However admirable the fruit may be,' said the abbot

drily, 'it does not justify priding oneself on a sin, nor calling a sin by any other name. But neither is there any profit in passing today's judgement upon a sin some thirty years past. Since your avowal I have very seldom found any fault to chasten in you, beyond the small daily failings in patience or diligence to which we are all prone. Let us deal, therefore, with what confronts us now. For I think you have somewhat to ask of me or to put to me concerning Olivier de Bretagne.'

'Father,' said Cadfael, choosing his words gravely and with deliberation, 'if I presume in supposing that father-hood imposes a duty upon me, wherever child of mine may be in trouble or misfortune, reprove me. But I do conceive of such a duty, and cannot heave it off my heart. I am bound to go and seek my son, and deliver him when found. I ask your countenance and your leave.'

'And I,' said Radulfus, frowning, but not wholly in dis-pleasure, rather in profound concentration, 'put to you the opposing view of what is now your duty. Your vows bind you here. Of your own will you chose to abandon the world and all your ties within it. That cannot be shed like a coat.'

'I took my vows in good faith,' said Cadfael, 'not then knowing that there was in the world a being for whose very existence I was responsible. From all other ties my vows absolved me. All other personal relationships my vows sev-ered. Not this one! Whether I would have resigned the world if I had known it contained my living seed, that I cannot answer, nor may you hazard at an answer. But he lives, and it was I engendered him. He suffers captivity and I am free. He may be in peril, and I am safe. Father, can the creator forsake the least of his creatures? Can a man turn away from his own imperilled blood? Is not procreation itself the undertaking of a sacred and inviolable

17

vow? Knowing or unknowing, before I was a brother I was a father.'

This time the silence was chiller and more detached, and lasted longer. Then the abbot said levelly: 'Ask what you have come to ask. Let it be plainly said.'

'I ask your leave and blessing,' said Cadfael, 'to go with Hugh Beringar and attend this conference at Coventry, there to ask before king and empress where my son is held, and by God's help and theirs see him delivered free.'

'And then?' said Radulfus. 'If there is no help there?'

'Then by whatever means to pursue that same quest, until I do find and set him free.'

The abbot regarded him steadily, recognizing in the voice some echo from far back and far away, with the steel in it that had been blunted and sheathed as long as he had known this elderly brother. The weathered face, brown-browed and strongly boned, and deeply furrowed now by the wear and tear of sixty-five years, gazing back at him from wide-set and wide open eyes of a dark, autumnal brown, let him in honestly to the mind within. After years of willing submission to the claims of community, Cadfael stood suddenly erect and apart, again solitary. Radulfus recognized finality.

'And if I forbid,' he said with certainty, 'you will still go.'

'Under God's eye, and with reverence to you, Father, yes.'

'Then I do not forbid,' said Radulfus. 'It is my office to keep all my flock. If one stray, the ninety and nine left are also bereft. I give you leave to go with Hugh, and see this council meet, and I pray some good may come of it. But once they disperse, whether you have learned what you need or no, there your leave of absence ends. Return with Hugh, as you go with Hugh. If you go further and delay

18

longer, then you go as your own man, none of mine. With-out my leave or my blessing.'

'Without your prayers?' said Cadfael.

'Have I said so?'

'Father,' said Cadfael, 'it is written in the Rule that the brother who by his own wrong choice has left the monastery may be received again, even to the third time, at a price. Even penance ends when you shall say: It is enough!'

Chapter Two

HE DAY of the council at Coventry was fixed as the last day of November. Before that date there had been certain evidences that the prospect of agreement and peace was by no means universally welcome, and there were powerful interests ready and willing to wreck it. Philip FitzRobert had seized and held prisoner Reginald FitzRoy, another of the empress's half-brothers and Earl of Cornwall, though the earl was his kinsman, on the empress's business, and bearing the king's safe conduct. The fact that Stephen ordered the earl's release on hearing of it, and was promptly and correctly obeyed, did not lessen the omen.

'If that's his mind,' said Cadfael to Hugh, the day they heard of it, 'he'll never come to Coventry.'

'Ah, but he will,' said Hugh. 'He'll come to drop all manner of caltrops under the feet of all those who talk peace. Better and more effective within than without. And he'll come, from all that I can make of him, to confront his father brow to brow, since he's taken so bitter a rage against him. Oh, Philip will be there.' He regarded his friend with searching eyes; a face he could usually read clearly, but its grey gravity made him a little uneasy now. 'And you? Do you really intend to go with me? At the risk of trespassing too far for return? You know I would do your errand for you gladly. If there's word to be had there of Olivier, I will uncover it. No need for you to stake what I know you value as your life itself.'

'Olivier's life,' said Cadfael, 'has more than half its race to run, by God's grace, and is of higher value than my spent years. And you have a duty of your own, as I have mine. Yes, I will go. He knows it. He promises nothing and threatens nothing. He has said I go as my own man if I go beyond Coventry, but he has not said what he would do, were he in my shoes. And since I go without his bidding, I will go without any providing of his, if you will find me a mount, Hugh, and a cloak, and food in my scrip.'

'And a sword and a pallet in the guardroom afterwards,' said Hugh, shaking off his solemnity, 'if the cloister discards you. After we have recovered Olivier, of course.'

The very mention of the name always brought before Cadfael's eyes the first glimpse he had ever had of his unknown son, seen over a girl's shoulder through the open wicket of the gate of Bromfield Priory in the snow of a cruel winter. A long, thin but suave face, wide browed, with a scimitar of a nose and a supple bow of a mouth, proud and vivid, with the black and golden eyes of a hawk, and a close, burnished cap of blue-black hair. Olive-gold, cast in fine bronze, very beautiful. Mariam's son wore Mariam's face, and did honour to her memory. Fourteen years old when he left Antioch after her funeral rites, and went to Jerusalem to join the faith of his father, whom he had never seen but through Mariam's eyes. Thirty years old now, or close. Perhaps himself a father, by the girl

21

Ermina Hugonin, whom he had guided through the snow to Bromfield. Her noble kin had seen his worth, and given her to him in marriage. Now she lacked him, she and that possible grandchild. And that was unthinkable, and could not be left to any other to set right.

'Well,' said Hugh, 'it will not be the first time you and I have ridden together. Make ready, then, you have three days yet to settle your differences with God and Radulfus. And at least I'll find you the best of the castle's stables instead of an abbey mule.'

Within the enclave there were mixed feelings among the brothers concerning Cadfael's venture, undertaken thus with only partial and limited sanction, and with no promise of submission to the terms set. Prior Robert had made known in chapter the precise provisions laid down for Cadfael's absence, limited to the duration of the conference at Coventry, and had emphasized that strict injunction as if he had gathered that it was already threatened. Small blame to him, the implication had certainly been there in the abbot's incomplete instruction to him. As for the reason for this journey to be permitted at all, even grudgingly, there had been no explanation. Cadfael's confidence was between Cadfael and Radulfus.

Curiosity unsatisfied put the worst interpretation upon such facts as had been made public. There was a sense of shock, grieved eyes turning silently upon a brother already almost renegade. There was dread in the reactions of some who had been monastic from infancy, and jealousy among some come later, and uneasy at times in their confinement. Though Brother Edmund the infirmarer, himself an oblate at four years old, accepted loyally what puzzled him in his brother, and was anxious only at losing his apothecary for a time. And Brother Anselm the precentor, who acknowledged few disruptions other than a note offkey, or a sore throat among his best voices, accepted all other events with utter serenity, assumed the best, wished all men well, and gave over worrying.

Prior Robert disapproved of any departure from the strict Rule, and had for years disapproved of what he considered privileges granted to Brother Cadfael, in his freedom to move among the people of the Foregate and the town when there was illness to be confronted. And time had been when his chaplain, Brother Jerome, would have been assiduous in adding fuel to the prior's resentment; but Brother Jerome, earlier in the year, had suffered a shattering shock to his satisfaction with his own image, and emerged from a long penance deprived of his office as one of the confessors to the novices, and crushed into surprising humility. For the present, at least, he was much easier to live with, and less vociferous in denouncing the faults of others. In time, no doubt, he would recover his normal sanctimony, but Cadfael was spared any censure from him on this occasion.

So in the end Cadfael's most challenging contention was with himself. He had indeed taken vows, and he felt the bonds they wound about him tightening when he contemplated leaving this chosen field. He had told only truth in his presentation of his case to the abbot; everything was done and stated openly. But did that absolve him? Brother Edmund and Brother Winfrid between them would now have to supply his place, prepare medicines, provision the leper hospital at Saint Giles, tend the herb-garden, do not only their own work, but also his.

All this, if his defection lasted beyond the time allotted to him. By the very act of contemplating that possibility, he knew he was expecting it. So this decision, before ever he left the gates, had the gravity of life and death in it.

But all the while he knew that he would go.

Hugh came for him on the morning appointed, immediately after Prime, with three of his officers in attendance, all well mounted, and a led horse for Cadfael. Hugh remarked with satisfaction that his friend's sternly preoccupied eyes perceptibly brightened approvingly at the sight of a tall, handsome roan, almost as lofty as Hugh's raking grey, with a mettlesome gait and an arrogant eye, and a narrow white blaze down his aristocratic nose. Cloaked and booted and ready, Cadfael buckled his saddle-bags before him, and mounted a little stiffly, but with plain pleasure. Considerately, Hugh refrained from offering help. Sixty-five is an age deserving of respect and reverence from the young, but those who have reached it do not always like to be reminded.

There was no one obviously watching as they rode out from the gate, though there may have been eyes on them from the shelter of cloister or infirmary, or even from the abbot's lodging. Better to pursue the regular routine of the day as though this was merely a day like any other, and nowhere in any mind a doubt that the departing brother would come back at the due time, and resume his duties as before. And if peace came home with him, so much the more welcome.

Once out past Saint Giles, with the town and Foregate behind them, and the hogback of the Wrekin looming ahead, Cadfael's heart lifted into eased resignation, open without grudging to whatever might come. There were consolations. With December on the doorstep the fields were still green, the weather mild and windless, he had a good horse under him, and riding beside Hugh was a pleasure full of shared memories. The highroad was open and safe, and the way they must take familiar to them both, at least as far as the forest of Chenet, and Hugh had set out three days before the council was due to meet formally.

24

'For we'll take it gently along the way,' he said, 'and be there early. I could do with a word with Robert Bossu before anything is said in session. We may even run into Ranulf of Chester when we halt overnight at Lichfield. I heard he had some last-minute advice to pour into the ears of his half-brother of Lincoln. William is minding the winnings of both of them in the north while Ranulf comes demurely to council in Coventry.'

'He'll be wise,' said Cadfael thoughtfully, 'not to flaunt his successes. There must be a good number of his enemies gathering.'

'Oh, he'll still be courting. He's handed out several judicious concessions these last few weeks, to barons he was robbing of lands or privileges only last year. It costs,' said Hugh cynically, 'to change sides. The king is only the first he has to charm, and the king is apt to welcome allies with his eyes shut and his arms open, and be the giver rather than the getter. All those who have held by him throughout, and watched Ranulf flout him, won't come so cheaply. Some of them will take the sweets he offers, but forbear from delivering the goods he thinks he's buying. If I were Ranulf, I would walk very meekly and humbly for a year or so yet.'

When they rode into the precinct of the diocesan guest-halls at Lichfield, early in the evening, there was certainly a lively bustle to be observed, and several noble devices to be seen among the grooms and servants in the common lodging where Hugh's men-at-arms rested. But none from Chester. Either Ranulf had taken another route, perhaps straight from his half-brother in Lincoln, or else he was ahead of them, already back in his castle of Mountsorrel, near Leicester, making his plans for the council. For him it was not so much an attempt at making peace as an opportunity to secure his acceptance on what he hoped and calculated would be the winning side in a total victory.

Cadfael went out before Compline into the chill of the dusk, and turned southward from the close to where the burnished surfaces of the minster pools shone with a sullen leaden light in the flat calm, and the newly cleared space where the Saxon church had stood showed as yet like a scar slow to heal. Roger de Clinton, continuing work on foundations begun years before, had approved the choice of a more removed and stable site for a projected weight far greater than Saint Chad, the first bishop, had ever contemplated. Cadfael turned at the edge of the holy ground blessed by the ministry of one of the gentlest and most beloved of prelates, and looked back to the massive bulk of the new stone cathedral, barely yet finished, if indeed there could ever be an end to adorning and enlarging it. The long roof of the nave and the strong, foursquare central tower stood razor-edged against the paler sky. The choir was short, and ended in an apse. The tall windows of the west end caught a few glimpses of slanted light through walls strong as a fortress. Invisible under those walls, the marks of the masons' lodges and the scars of their stored stone and timber still remained, and a pile of stacked ashlar where the bankers had been cleared away. Now the man who had built this castle to God had Christendom heavy on his mind, and was already away in the spirit to the Holy Land.

Faint glints of lambent light pricked out the edge of the pool as Cadfael turned back to Compline. As he entered the close he was again among men, shadowy figures that passed him on their various occasions and spoke to him courteously in passing, but had no recognizable faces in the gathering dark. Canons, acolytes, choristers, guests from the common lodging and the hall, devout townspeople coming in to the late office, wanting the day completed and crowned. He felt himself compassed about with a great cloud of witnesses, and it mattered not at all that the whole soul of every one of these might be intent upon other anxieties, and utterly unaware of him. So many passionate needs brought together must surely shake the heavens.

Within the great barn of the nave a few spectral figures moved silently in the dimness, about the Church's evening business. It was early yet, only the constant lamps on the altars glowing like small red eyes, though in the choir a deacon was lighting the candles, flame after steady flame growing tall in the still air.

There was an unmistakably secular young man standing before a side altar where the candles had just been lighted. He bore no weapon here, but the belt he wore showed the fine leather harness for sword and dagger, and his coat, dark-coloured and workmanlike, was none the less of fine cloth and well cut. A square, sturdy young man who stood very still and gazed unwaveringly at the cross, with a regard so earnest and demanding that he was surely praying, and with grave intent. He stood half turned away, so that Cadfael could not see his face, and certainly did not recall that he had ever seen the man before; and yet there seemed something curiously familiar about the compact, neat build, and the thrust of the head upward and forward, as though he jutted his jaw at the God with whom he pleaded and argued, as at an equal of whom he had a right to demand help in a worthy cause.

Cadfael shifted his ground a little to see the fixed profile, and at the same moment one of the candles, the flame reaching some frayed thread, flared suddenly sidelong, and cast an abrupt light on the young man's face. It lasted only an instant, for he raised a hand and pinched away the fault briskly between finger and thumb, and the flame dimmed

27

and steadied again at once. A strong, bright profile, straight-nosed and well chinned, a young man of birth, and well aware of his value. Cadfael must have made some small movement at the edge of the boy's vision when the candle flared, for suddenly he turned and showed his full face, still youthfully round of cheek and vulnerably honest of eye, wide-set brown eyes beneath a broad forehead and a thick thatch of brown hair.

The startled glance that took in Cadfael was quickly and courteously withdrawn. In the act of returning to his silent dialogue with his maker the young man as suddenly stiffened, and again turned, this time to stare as candidly and shamelessly as a child. He opened his mouth to speak, breaking into an eager smile, recoiled momentarily into doubt, and then made up his mind.

'Brother Cadfael? It *is* you?'

Cadfael blinked and peered, and was no wiser.

'You can't have forgotten,' said the young man blithely, certain of his memorability. 'You brought me to Bromfield. It's six years ago now. Olivier came to fetch me away, Ermina and me. I'm changed, of course I am, but not you – not changed at all!'

And the light of the candles was steady and bright between them, and six years melted away like mist, and Cadfael recognized in this square, sturdy young fellow the square, sturdy child he had first encountered in the forest between Stoke and Bromfield in a bitter December, and helped away with his sister to safety in Gloucester. Thirteen years old then, now almost nineteen, and as trim and assured and bold as he had promised from that first meeting.

'Yves? Yves Hugonin! Ah, now I do see . . . And you are not so changed after all. But what are you doing here? I

28

thought you were away in the west somewhere, in Gloucester or Bristol.'

'I've been on the empress's errand to Norfolk, to the earl. He'll be on his way to Coventry by now. She needs all her allies round her, and Hugh Bigod carries more weight than most with the baronage.'

'And you're joining her party there?' Cadfael drew delighted breath. 'We can ride together. You are here alone? Then alone no longer, for it's a joy to see you again, and in such good fettle. I am here with Hugh, he'll be as glad to see you as I am.'

'But how,' demanded Yves, glowing, 'did you come to be here at all?' He had Cadfael by both hands, wringing them ardently. 'I know you were sent out by right, that last time, to salve a damaged man, but what art did you use to be loosed out to a state conference like this one? Though if there were more of you, and all delegates,' he added ruefully, 'there might be more hope of accord. God knows I'm happy to see you, but how did you contrive it?'

'I have leave until the conference ends,' said Cadfael.

'On what grounds? Abbots are not too easily persuaded.'

'Mine,' said Cadfael, 'allows me limited time, but sets a period to it that I may not infringe. I am given leave to attend at Coventry for one reason, to seek for news of one of the prisoners from Faringdon. Where princes are gathered together I may surely get word of him.'

He had not spoken a name, but the boy had stiffened into an intensity that tightened all the lines of his young, fresh face into a formidable maturity. He was not yet quite at the end of his growing, not fully formed, but the man was already there within, burning through like a stirred fire when some partisan passion probed deep into his heart.

'I think we are on the same quest,' he said. 'If you are looking for Olivier de Bretagne, so am I. I know he was in

29

Faringdon, I know as all who know him must know that he would never change his allegiance, and I know he has been hidden away out of reach. He was my champion and saviour once, he is my brother now, my sister carries his child. Closer to me than my skin, and dear as my blood, how can I ever rest,' said Yves, 'until I know what they have done with him, and have haled him out of captivity?'

'I was with him,' said Yves, 'until they garrisoned Faringdon. I was with him from the time I first bore arms, I would not willingly be parted from him, and he of his kindness kept me close. Father and brother both he has been to me, since he and my sister married. Now Ermina is solitary in Gloucester, and with child.'

They sat together on a bench beneath one of the torches in the guesthall, Hugh and Cadfael and the boy, in the last hush of the evening after Compline, with memories all about them in the dimness where the torchlight could not reach. Yves had pursued his quest alone since the fall of Faringdon had cast his friend into limbo, unransomed, unlisted, God knew where. It was relief now to open his heart and pour out everything he knew or guessed, to these two who valued Olivier de Bretagne as he did. Three together might surely do more than one alone.

'When Faringdon was finished, Robert of Gloucester took his own forces away and left the field to his son, and Philip made Brien de Soulis castellan of Faringdon, and gave him a strong garrison drawn from several bases. Olivier was among them. I was in Gloucester then, or I might have gone with him, but for that while I was on an errand for the empress, and she kept me about her. Most of her household were in Devizes still, she had only a few of us with her. Then we heard that King Stephen had brought a great host to lay siege to the new castle, and ease the pressure on Oxford and Malmesbury. And the next we knew was of Philip sending courier after courier to his father to come with reinforcements and save Faringdon. But he never came. Why?' demanded Yves helplessly. 'Why did he not? God knows! Was he ill? Is he still a sick man? Very weary I well understand he may be, but to be inactive then, when most he was needed!'

'From all I heard,' said Hugh, 'Faringdon was strongly held. Newly armed, newly provisioned. Even without Robert, surely it could have held out. My king, with all the liking I have for him, is not known for constancy in sieges. He would have sickened of it and moved on elsewhere. It takes a long time to starve out a newly supplied fortress.'

'It could have held,' Yves said bleakly. 'There was no need for that surrender, it was done of intent, of malice. Whether Philip was in it then or not, is something no man knows but Philip. For what happened certainly happened without his presence, but whether without his will is another matter. De Soulis is close in his counsels. However it was, there was some connivance between the leaders who had personal forces within, and the besiegers without, and suddenly the garrison was called to witness that all their six captains had come to an agreement to surrender the castle, and their men were shown the agreement inscribed and sealed by all six, and perforce they accepted what their lords decreed. And that left the knights and squires without following, to be disarmed and made prisoner unless they also accepted the fiat. The king's forces were already within the gates. Thirty young men were doled out like pay to Stephen's allies, and vanished. Some have reappeared, bought free by their kin and friends. Not Olivier.'

'This we do know,' said Hugh. 'The Earl of Leicester has the full list. No one has offered Olivier for ransom. No one has said, though someone must know, who holds him.'

'My Uncle Laurence has been enquiring everywhere,' agreed Yves, 'but can learn nothing. And he grows older, and is needed in Devizes, where she mainly keeps her court these days. But in Coventry I intend to bring this matter into the open, and have an answer. They cannot deny me.'

Cadfael, listening in silence, shook his head a little, almost fondly, at such innocent confiding. King and empress, with absolute if imagined victory almost within sight, were less likely to give priority to a matter of simple individual justice than this boy supposed. He was young, candid, born noble, and serenely aware of his rights to fair dealing and courteous consideration. He had some rough awakenings coming to him before he would be fully armoured against the world and the devil.

'And then,' said Yves bitterly, 'Philip handed over Crick-lade whole and entire to King Stephen, himself, his garrison, arms, armour and all. I can't for my life imagine why, what drove him to it. I've worn my wits out trying to fathom it. Was it a simple calculation that he was labouring more and more on the losing side, and could better his fortunes by the change? In cold blood? Or in very hot blood, bitter against his father for leaving Faringdon to its fate? Or was it he who betrayed Faringdon in the first place? Was it by his orders it was sold? I cannot see into his mind.'

'But you at least have seen him,' said Hugh, 'and served with him. I have never set eyes on him. If you cannot account for what he has done now, yet you have worked alongside him, you must have some view of him, as one man of another in the same alliance. How old can he be? Surely barely ten years your elder.'

Yves shook the baffled bewilderment impatiently from him, and took time to think. 'Around thirty. Robert's heir, William, must be a few years past that. A quiet man, Philip

– he had dark moods, but a good officer. I would have said I liked him, if ever I had considered to answer that at all. I never would have believed he would change his coat – certainly never for gain or for fear. . . .'

'Let it be,' said Cadfael placatingly, seeing how the boy laboured at the thing he could not understand. 'Here are three of us not prepared to let Olivier lie unransomed. Wait for Coventry, and we shall see what we can uncover there.'

They rode into Coventry in mid-afternoon of the following day, a fine, brisk day with gleams of chilly sunshine. The pleasure of the ride had diverted Yves for a while from his obsession, brightened his eyes and stung high colour into his cheeks. Approaching the city from the north, they found Earl Leofric's old defences still in timber, but sturdy enough, and the tangle of streets within well paved and maintained since the bishops had made this city their main base within the see. Roger de Clinton had continued the practice, though Lichfield was dearer to his own heart, for in these disturbed times Coventry was nearer the seat of dissension, and in more danger from the sporadic raids of rival armies, and he was not a man to steer clear of perils himself while his flock endured them.

And certainly his redoubtable presence had afforded the city a measure of protection, but for all that there were some scars and dilapidations to be seen along the streets, and an occasional raw-edged gap where a house had been stripped down to its foundations and not yet replaced. In a country which for several years now had been disputed in arms between two very uncousinly cousins, it was no wonder if private enemies and equally acquisitive neighbours joined in the plundering for themselves, independently of either faction. Even the Earl of Chester's small timber castle within the town had its scars to show, and would hardly be suitable for his occupation with the kind of retinue he intended to bring to the conference table, much less for entertaining his newly appeased and reconciled king. He would prefer the discreet distance of Mountsorrel in which to continue his careful wooing.

The city was divided between two lordships, the prior's half and the earl's half, and from time to time there was some grumbling and discontent over privileges varying between the two, but there was a shared and acknowledged town moot for all, and by and large they rubbed shoulders with reasonable amity. There were few more prosperous towns in England, and none more resilient and alert to opportunity. It was to be seen in the bustle in the streets. Merchants and tradesmen were busy setting out their wares to the best advantage, to catch the eyes of the assembling nobility. Whether they expected that the gathering would last long or produce any advance towards peace might be doubtful, but trade is trade, and where earls and barons were massing there would be profits to be made.

There were illustrious pennants afloat against the leaning house fronts, and fine liveries passing on horseback towards the gates of the priory and the houses of rest for pilgrims. Coventry possessed the relics of its own Saint Osburg, as well as an arm of Saint Augustine and many minor relics, and had thrived on its pilgrims ever since its founding just over a hundred years previously. This present crop of the wealthy and powerful, thought Cadfael, eyeing the evidences of their presence all about him, could hardly, for reputation's sake, depart without giving profitable reward for their entertainment and the Church's hospitality.

They wove their way at an easy walk through the murmur and bustle of the streets, and long before they reached the gateway of Saint Mary's Priory Yves had begun to flush into eagerness, warmed by the air of excitement and hope

34

that made the town seem welcoming and the possibility of conciliation a little nearer. He named the unfamiliar badges and banneroles they encountered on the way, and exchanged greetings with some of his own faction and status, young men in the service of the empress's loyal following.

'Hugh Bigod has made haste from Norfolk, he's here before us . . . Those are some of his men. And there, you see the man on the black horse yonder? That's Reginald FitzRoy, half-brother to the empress, the younger one, the one Philip seized not a month ago, and the king made him set him free. I wonder,' said Yves, 'how Philip dared touch him, with Robert's hand always over him, for they do show very brotherly to each other. But give him his due, Stephen does play fair. He'd granted safe conducts, he stood by them.'

They had reached the broad gate of the priory enclave, and turned into a great court alive with colour and quivering with movement. The few habited Benedictine brothers who were doing their best to go about their duties and keep the horarium of the day were totally lost among this throng of visiting magnates and their servitors, some arriving, some riding out to see the town or visit acquaintances, grooms coming and going with horses nervous and edgy in such a crowd, squires unsaddling and unloading their lords' baggage. Hugh, entering, drew aside to give free passage to a tall horseman, splendid in his dress and well attended, who was just mounting to ride forth.

'Roger of Hereford,' said Yves, glowing, 'the new earl. He whose father was killed by mishap, out hunting, a couple of years ago. And the man just looking back from the steps yonder – that's the empress's steward, Humphrey de Bohun. She must be already arrived—'

He broke off abruptly, stiffening, his mouth open on the unfinished sentence, his eyes fixed in an incredulous stare.

Cadfael, following the direction of the boy's fixed gaze, beheld a man striding down the stone steps of the guesthall opposite, for once the sole figure on the wide staircase, and in clear sight above the moving throng below. A very personable man, trimly built and moving with an elegant arrogance, his fair head uncovered, a short cloak swinging on one shoulder. Thirty-five years old, perhaps, and well assured of his worth. He reached the cobbles of the court, and the crowd parted to give him passage, as if they accepted him at his own valuation. But nothing there, surely, to cause Yves to check and stare, gathering dark brows into a scowl of animosity.

'He?' said Yves through his teeth. 'Dare *he* show his face here?' And suddenly his ice melted into fire, and with a leap he was out of the saddle and surging forward into the path of the advancing stranger, and his sword was out of the scabbard and held at challenge, spinning grooms and horses aside out of his way. His voice rose loud and hard.

'You, de Soulis! Betrayer of your cause and your comrades. Dare *you* come among honest men?'

For one shocked instant every other voice within the court was stunned into silence; the next, every voice rose in a clamour of alarm, protest and outrage. And as the first clash had sent people scurrying out of the vortex, so an immediate reaction drew many inward in recoil, to attempt to prevent the threatened conflict. But de Soulis had whirled to confront his challenger, and had his own sword naked in his hand, circling about him to clear ground for his defence. And then they were at it in earnest, steel shrieking against steel.

Chapter Three

UGH SPRANG down, flinging his bridle on his horse's neck for a groom to retrieve, and plunged into the ring of affrighted people surrounding the contestants, out of range of the flashing swords. Cadfael followed suit, with resigned patience but without haste, since he could hardly do more or better to quiet this disturbance than Hugh would be able to do. It could not go on long enough to be mortal, there were too many powers, both regal and clerical, in residence here to permit anything so unseemly, and by the noise now reverberating on all sides from wall to wall around the court, every one of those powers would be present and voluble within minutes.

Nevertheless, once on his feet he made his way hastily enough into the heaving throng, thrusting through to where he might at least be within reach, should any opportunity offer of catching at a whirling sleeve and hauling one of the combatants back out of danger. If this was indeed de Soulis, the renegade of Faringdon, he had a dozen years the advantage of Yves, and showed all too alert and practised with the sword. Experience tells. Cadfael burrowed sturdily, distantly aware of a great voice bellowing from behind him, somewhere in the gateway, and of a flashing of lustrous colours above him in the doorway of the guesthall, but so intent on breaking through the circle that he missed the most effective intervention of all, until it was launched without warning over his left shoulder, shearing through clean into the circling sword play.

A long staff was thrust powerfully past him, prising bodies apart to shear a way through. A long arm followed it, and a long, lean, vigorous body, and silver flashed at the head of the stave, striking the locked swords strongly upward, bruising the hands that held them. Yves lost his grip, and the blade rang and re-echoed on the cobbles. De Soulis retrieved his hold with a lunge, but the hilt quivered in his hand, and he sprang back out of range of the heavy silver mount crowning the staff now upright between them. A breathless silence fell.

'Put up your weapons,' said Bishop Roger de Clinton, without so much as raising his voice. 'Think shame to bare your swords within this precinct. You put your souls in peril. Our intent here is peace.'

The antagonists stood breathing hard, Yves flushed and half rebellious still, de Soulis eyeing his attacker with a chill smile and narrowed eyes.

'My lord,' he said with smooth civility, 'I had no thought of offending until this rash young man drew on me. For no sane reason that I know of, for I never set eyes on him before.' He slid his blade coolly into the scabbard, with a deliberately ceremonious gesture of reverence towards the bishop. 'He rides in here from the street, stranger to me, and begins to abuse me like a kennel brawler. I drew to keep my head.'

'He well knows,' flashed Yves, burning, 'why I call him turncoat, renegade, betrayer of better men. Good knights lie in castle dungeons because of him.'

'Silence!' said the bishop, and was instantly obeyed. 'Whatever your quarrels, they have no place within these walls. We are here to dispose of all such divisions between honourable men. Pick up your sword. Sheathe it! Do not draw it again on this sacred ground. Not upon any provocation! I so charge you, as for the Church. And here are also those who will lay the same charge on you, as your sovereigns and liege lords.'

The great voice that had bellowed orders on entering the gate upon this unseemly spectacle had advanced upon the suddenly muted circle in the shape of a big, fair, commanding and very angry man. Cadfael knew him at once, from a meeting years past, in his siege camp in Shrewsbury, though the years between had sown some ashen threads in his yellow hair, and seams of anxiety and care in his handsome, open face. King Stephen, soon roused, soon placated, brave, impetuous but inconstant, a good-natured and generous man who had yet spent all the years of his reign in destructive warfare. And that flash of bright colours in the doorway of the guesthall, Cadfael realized at the same moment, was, must be, the other one, the woman who challenged Stephen's sovereignty. Tall and erect against the dimness within the hall, splendidly apparelled and in her proud prime, there stood old King Henry's sole surviving legitimate child, Empress Maud by her first marriage, countess of Anjou by her second, the uncrowned Lady of the English.

She did not condescend to come down to them, but stood quite still and viewed the scene with a disinterested and slightly disdainful stare, only inclining her head in acknowledgement of the king's reverence. She was regally handsome, her hair dark and rich under the gilded net of her coif, her eyes large and direct, as unnerving as the straight stare of a Byzantine saint in a mosaic, and as indifferent. She was past forty, but as durable as marble.

'Say no word, either of you,' said the king, towering over the offenders, even over the bishop, who was tall by most men's standards, 'for we'll hear none. Here you are in the Church's discipline, and had best come to terms with it. Keep your quarrels for another time and place, or better still, put them away for ever. They have no place here. My lord bishop, give your orders now as to this matter of bearing arms, and announce it formally when you preside in hall tomorrow. Banish all weapons if you will, or let us have some firm regulation as to their wear, and I will see to it that who ever offends against your rule shall pay his dues in full.'

'I would not presume to deprive any man of the right to bear arms,' said the bishop firmly. 'I can, with full justification, take measures to regulate their use within these walls and during these grave discussions. In going about the town, certainly swords may be worn as customary, a man might well feel incomplete without his sword.' His own vigorous form and aquiline face could as well have belonged to a warrior as a bishop. And was it not said of him that his heart was already set on playing more than a passive role in the defence of the Christian kingdom of Jerusalem? 'Within these walls,' he said with deliberation, 'steel must not be drawn. Within the hall in session, not even worn, but laid by in the lodgings. And no weapon must ever be worn to the offices of the Church. Whatever the outcome, no man shall challenge another man in arms, for any reason soever, until we who are met here again separate. If your Grace is content so?'

'I am content,' said Stephen. 'This does well. You,

gentlemen, bear it in mind, and see to it you keep faith.' His blue, bright gaze swept over them both with the like broad, impersonal warning. Neither face meant anything to him, not even to which faction they belonged. Probably he had never seen either of them before, and would forget their faces as soon as he turned his back on them.

'Then I will put the case also to the lady,' said Roger de Clinton, 'and declare terms when we gather tomorrow morning.'

'Do so, with my goodwill!' said the king heartily, and strode away towards the groom who was holding his horse within the gate.

The lady, Cadfael observed when he looked again towards the doorway of the guesthall, had already withdrawn her aloof and disdainful presence from the scene, and retired to her own apartments within.

Yves fumed his way in black silence to their lodging in one of the pilgrim houses within the precinct, half in a boy's chagrin at being chastened in public, half in a man's serious rage at having to relinquish his quarrel.

'Why should you fret?' Hugh argued sensibly, humouring the boy but warily considering the man. 'De Soulis, if that was de Soulis, has had his ears clipped, too. There's no denying it was you began it, but he was nothing loth to spit you, if he could have done it. Now you've brought about your own deprivation. You might have known the Church would take it badly having swords drawn here on their ground.'

'I did know it,' Yves admitted grudgingly, 'if I'd ever stopped to think. But the sight of him, striding around as if in his own castle wards ... I never thought he would show here. Good God, what must she feel, seeing him so brazen, and the wrong he has done her! She favoured him, she gave him office!'

'She gave office to Philip no less,' said Hugh hardly. 'Will you fly at his throat when he comes into the conference hall?'

'Philip is another matter,' said Yves, flaring. 'He gave over Cricklade, yes, that we know, but that whole garrison went willingly. Do you think I do not know there could be good reasons for a man to change his allegiance? Honest reasons? Do you think she is easy to serve? I have seen her turn cold and insolent even to Earl Robert, seen her treat him like a peasant serf when the mood was on her. And he her sole strength, and enduring all for her sake!'

He wrung momentarily at a grief Cadfael had already divined. The Lady of the English was gallant, beautiful, contending for the rights of her young son rather than for her own. All these innocent young men of hers were a little in love with her, wanted her to be perfect, turned indignant backs on all manifestations that she was no such saint, but knew very well in their sore hearts all her arrogance and vindictiveness, and could not escape the pain. This one, at least, had got as far as blurting out the truth of his knowledge of her.

'But this de Soulis,' said Yves, recovering his theme and his animosity, 'conspired furtively to let the enemy into Faringdon, and sold into captivity all those honest knights and squires who would not go with him. And among them Olivier! If he had been honest in his own choice he would have allowed them theirs, he would have opened the gates for them, and let them go forth honourably in arms, to fight him again from another base. No, he sold them. He sold Olivier. That I do not forgive.'

'Possess your soul in patience,' said Brother Cadfael, 'until we know what we most need to know, where to look

42

for him. Fall out with no one, for who knows which of them here may be able to give us an answer?' And by the time we get that answer, he thought, eyeing Yves' lowering brows and set jaw tolerantly, revenges may well have gone by the board, no longer of any significance.

'I have no choice now but to keep the peace,' said Yves, resentfully but resignedly. None the less, he was still brooding when a novice of the priory came looking for him, to bid him to the empress's presence. In all innocence the young brother called her the Countess of Anjou. She would not have liked that. After the death of her first elderly husband she had retained and insisted on her title of empress still; the descent to mere countess by her second husband's rank had displeased her mightily.

Yves departed in obedience to the summons torn between pleasure and trepidation, half expecting to be taken to task for the unbecoming scene in the great court. She had never yet turned her sharp displeasure on him, but once at least he had witnessed its blistering effect on others. And yet she could charm the bird from the tree when she chose, and he had been thrown the occasional blissful moment during his brief sojourn in her household.

This time one of her ladies was waiting for him on the threshold of the empress's apartments in the prior's own guesthouse, a young girl Yves did not know, dark-haired and bright-eyed, a very pretty girl who had picked up traces of her mistress's self-confidence and boldness. She looked Yves up and down with a rapid, comprehensive glance, and took her time about smiling, as though he had to pass a test before being accepted. But the smile, when it did come, indicated that she found him something a little better than merely acceptable. It was a pity he hardly noticed.

'She is waiting for you. The earl of Norfolk commended you, it seems. Come within.' And crossing the threshold

43

into the presence she lowered her eyes discreetly, and made her deep reverence with practised grace. 'Madame, Messire Hugonin!'

The empress was seated in a stall-like chair piled with cushions, her dark hair loosed from its coif and hanging over her shoulder in a heavy, lustrous braid. She wore a loose gown of deep blue velvet, against which her ivory white skin glowed with a live sheen. The light of candles was kind to her, and her carriage was always that of a queen, if an uncrowned queen. Yves bent the knee to her with unaffected fervour, and stood to wait her pleasure.

'Leave us!' said Maud, without so much as a glance at the lingering girl, or the older lady who stood at her shoulder. And when they were gone from the room: 'Come closer! Here are all too many stretched ears at too many doors. Closer still! Let me look at you.'

He stood, a little nervously, to be studied long and thoughtfully, and the huge, Byzantine eyes passed over him at leisure, like the first stroking caress of the flaying knife.

'Norfolk says you did your errand well,' she said then. 'Like a natural diplomat. It's true I was in some doubt of him, but he is here. I marked little of the diplomat about you this afternoon in the great court.'

Yves felt himself flushing to the hair, but she hushed any protest or excuse he might have been about to utter with a raised hand and a cool smile. 'No, say nothing! I admired your loyalty and your spirit, if I could not quite compliment you on your discretion.'

'I was foolish,' he said. 'I am sensible of it.'

'Then that is quickly disposed of,' said the empress, 'for at this moment I am, officially, reproving you for the folly, and repeating the bishop's orders to you, as the aggressor, to curb your resentment hereafter. For the sake of appearances, as no doubt Stephen is chastising the other fool.

Well, now you have understood me, and you know you may not offer any open affront or injury to any man within these walls. With that in agreement between us, you may leave me.'

He made his obeisance, somewhat confused in mind, and turned again to the closed door. Behind him the incisive voice, softened and still, said clearly: 'All the same, I must confess I should not be greatly grieved to see Brien de Soulis dead at my feet.'

Yves went out in a daze, the soft, feline voice pursuing him until he had closed the door between. And there, standing patiently a few yards away, waiting with folded hands to be summoned back to her mistress, the elder lady turned her thin oval face and dark, incurious eyes upon him, asking nothing, confiding nothing. No doubt she had seen many young men emerge from that imperial presence, in many states of mortification, elation, devotion and despair, and refrained, as she did now, from making them aware how well she could read the signs. He drew his disrupted wits together, and made the best he could of his withdrawal, passing by her with a somewhat stiff reverence. Not until he was out in the darkened court, with the chill of the November twilight about him, did he pause to draw breath, and recall, with frightening clarity, every word that had been said in that brief encounter.

Had the empress's gentlewoman overheard the valedictory words? Could she have heard them, or any part of them, as the door opened to let him out? And would she, even for an instant, have interpreted them as he had? No, surely impossible! He remembered now who she was, closer than any other to her liege lady: the widow of a knight in the earl of Surrey's following, and herself born a de Redvers, from a minor branch of the family of Baldwin de Redvers, the empress's earl of Devon. Impeccably noble, fit to serve an empress. And old enough and wise enough to be a safe repository for an empress's secrets. Perhaps too wise to hear even what she heard! But if she had caught the last words, how did she read them?

He crossed the court slowly, hearing again the soft, insistent voice. No, it was he who was mangling the sense of her words. Surely she had been doing no more than giving bitter expression to a perfectly natural hatred of a man who had betrayed her. What else could be expected of her? No, she had not been even suggesting a course of action, much less ordering. We say these things in passion, into empty air, not with intent.

And yet she had quite deliberately instructed him: You may not offer any *open* affront or injury . . . And then: But all the same, I should not be greatly grieved . . . And with that you may leave me. Yves Hugonin! You have wit enough to get my meaning.

Impossible! He was doing her great wrong, it was he who had the devious mind, seeing her words twisted and askew. And he must and would put this unworthiness clean out of his mind and his memory.

He said no word to Hugh or to Cadfael, he would have been ashamed to probe the wound openly. He shrugged off Hugh's teasing: 'Well, at any rate she did not eat you!' with an arduous smile, and declined to be drawn. But not even Compline, in solemn state among bishops and magnates in preparation for the next day's conference, could quite cleanse the disquiet from his mind.

In the chapter-house of Saint Mary's Priory, after solemn Mass, the sovereignty and nobility of England met in full session. Three bishops presided, Winchester, Ely, and Roger de Clinton of Coventry and Lichfield. All three, inevitably, had partisan inclination towards one or other of the contending parties, but it appeared that they made a genuine effort to put all such interest aside, and concentrate with profound prayer on the attempt to secure agreement. Brother Cadfael, angling for a place outside the open door, where observers might at least glimpse and overhear the exchanges within, took it as a warning against any great optimism that those attending tended to group defensively together with their own kind, the empress and her allies on one side in solid phalanx, King Stephen and his magnates and sheriffs on the other. So marked a tendency to mass as for battle boded no good, however freely friends might come together across the divide once out of the chapter-house. There was Hugh, shoulder to shoulder with the Earl of Leicester and only four or five places from the king's own seat, and Yves upon the other side, in attendance on Hugh Bigod, earl of Norfolk, who had commended him to the empress for an errand well done. Once loosed from this grave meeting they would come together as naturally as right hand and left on a job to be done; within, they were committed to left and right in opposition.

Cadfael viewed the ranks of the great with intent curiosity, for most of them he had never seen before. Leicester he already knew: Robert Beaumont, secure in his earldom since the age of fourteen, intelligent, witty and wise, one of the few, perhaps, who were truly working behind the scenes towards a just and sensible compromise. Robert Bossu they called him, Robert the Hunchback, by reason of his one misshapen shoulder, though in action the flaw impeded him not at all, and scarcely affected the compact symmetry of his body. Beside him was William Martel, the king's steward, who had covered Stephen's retreat a few years back at Wilton, and himself been made prisoner, and bought free by Stephen at the cost of a valuable castle.

William of Ypres was beside him, the chief of the king's Flemings, and beyond him Cadfael, craning and peering in the doorway between the heads of others equally intent, could just see Nigel, Bishop of Ely, newly reconciled to the king after some years of disfavour, and no doubt wishful to keep his recovered place among the approved.

On the other side Cadfael had in full view the man who was the heart and spirit of the empress's cause, Robert, earl of Gloucester, constant at his half-sister's side here as he fought her battles in the field. A man of fifty, broad built, plain in his clothing and accoutrements, a lacing of grey in his brown hair, lines of weariness in his comely face. Grey in his short beard, too, accentuating the strong lines of his jaw in two silver streaks. His son and heir, William, stood at his shoulder. The younger son, Philip, if he was present here, would be among those on the opposing side. This one was built sturdily, like his father, and resembled him in the face. Humphrey de Bohun was there beside them, and Roger of Hereford. Beyond that Cadfael could not see.

But he could hear the voices, even identify some whose tones he had heard on rare occasions before. Bishop de Clinton opened the session by welcoming all comers in goodwill to the house of which he was titular abbot as well as bishop, and asserting, as he had promised, the ban on the carrying of weapons either here in hall, or, under any circumstances, when attending the office of the Church, then he handed over the opening argument to Henry of Blois, King Stephen's younger brother and bishop of Winchester. This high, imperious voice Cadfael had never heard before, though the effects of its utterances had influenced the lives of Englishmen for years, both secular and monastic.

It was not the first time that Henry of Blois had attempted to bring his brother and his cousin to sit down together and work out some compromise that would at least put a stop to active warfare, even if it meant maintaining a divided and guarded realm, for ever in danger of local eruptions. Never yet had he had any success. But he approached this latest endeavour with the same vigour and force, whatever his actual expectations. He drew for his audience the deplorable picture of a country wracked and wasted in senseless contention, through years of struggle without positive gain to either party, and a total loss to the common people. He painted a battle which could neither be won by either party nor lost by either, but would be solved only by some compounding that bound them both. He was eloquent, trenchant, and brief. And they listened; but they had always listened, and either never really heard, never understood, or never believed him. He had sometimes wavered and shifted in his own allegiance, and everyone knew it. Now he challenged both combatants with equal asperity. When he ended, by his rising cadence inviting response, there was a brief silence, but with a curious suggestion in its hush that two jealous presences were manoeuvring for the advantage. No good omen there!

It was the empress who took up the challenge, her voice high and steely, raised to carry. Stephen, thought Cadfael, had left her the opening of the field not out of policy, as might have been supposed, since the first to speak is the first to be forgotten, but out of his incorrigible chivalry towards all women, even this woman. She was declaring, as yet with cautious mildness, her right to be heard in this or any other gathering purporting to speak for England. She was chary of revealing all her keenest weapons at the first assay, and went, for her, very circumspectly, harking back to old King Henry's lamentable loss of his only remaining legitimate son in the wreck of the White Ship off Barfleur, years previously, leaving her as unchallenged heiress to his kingdom. A status which he had taken care to ensure while he lived, by summoning all his magnates to hear his will and swear fealty to their future queen. As they had done, and afterwards thought better of acknowledging a woman as sovereign, and accepted Stephen without noticeable reluctance, when for once he moved fast and decisively, installed himself, and assumed the crown. The small seed which had proliferated into all this chaos.

They talked, and Cadfael listened. Stephen asserted with his usual vulnerable candour his own right by crowning and coronation, but also refrained as yet from inviting anger. A few voices, forcefully quiet, argued the case of those lower in the hierarchies, who were left to bear the heaviest burden. Robert Bossu, forbearing from this seldom regarded plea, bluntly declared the economic idiocy of further wasting the country's resources, and a number of his young men, Hugh among them, echoed and reinforced his argument by reference to their own shires. Enough words were launched back and forth to supply a Bible, but not too often mentioning 'agreement', 'compromise', 'reason' or 'peace'. The session was ending before an unexpected minor matter was raised.

Yves had chosen his time. He waited until Roger de Clinton, scanning the ranks which had fallen silent, rose to declare an end to this first hearing, relieved, perhaps even encouraged, that it had passed without apparent rancour. Yves' voice rose suddenly but quietly, with deferential mildness; he had himself well in hand this time. Cadfael shifted his position vainly to try and get a glimpse of him, and clasped his hands in a fervent prayer that this calm should survive.

'My lords, your Grace . . .'

The bishop gave way courteously and let him speak.

'My lords, if I may raise a point, in all humility . . .'

The last quality the young and impetuous should lay claim to, but at least he was trying.

'There are some outstanding minor matters which might tend to reconciliation, if they could be cleared up now. Even agreement on a detail must surely tend to agreement on greater things. There are prisoners held on both sides. While we are at truce for this good purpose would it not be just and right to declare a general release?'

A murmur arose from partisans of both factions, and grew into a growl. No, neither of them would concede that, to put back into the opposing ranks good fighting men at present disarmed and out of the reckoning. The empress swept the idea aside with a gesture of her hand. 'These are matters to be dealt with in the terms of peace,' she said, 'not priorities.'

The king, for once in agreement upon not agreeing, said firmly: 'We are here first to come to terms upon the main issue. This is a matter to be discussed and negotiated afterwards.'

'My lord bishop,' said Yves, fixing sensibly upon the one ally upon whom he could rely in considering the plight of captives, 'if such an exchange must be deferred, at least may I ask for information concerning certain knights and squires made prisoner at Faringdon this past summer. There are some among them held by unnamed captors. Should not their friends and kin, who wish to ransom them, at least be provided that opportunity?'

'If they are held for gain,' said the bishop, with a slight edge of distaste in his voice, 'surely the holder will be the first to offer them for his profit. Do you say this has not been done?'

'Not in all cases, my lord. I think,' said Yves clearly, 'that some are held not for gain but for hate, in personal revenge

51

for some real or imagined offence. There are many private feuds bred out of faction.'

The king shifted in his chair impatiently, and repeated loudly: 'With private feuds we are not concerned. This is irrelevant here. What is one man's fate beside the fate of the realm?'

'Every man's fate *is* the fate of the realm,' cried Yves boldly. 'If injustice is done to one, it is one too many. The injury is to all, and the whole realm suffers.'

Over the growing hubbub of many voices busily crying one another down, the bishop raised authoritative hands. 'Silence! Whether this is the time and place or no, this young man speaks truth. A fair law should apply to all.' And to Yves, standing his ground apprehensive but determined: 'You have, I think, a particular case in mind. One of those made prisoner after Faringdon fell.'

'Yes, my lord. And held in secret. No ransom has been asked, nor do his friends, or my uncle, his lord, know where to enquire for his price. If his Grace would but tell me who holds him . . .'

'I did not parcel out my prisoners under my own seal,' blared the king, growing louder and more restive, but as much because he wanted his dinner, Cadfael judged, as because he had any real interest in what was delaying him. It was characteristic of him that, having gained a large number of valuable prizes, he should throw the lot of them to his acquisitive supporters and walk away from the bargaining, leaving them to bicker over the distribution of the booty. 'I knew few of them, and remember no names. I left them to my castellan to hand out fairly.'

Yves took that up eagerly, before the point could be lost. 'Your Grace, your castellan of Faringdon is here present. Be so generous as to let him give me an answer.' And he launched the question before it could be forbidden. 'Where is Olivier de Bretagne, and in whose keeping?'

He had kept his voice deliberate and cool, but he hurled the name like a lance for all that, and not at the king, but clean across the open space that divided the factions, into the face of de Soulis. Stephen's tolerance he needed if he was to get an answer. Stephen could command where no one else could do more than request. And Stephen's patience was wearing thin, not so much with the persistent squire as with the whole process of this overlong session.

'It is a reasonable request,' said the bishop, with the sharp edge still on his voice.

'In the name of God,' agreed the king explosively, 'tell the fellow what he wants to know, and let us be done with the matter.'

The voice of de Soulis rose in smooth and prompt obedience, from among the king's unseen minor ranks, well out of Cadfael's sight, and so modestly retired from prominence that it sounded distant. 'Your Grace, I would willingly, if I knew the answer. At Faringdon I made no claim for myself, but withdrew from the council and left it to the knights of the garrison. Those of them who returned to your Grace's allegiance, of course,' he said with acid sweetness. 'I never enquired as to their decisions, and apart from such as have already been offered for ransom and duly redeemed, I have no knowledge of the whereabouts of any. The clerks may have drawn up a list. If so, I have never asked to see it.'

Long before he ended, the deliberate sting against those of the Faringdon garrison who had remained true to their salt had already raised an ominous growl of rage among the empress's followers, and a ripple of movement along the ranks, that suggested swords might have been half out of scabbards if they had not been forbidden within the hall.

Yves' raised voice striking back in controlled but passionate anger roused a counter roar from the king's adherents. 'He lies, your Grace! He was there every moment, he ordered all. He lies in his teeth!'

Another moment, and there would have been battle, even without weapons, barring the common man's weapons of fists, feet and teeth. But the Bishop of Winchester had risen in indignant majesty to second Roger de Clinton's thunderous demand for order and silence, king and empress were both on their feet and flashing menacing lightnings, and the mounting hubbub subsided gradually, though the acrid smell of anger and hatred lingered in the quivering air.

'Let us adjourn this session,' said Bishop de Clinton grimly, when the silence and stillness had held good for uneasy and shaming minutes, 'without further hot words that have no place here. We will meet again after noon, and I charge you all that you come in better and more Christian condition, and further, that after that meeting, whatever it brings, you who truly mean in the heart what your mouths have uttered, that you seek peace here, shall attend at Vespers, unarmed, in goodwill to all, in enmity towards none, to pray for that peace.'

Chapter Four

‘E IS lying,’ repeated Yves, still flushed and scowling over the priory’s frugal board, but eating like a hungry boy nevertheless. ‘He never left that council for a moment. Can you conceive of him forgoing any prize for himself, or being content with less than the best? He knows very well who has Olivier in hold. But if Stephen cannot force him to speak out – or will not! – how can any other man get at him?’

‘Even a liar,’ reflected Hugh judicially, ‘for I grant you he probably is that! – may tell truth now and again. For I tell you this, there seem to be very few, if any, who do know what happened to Olivier. I’ve been probing where I could, but with no success, and I daresay Cadfael has been keeping his ears open among the brothers. Better, I do believe the bishop will be making his own enquiries, having heard what he heard from you this morning.’

‘If I were you,’ said Cadfael, profoundly pondering, ‘I would keep the matter out of the chapter-house. It’s certain king and empress will have to declare themselves, and neither will relish being pestered to go straying after the fate of one squire, when their own fortunes are in the balance. Go round about, if there are any others here who were in Faringdon. And I will speak to the prior. Even monastic ears can pick up whatever rumours are passed around, as fast as any, and all the better for being silent themselves.'

But Yves remained blackly brooding, and would not be deflected. 'De Soulis knows, and I will have it out with him, if I must carve it out of his treacherous heart. Oh, say no word!' he said, waving away whatever Cadfael might have had on the tip of his tongue. 'I know I am hobbled within here, I cannot touch him.'

Now why, thought Cadfael, should he state the obvious with so much lingering emphasis, yet so quietly, as if to remind himself rather than reassure anyone else. And why should his normally wide-eyed, candid gaze turn dubiously inward, looking back, very wearily, on something imperfectly understood and infinitely disquieting?

'But both he and I will have to leave the pale of the Church soon,' said Yves, shaking himself abruptly out of his brooding, 'and then nothing hinders but I should meet him in arms, and have the truth out of his flesh.'

Brother Cadfael went out through the crowds in the great court, and made his way into the priory church. The grandees would not yet have left their high table to resume discussions so little likely to produce profitable results; he had time to retire into some quiet corner and put the world away from him for a while. But quiet corners were few, even in the church. Numbers of the lesser partisans had also found it convenient to gather where they could confer without being overheard, and had their heads together in the shelter of altars and in the carrels of the cloister. Visiting clergy were parading nave and choir and studying the dressing of the altars, and a few of the brothers, returning to their duties after the half-hour of rest, threaded their way silently among the strangers.

There was a girl standing before the high altar, with modestly folded hands and lowered eyes. In prayer? Cadfael doubted it. The altar lamp shed a clear, rosy light over her slight, confident smile, and the man who stood close at her shoulder was speaking very discreetly and respectfully into her ear, but with something of the same private smile in the curve of his lips. Ah, well! A young girl here among so many personable young men, and herself virtually the only one of her sex and years in this male assemblage, might well revel in her privileges while they lasted, and exploit her opportunities. Cadfael had seen her before, blithely following the empress to Mass that morning, bearing the imperial prayer-book and a fine wool shawl in case the lady felt the cold in this vast stony cavern before the service ended. The niece of the older gentlewoman, he had been told. And those three, one royal, two from the ranks of the baronage, the only women in this precinct among the entire nobility of the land. Enough to turn any girl's head. Though by her pose and her carriage, and the assurance with which she listened and made no response, Cadfael judged that this one would not lightly make any concessions, or ever lose sight of her real advantages. She would listen and she would smile, and she might even suggest the possibility of going further, but her balance was secure. With a hundred or more young men here to see and admire, and flatter her with enjoyable attentions, the first and boldest was not likely to advance very far until others had shown their paces. She was young enough to take delight in the game, and shrewd enough to survive it untouched.

Now she had recalled the approaching hour and the exigence of her service, and turned to depart, to attend her mistress again to the door of the chapter-house. She moved decisively, walking briskly enough to indicate that she did not care whether her courtier followed her or not, but not so rapidly as to leave him behind. Until that moment Cadfael had not recognized the man. The first and boldest – yes, so he would be. The fair head, the elegant, self-assured stride, the subtle, half-condescending smile of Brien de Soulis followed the girl out of the church with arrogant composure, to all appearances as certain that there was no haste, that she would come his way whenever he chose, as she was certain she could play him and discard him. And which of two such overweening creatures would prevail was a matter for serious speculation.

Cadfael felt curious enough to follow them out into the court. The older gentlewoman had come out from the guesthall looking for her niece. She contemplated the pair of them without any perceptible emotion, her face impassive, and turned to re-enter the hall, looking back for the girl to follow her. De Soulis halted to favour them both with a courtly reverence, and withdrew at leisure towards the chapter-house. And Cadfael turned back into the cloister garth, and paced the bleached wintry sward very thoughtfully.

The empress's gentlewoman could hardly approve her niece's dalliance, however restrained, with the empress's traitor and renegade. She would be concerned to warn the girl against any such foolishness. Or perhaps she knew her own kin better, and saw no reason for concern, being well aware that this was a shrewd young woman who would certainly do nothing to compromise her own promising future in the empress's household.

Well, he had better be turning his mind to graver matters

than the fortunes of young women he had never seen before. It was almost time for the feuding factions to meet yet again in session. And how many of them on either side were genuinely in search of peace? How many in pursuit of total victory with the sword?

When Cadfael manoeuvred his way as close as he could to the doorway of the chapter-house, it seemed that Bishop de Clinton had ceded the presidium on this occasion to the Bishop of Winchester, perhaps hopeful that so powerful a prelate would exert more influence upon obdurate minds, by virtue of his royal blood, and his prestige as recently filling the office of papal legate to the realm of England. Bishop Henry was just rising to call the assembly to order, when hasty footsteps and a brusque but civil demand for passage started the crowding watchers apart, and let through into the centre of the chapter-house a tall new-comer, still cloaked and booted for riding. Behind him in the court a groom led away the horse from which he had just dismounted, the hoofbeats receding slowly towards the stables. Eased to a walk now after a long ride, and the horseman dusty from the wind-dried roads.

The latecomer crossed the open space between the partisans with a long, silent stride, made a deferential obeisance to the presiding bishop, who received it with a questioning frown and the merest severe inclination of his head, and bent to kiss the king's hand, all without compromising for an instant his own black dignity. The king smiled on him with open favour.

'Your Grace, I ask pardon for coming late. I had work to do before I could leave Malmesbury.' His voice was pitched low, and yet had a clear, keen edge to it. 'My lords, forgive my travel-stained appearance, I hoped to come

59

before this assembly with better grace, but am come too late to delay the proceedings longer.'

His manner towards the bishops was meticulously courteous. To the empress he said no word, but made her a bow of such ceremonious civility and with such an aloof countenance that its arrogance was plainly apparent. And his father he had passed by without a glance, and now, turning, confronted with a steady, distant stare, as though he had never seen him before.

For this was certainly Philip FitzRobert, the earl of Gloucester's younger son. There was even a resemblance, though they were built differently. This man was not compact and foursquare, but long and sinewy, abrupt but graceful of movement and dark of colouring. Above the twin level strokes of his black brows the cliff of forehead rose loftily into thick, waving hair, and below them his eyes were like damped-down fires, muted but alive. Yet the likeness was there, stressed most strongly by the set of long, passionate lips and formidable jaw. It was the image carried one generation further into extremes. What would be called constant in the father would be more truly stubborn in the son.

His coming, it seemed, had cast a curious constraint upon the company, which could not be eased without his initiative. He took pains to release them from the momentary tension, with an apologetic gesture of hand and head in deference to the bishops. 'My lords, I beg you'll proceed, and I'll withdraw.' And he drew back into the ranks of King Stephen's men, and melted smoothly through them to the rear. Even so, his presence was almost palpable in the air, stiffening spines, causing ears to prick and hackles to rise in the nape of the neck, all about him. Many there had held that he would not dare to come where his affronted father and his betrayed liege lady were. It appeared, after all, that there was very little this man would not dare, nor much that he could not carry off with steely composure, too commanding to be written off lightly as effrontery.

He had somewhat discomposed even the bishop of Winchester, but the hesitation was only a moment long and the impressive voice rose with authority, calling them peremptorily to prayer, and to the consideration of the grave matters for which they were gathered together.

As yet the principals had done no more than state, with caution, the bases of their claims to sovereignty. It was high time to elicit from them some further consideration of how far they were willing to go, by way of acknowledging each the other's claim. Bishop Henry approached the empress very circumspectly; he had long experience of trying to manipulate her, and breaking his forehead against the impregnable wall of her obstinacy. Above all, avoid ever referring to her as the countess of Anjou. Accurate enough, that was yet a title she regarded as derogatory to her status as a king's daughter and an emperor's consort.

'Madam,' said the bishop weightily, 'you know the need and the urgency. This realm has suffered dissension all too long, and without reconciliation there can be no healing. Royal cousins should be able to come together in harmony. I entreat you, search your heart and speak, give a lead to your people as to the way we should take from this day and this place, to put an end to the wastage of life and land.'

'I have given years of consideration already,' said the empress crisply, 'to these same matters, and it seems to me that the truth is plain, and no amount of gazing can change it, and no amount of argument make it untrue. It is exactly as it was when my father died. He was king unquestioned, undisputed, and by the loss of a brother, I was left the sole living child of my father by his lawful wife, Matilda, his queen, herself daughter to the king of Scots. There is no man here present who does not know these things. There is no man in England who dare deny them. How then could there be any other heir to this kingdom when the king my father died?'

Not a word, of course, reflected Cadfael, stretching his ears outside the doorway, of the dozen or so children the old king had left behind, scattered about his realm, by other mothers. They did not count, not even the best of them, who stood patient and steadfast at her shoulder, and could have out-royalled both these royal rivals had his pedigree accorded with Norman law and custom. In Wales he would have had his rights, the eldest son of his father, and the most royal.

'Yet to make all sure,' pursued the dominant voice proudly, 'my father the king himself broached the matter of succession, at his Christmas court, nine years before his death, and called on all the magnates of his realm to take a solemn oath to receive me, descendant of fourteen kings, as his heiress, and their queen after him. And so they did, every man. My lords bishops, it was William of Corbeil, then Archbishop of Canterbury, who first took the oath. My uncle, the king of Scots, was the second, and the third who swore his allegiance to me,' she said, raising her voice and honing it like a dagger, 'was Stephen, my cousin, who now comes here with argument of royalty against me.'

A dozen voices were murmuring by then, deprecatory and anxious on one side, in rumbling anger on the other. The bishop said loudly and firmly: 'It is no place here to bring forward all the deeds of the past. There have been enough, not all upon one part. We stand now where these faults and betrayals, from whatever source, have left us, and from where we stand we must proceed, we have no other choice. What is to be done *now*, to undo such ills as may be undone, is what we have to fathom. Let all be said with that in mind, and not revenges for things long past.'

'I ask only that truth be recognized as truth,' she said inflexibly. 'I am lawful queen of England by hereditary right, by my father's royal decree and by the solemn oaths of all his magnates to accept and acknowledge me. If I wished, I cannot change my status, and as God sees me, I will not. That I am denied my right alters nothing. I have not surrendered it.'

'You cannot surrender what you do not possess,' taunted a voice from the rear ranks of Stephen's supporters. And instantly there were a dozen on either side crying out provocation, insult and mockery, until Stephen crashed his fist down on the arms of his chair and bellowed for order even above the bishop's indignant plea.

'My imperial cousin is entitled to her say,' he proclaimed firmly, 'and has spoken her mind boldly. Now for my part I have somewhat to say of those symbols which not so much decree or predict sovereignty, but confer it and confirm it. For the countess of Anjou to inherit that crown to which she lays claim by inheritance, it would be needful to deprive me of what I already hold. I hold by coronation, by conse-cration, by anointing. That acceptance she was promised, I came, I asked for, I won fairly. The oil that consecrated me cannot be washed away. That is the right by which I claim what I hold. And what I hold I will not give up. No part of anything I have won, in any way soever, will I give up. I make no concession, none.'

And with that said, upon either part, the one pleading by blood-right, the other by both secular and clerical acknowledgement and investiture, what point was there in saying anything further? Yet they tried. It was the turn of the moderate voices for a while, and not urging brotherly or cousinly forgiveness and love, but laying down bluntly the brutal facts; for if this stalemate, wrangling and waste continued, said Robert Bossu with cold, clear emphasis, there would eventually be nothing worth annexing or retaining, only a desolation where the victor, if the survivor so considered himself, might sit down in the ashes and moulder. But that, too, was ignored. The empress, confident in her knowledge that her husband and son held all Normandy in their grasp, and most of these English magnates had lands over there to protect, and must cling to what favour they had with the house of Anjou to accomplish that feat, felt certain of eventual victory in England no less. And Stephen, well aware that his star was in the ascendant here in England, what with this year's glittering gains, was equally sure the rest must fall into his hands, and was willing to risk what might be happening overseas, and leave it to be dealt with later.

The voices of cold reason were talking, as usual, to deaf ears. The bulk of the talk now was little more than an exchange of accusations and counter accusations. Henry of Winchester held the balance gallantly enough, and fended off actual conflict, but could do no better than that. And there were many, Cadfael noted, who listened dourly and said nothing at all. Never a word from Robert of Gloucester, never a word from his son and enemy, Philip FitzRobert. Mutually sceptical, they refrained from waste of breath and effort, in whatever direction.

'Nothing will come of it,' said Robert Bossu resignedly in Hugh Beringar's ear, when the two monodies had declined at last into one bitter threnody. 'Not here. Not yet. This is how it must end at last, and in an even bleaker desolation. But no, there'll be no end to it yet.'

They were adjured, when the fruitless session finally closed, at least to keep this last evening together in mutual tolerance, and to observe the offices of the Church together at Vespers and Compline before parting the next morning to go their separate ways. A few, not far from home, left the priory this same evening, despairing of further waste of time, and perhaps even well satisfied that nothing had resulted from the hours already wasted. Where most men are still dreaming of total victory, the few who would be content with an economical compromise carry no weight. And yet at the last, as Robert Bossu had said, this was the way it must go, there could be no other ending. Neither side could ever win, neither side lose. And they would sicken at last of wasting their time, their lives and their country.

But not here. Not yet.

Cadfael went out into the stillness of early dusk, and watched the empress sweep across the court towards her lodging, with the slender, elderly figure of Jovetta de Montors at her elbow, and the girl Isabeau demurely following, a pace or two behind them. There was an hour left before Vespers for rest and thought. The lady would probably content herself with the services of her own chaplain instead of attending the offices in the priory church, unless, of course, she saw fit to make a final splendid state appearance in vindication of her legitimate right, before shaking off the very dust of compromise and returning to the battlefield.

For that, Cadfael thought sadly, is where they are all bound, after this regrouping of minds and grudges. There will be more of siege and raid and plunder, they will even have stored up reserves of breath and energy and hatred during this pause. For a while the fires will be refuelled, though the weariness will come back again with the turn of another year. And I am no nearer knowing where my son lies captive, let alone how to conduct the long journey to his deliverance.

He did not look for Yves or for Hugh, but went alone into the church. There were now quiet corners enough within there for every soul who desired a holy solitude and the peopled silence of the presence of God. In entering any other church but his own he missed, for one moment, the small stone altar and the chased reliquary where Saint Winifred was not, and yet was. Just to set eyes on it was to kindle a little living fire within his heart. Here he must forego that particular consolation, and submit to an unfamiliar benediction. Nevertheless, there was an answer here for every need.

He found himself a dim place in a transept corner, on a narrow stone ridge that just provided room to sit, and there composed himself into patient stillness and closed his eyes, the better to conjure up the suave olive face and startling eyes, black within gold, of Mariam's son. Other men engendered sons, and had the delight of their infancy and childhood, and then the joy of watching them grow into manhood. He had had only the man full grown and marvellous, launched into his ageing life like the descent of an angelic vision, as sudden and as blinding; and that only in two brief glimpses, bestowed and as arbitrarily withdrawn. And he had been glad and grateful for that, as more than his deserving. While Olivier went free and fearless and blessed about the world, his father needed nothing more. But Olivier in captivity, stolen out of the world, hidden from the light, that was not to be borne. The darkened void where he had been was an offence against truth.

He did not know how long he had sat silent and apart, contemplating that aching emptiness, unaware of the few people who came and went in the nave at this hour. It had grown darker in the transept, and his stillness made him invisible to the man who entered from the mild twilight of the cloister into his chosen and shadowy solitude. He had

not heard footsteps. It startled him out of his deep withdrawal when a body brushed against him, colliding with arm
and knee, and a hand was hurriedly reached to his shoulder
to steady them both. There was no exclamation. A
moment's silence while the stranger's eyes took time to
adjust to the dimness within, then a quiet voice said: 'I ask
pardon, brother, I did not see you.'

'I was willing,' said Cadfael, 'not to be seen.'

'There have been times,' agreed the voice, unsurprised,
'when I would have welcomed it myself.'

The hand on Cadfael's shoulder spread long, sinewy
fingers strongly into his flesh, and withdrew. He opened
his eyes upon a lean, dark figure looming beside him, and
a shadowed oval face, high-boned and aquiline, looking
down at him impersonally, with a grave and slightly unnerving intelligence. Eyes intent and bright studied him unhurriedly, without reticence, without mercy. Confronted with a
mere man, neither ally nor enemy to him, Philip FitzRobert
contemplated humanity with a kind of curious but profound perception, hard to evade.

'Are there griefs, brother, even here within the pale?'

'There are griefs everywhere,' said Cadfael, 'within as
without. There are few hiding-places. It is the nature of
this world.'

'I have experienced it,' said Philip, and drew a little
aside, but did not go, and did not release him from the
illusionless penetration of the black, aloof stare. In his own
stark way a handsome man, and young, too young to be
quite in control of the formidable mind within. Not yet
quite thirty, Olivier's own age, and thus seen in semi-
darkness the clouded mirror image of Olivier.

'May your grief be erased from memory, brother,' said
Philip, 'when we aliens depart from this place, and leave

you at least in peace. As we shall be erased when the last hoofbeat dies.'

'If God wills,' said Cadfael, knowing by then that it would not be so.

Philip turned and went away from him then, into the comparative light of the nave, a lithe, light-stepping youth as soon as the candles shone upon him; round into the choir, up to the high altar. And Cadfael was left wondering why, in this moment of strange fellowship, mistaken, no doubt, for a brother of this house, he had not asked Gloucester's son, face to face, who held Olivier de Bretagne; wondering also whether he had held his tongue because this was not the time or the place, or because he was afraid of the answer.

Compline, the last office of the day, which should have signified the completion of a cycle of worship, and the acknowledgement of a day's effort, however flawed, and a day's achievement, however humble, signified on this night only a final flaunting of pride and display, rival against rival. If they could not triumph on the battlefield, not yet, they would at least try to outdo each other in brilliance and piety. The Church might benefit by the exuberance of their alms. The realm would certainly gain nothing.

The empress, after all, was not content to leave even this final field to her rival. She came in sombre splendour, attended not by her gentlewomen, but by the youngest and handsomest of her household squires, and with all her most powerful barons at her back, leaving the commonalty to crowd in and fill the last obscure corners of the nave. Her dark blue and gold had the sombre, steely sheen of armour, and perhaps that was deliberate, and she had left the women out of her entourage as irrelevant to a battlefield on which she was the equal of any man, and no other woman was fit to match her. She preferred to forget Stephen's able and heroic queen, dominant without rival in the south-east, holding inviolable the heart and source of her husband's sovereignty.

And Stephen came, massively striding, carelessly splendid, his lofty fair head bared, to the eye every inch a king. Ranulf of Chester, all complacent smiles, kept his right flank possessively, as if empowered by some newly designed royal appointment specially created for a new and valuable ally. On his left William Martel, his steward, and Robert de Vere, his constable, followed more staidly. Long and proven loyalty needs no sleeve-brushing and hand-kissing. It was some minutes, Cadfael observed from his remote dark corner of the choir, before Philip FitzRobert came forward unhurriedly from wherever he had been waiting and brooding, and took his place among the king's adherents; nor did he press close, to be certain of royal notice as in correct attendance, but remained among the rearguard. Reticence and withdrawal did not diminish him.

Cadfael looked for Hugh, and found him among the liegemen of the earl of Leicester, who had collected about him a number of the more stable and reliable young. But Yves he did not find. There were so many crowding into the church by the time the office began that latecomers would be hard put to it to find a corner in nave or porch. Faces receded into a dappled dimness. The windows were darkening, banishing the outer world from the dealings within. And it seemed that the bishops had accepted, with sadness, the failure of their efforts to secure any hope of peace, for there was a valedictory solemnity about the terms in which Roger de Clinton dismissed his congregation.

'And I adjure you, abide this last night before you disperse and turn your faces again to warfare and contention. You were called here to consider on the sickness of the land, and though you have despaired of any present cure, you cannot therefore shake off from your souls the burden of England's sorrows. Use this night to continue in prayer and thought, and if your hearts are changed, know that it is not too late to speak out and change the hearts of others. You who lead – we also to whom God has committed the wellbeing of souls – not one of us can evade the blame if we despoil and forsake our duties to the people given into our care. Go now and consider these things.'

The final blessing sounded like a warning, and the vault cast back echoes of the bishop's raised and vehement voice like distant minor thunders of the wrath of God. But neither king nor empress would be greatly impressed. Certainly the reverberations held them motionless in their places until the clergy had almost reached the door of their vestry, but they would forget all warnings once they were out of the church and into the world, with all their men of war about them.

Some of the latecomers had withdrawn quietly to clear the way for the brothers' orderly recession, and the departure of the princes. They spilled out from the south porch into the deep dusk of the cloister and the chill of nightfall. And somewhere among the first of them, a few yards beyond into the north walk, a sudden sharp cry arose, and the sound of a stumble, recovered just short of the fall. It was not loud enough to carry into the church, merely a startled exclamation, but the shout of alarm and consternation that followed it next moment was heard even in the sanctity of the choir. And then the same voice was raised urgently, calling: 'Help here! Bring torches! Someone's hurt . . . A man lying here . . .'

The bishops heard it, and recoiled from their robing-room threshold to stand stockstill for a moment, ears stretched, before bearing down in haste upon the south door. All those nearest to it were already jamming the doorway in their rush to get out, and bursting forth like seeds from a dehiscent pod in all directions as the pressure behind expelled them into the night. But the congestion was miraculously stricken apart like the Red Sea when Stephen came striding through, not even yielding the precedence to the empress, though she was not far behind him, swept along in the momentum of his passage. She emerged charged and indignant, but silent, Stephen loud and peremptory.

'Lights, some of you! Quickly! Are you deaf?' And he was off along the north walk of the cloister, towards the alarm that had now subsided into silence. The dimness under the vault halted him long enough for someone to run with a guttering torch, until a gust of wind, come with the evening chill, cast a sudden lick of flame down to the holder's fingers, and he dropped it with a yell, to sputter out against the flags.

Brother Cadfael had discarded the idea of candles, aware of the sharp evening wind, but recalled that he had seen a horn lantern in the porch, and carried one of the candlesticks with him to retrieve and light it. One of the brothers was beside him with a torch plucked from its sconce, and one of Leicester's young men had possessed himself of one of the iron fire-baskets from the outer court, on its long pole. Together they bore down on the congestion in the north walk of the cloister, and thrust a way through to shed light upon the cause of the outcry.

On the bare flags outside the third carrel of the walk a man lay sprawled on his right side, knees slightly drawn up, a thick fell of light brown hair hiding his face, his arms spilled helplessly along the stones. Rich dark clothing marked his status, and a sheathed sword slanted from his left hip, its tip just within the doorway of the carrel, as

71

his toes just brushed the threshold. And stooped over him, just rising from his knees, Yves Hugonin stared up at them with shocked, bewildered eyes and white face.

'I stumbled over him in the dark. He's wounded . . .'

He stared at his own hand, and there was blood on his fingers. The man at his feet lay more indifferently still than any living thing should be, with king and empress and half the nobility of the land peering down at him in frozen fascination. Then Stephen stooped and laid a hand on the hunched shoulder, and rolled the body over on to its back, turning up to the light of the torches a face now fixed in blank astonishment, with half-open eyes glaring, and a broad breast marred by a blot of blood that spread and darkened slowly before their eyes.

From behind Stephen's shoulder issued a muted cry, not loud, but low, tightly controlled and harsh, as brief as it was chilling; and Philip FitzRobert came cleaving through the impeding crowd to kneel over the motionless body, stooping to lay a hand on the still warm flesh at brow and throat, lift one upper eyelid and glare into an eye that showed no reaction to light or darkness, and then as brusquely, almost violently, sweep both lids closed. Over dead Brien de Soulis he looked up to confront Yves with a bleak, glittering stare.

'Through the heart, and he had not even drawn! We all know the hate that you had for him, do we not? You were at his throat the moment you entered here, as I have heard from others who witnessed it. Your rage against him after, that I have seen with my own eyes. Your Grace, you see here murder! Murder, my lords bishops, in a holy place, during the worship of God! Either lay hold on this man for the law to deal with him, or let me take him hence and have his life fairly for this life he has taken!'

Chapter Five

VES HAD recoiled a stumbling pace backward from the whiplash voice and ferocious glare, gaping in blank shock and disbelief. In the confident armour of his status and privilege it had not even dawned on him that he had put himself in obvious peril of such suspicions. He stared open-mouthed, fool innocent that he was, he was even tempted into a grin of incredulity, almost into laughter, before the truth hit home, and he blanched whiter than his shirt, and flashed a wild glance round to recognize the same wary conviction in a dozen pairs of eyes, circling him every way. He heaved in breath gustily, and found a voice.

'I? You think that *I* . . .? I came from the church this moment. I stumbled over him. He lay here as you see him . . .'

'There's blood on your hand,' said Philip through set teeth. 'And on your hands by right! Who else? Here you stand over his body, and no man else abroad in the night but you. You, who bore a blood grudge against him, as every soul here knows.'

'I found him so,' protested Yves wildly. 'I kneeled to handle him, yes, it was dark, I did not know if he was dead or alive. I cried out when I stumbled over him. You heard me! I called you to come, to bring lights, to help him if help was possible . . .'

'What better way,' Philip demanded bitterly, 'to show as innocent, and bring witnesses running? We were on your heels, you had no time to vanish utterly and leave your dead man lying. This was my man, my officer, I valued him! And I will have his price out of you if there is any justice.'

'I tell you I had but just left the church, and fell over him lying here. I came late, I was just within the door.' He had grasped his dire situation by now, his voice had settled into a strenuous level, reasoning and resolute. 'There must be some here who were beside me in the church, latecomers like me. They can bear out that I have but just come forth into the cloister. De Soulis wears a sword. Am I in arms? Use your eyes! No sword, no dagger, no steel on me! Arms are forbidden to all who attend the offices of the Church. I came to Compline, and I left my sword in my lodging. How can I have killed him?'

'You are lying,' said Philip, on his feet now over the body of his friend. 'I do not believe you ever were in the church. Who speaks up for you? I hear none. While we were within you had time enough, more than enough, to clean your blade and bestow it in your quarters, while you waited for the office to end, to cry out to us and bring us running to discover him in his blood, and you unarmed and crying murder on some unknown enemy. You, the known enemy! Nothing hinders but this can be, must be, *is* your work.'

Cadfael, hemmed in among many bodies pressing close, could not thrust a way through towards king and empress, or make himself heard above the clamour of a dozen voices already disputing across the width of the cloister. He could see between the craning heads Philip's implacable face, sharply lit by the torchlight. Somewhere among the hubbub of partisan excitement and consternation, no doubt, the voices of the bishops were raised imploring reason and silence, but without effect, without even being heard. It took Stephen's imperious bellow to shear through the noise and cut off all other sound.

'Silence! Hush your noise!'

And the silence fell like a stone, crushingly; for one instant all movement froze, and every breath was held. A moment only, then almost stealthily feet shuffled, sleeves brushed, breath was drawn in gustily, and even comment resumed in hushed undertones and hissing whispers, but Stephen had his field, and bestrode it commandingly.

'Now let us have some room for thought before we accuse or exonerate any man. And before all, let someone who knows his business make good sure that the man is out of reach of help, or we are *all* guilty of his death. One lad falling over him in the dark, whether he himself struck the blow or not, can hardly give a physician's verdict. William, do you make sure.'

William Martel, long in experience of death by steel through many campaigns, kneeled beside the body, and turned it by the shoulder to lie flat, exposing to the torch-light the bloody breast, the slit coat, and the narrow, welling wound. He drew wide an eyelid and marked the unmoving stare.

'Dead. Through the heart, surely. Nothing to be done for him.'

'How long?' asked the king shortly.

'No telling. But very recently.'

'During Compline?' The office was not a long one,

though on this fateful evening it had been drawn out some-what beyond its usual time.

'I saw him living,' said Martel, 'only minutes before we went in. I thought he had followed us in. I never marked that he wore steel.'

'So if this young man is shown to have been within throughout the office,' said the king practically, 'he cannot be guilty of this murder. Not fair fight, for de Soulis never had time to draw. Murder.'

A hand reached softly for Cadfael's sleeve. Hugh had been worming his way inconspicuously through the press to reach him. In Cadfael's ear his voice whispered urgently: 'Can you speak for him? *Was* he within? Did you see him?'

'I wish to God I had! He says he came later. I was well forward in the choir. The place was full, the last would be pinned just within the doors.' In corners unlit, and possibly with none or few of their own acquaintance nearby to recognize or speak to them. All too easy not to be noticed, and a convincing reason why Yves should be one of the first to move out into the cloister and clear the way, to stumble over a dead man. The fact that his first cry had been a wordless one of simple alarm when he fell should speak for him. Only a minute later had he cried out the cause.

'No matter, let be!' said Hugh softly. 'Stephen has his finger on the right question. Someone surely will know. And if all else fails, the empress will never let Philip FitzRo-bert lay a finger on any man of hers. Not for the death of a man she loathes! Look at her!'

Cadfael had to crane and shift to do so, for tall though she was, for a woman, she was surrounded by men far taller. But once found, she shone fiercely clear under the torchlight, her handsome face composed and severe, but her large eyes glittering with a suggestion of controlled elation, and the corners of her lips drawn into the austere shadow of an exultant smile. No, she had no reason at all to grieve at the death of the man who had betrayed Faringdon, or to sympathize with the grief and anger of his lord and patron, who had handed over her castle of Cricklade to the enemy. And as Cadfael watched, she turned her head a little, and looked with sharp attention at Yves Hugonin, and the subtle shadows that touched the corners of her lips deepened, and for one instant the smile became apparent. She did not move again, not yet. Let other witnesses do all for her, if that was possible. No need to spend her own efforts until or unless they were needed. She had her half-brother beside her, Roger of Hereford at one shoulder, Hugh Bigod at the other, force enough to prevent any action that might be ventured against any protégé of hers.

'Speak up!' said Stephen, looking round the array of watchful faces, guarded and still now, side-glancing at near neighbours, eyeing the king's roused countenance. 'If any here can say he saw this man within the church throughout Compline, then speak up and declare it, and do him right. He says he came unarmed, in all duty, to the worship of God, and was with us to the end of the office. Who bears him out?'

No one moved, beyond turning to look for reaction from others. No one spoke. There was a silence.

'Your Grace sees,' said Philip at length, breaking the prolonged hush, 'there is no one willing to confirm what he says. And there is no one who believes him.'

'That is no proof that he lies,' said Roger de Clinton. 'Too often truth can bring no witness with it, and find no belief. I do not say he is proven true, but neither is he proven a liar. We have not here the testimony of every man who came to Compline this night. Even if we had, it would not be proof positive that he is lying. But if one man only

77

can come forward and say: I stood by him close to the door until the last prayer was said, and we went out to leave the doorway clear: then truth would be made manifest. Your Grace, we should pursue this further.'

'There is no time,' said the king, frowning. 'Tomorrow we leave Coventry. Why linger? Everything has been said.'

Back to the battlefield, thought Cadfael, despairing for a moment of his own kind, and with their fires refuelled by this pause.

'Within these walls,' said Roger de Clinton, roused, 'I forbid violence even in return for violence, and even outside these walls I charge you forswear all revenges. If there cannot be proper enquiry after justice, then even the guilty among us must go free.'

'They need not,' said Philip grimly. 'I require a blood price for my man. If his Grace wills justice, then let this man be left in fetters here, and let the constables of the city examine him, and hold him for trial. There is the means of justice in the laws of this land, is there not? Then use them! Give him to the law, as surely as death he has broken the law, and owes a death for a death. How can you doubt it? Who else was abroad? Who else had picked so fierce a quarrel with Brien de Soulis, or held so bitter a grudge against him? And we find him standing over the dead man, and barely another soul loose in the night, and you still doubt?'

And indeed it seemed to Cadfael that Philip's bitter conviction was carrying even the king with him. Stephen had no great cause to believe in an unknown youth's protestations of innocence against the odds, a youth devoted to the opposing cause, and suspect of robbing him of a useful fighting man who had recently done such signal service. He hesitated, visibly only too willing to shift the burden to other shoulders, and be off about his martial business again. The very suggestion that he was failing to maintain strict law in his own domain prompted him to commit Yves to the secular authorities, and wash his hands of him.

'I have a thing to say to that,' said the empress deliberately, her voice raised to carry clearly. 'This conference was convened upon the issue of safe conducts on both sides, that we might come together without fear. Whatever may have happened here, it cannot break that compact. I came here with a certain number of people in my following, and I shall go hence tomorrow with that same number, for all were covered by safe conduct, and against none of them has any wrong been proved, neither this young squire nor any other. Touch him, and you touch him unlawfully. Detain him, and you are forsworn and disgraced. We leave tomorrow as many as we came.'

She moved decisively then, brushing aside those who stood between, and held out her hand imperiously to Yves. Her sleeve brushed disdainfully past Philip's braced arm as the white-faced boy obeyed her gesture and turned to go with her wherever she directed. The ranks gave back and opened before her. Cadfael saw her turn to smile upon her escort, and marvelled that the boy's face should gaze back at her so blanched and empty of gratitude, worship or joy.

He came back to their lodging half an hour later. She did not even allow him to walk the short distance between without a guard, for fear Philip or some other aggrieved enemy would attempt revenge while he was here within reach. Though her interest in him, Yves reflected wretchedly, probably would not last long. She would keep him jealously from harm until her whole entourage was safely away on the road back to Gloucester, and then forget him.

It was to herself she owed it to demonstrate her power to hold him immune. The debt she owed, or believed she owed to him was thereby amply repaid. He was not of any permanent importance.

And yet the vital touch of her hand on his, leading him contemptuously out of the circle of his enemies, could not but fire his blood. Even though he felt it freeze again as he reminded himself what she believed of him, what she was valuing in him. Of all those who truly believed he had murdered Brien de Soulis, the Empress Maud was the most convinced. The soft voice he recalled, giving subtle orders by roundabout means, haunted him still. A loyal young man, clay in her hands, blindly devoted like all the rest, and nothing she could not ask of him, however circuitously, and be understood and obeyed. And of course he would deny it, even to her. He knew his duty. The death of de Soulis must not be spoken of, must never be acknowledged in any way.

He was short to question, that night, even by his friends; by his friends most of all. They were none too sure of his safety, either, and stayed close beside him, not letting him out of their sight until he should be embarked in the protective company of all the empress's escort next morning, and bound away for Gloucester.

He put together his few belongings before sleeping. 'I must go,' he said, and added nothing to explain the note of reluctance in his voice. 'And we are no nearer to finding out what they have done with Olivier.'

'With that matter,' said Cadfael, 'I have not finished yet. But for you, best get away from here, and let it lie.'

'And that cloud still over my name?' said Yves bitterly.

'I have not finished with that, either. The truth will be known in the end. Hard to bury truth for ever. Since you certainly did not kill Brien de Soulis, there's somewhere among us a man who did, and whoever uncovers his name removes the shadow from yours. If, indeed, there is anyone who truly believes you guilty.'

'Oh, yes,' said Yves, with a wry and painful smile. 'Yes, there is. One at least!'

But it was the nearest he got to giving that person a name; and Cadfael pressed him no more.

In the morning, group by group, they all departed. Philip FitzRobert was gone, alone as he had come, before ever the bell rang for Prime, making no farewells. King Stephen waited to attend High Mass before gathering all his baronage about him and setting forth briskly for Oxford. Some northern lords left for their own lands to make all secure, before returning their attention to either king or empress. The empress herself mustered for Gloucester in mid-morning, having lingered to be sure her rival was out of the city before her, and not delaying to use even this opportunity for recruiting support behind her back.

Yves had gone alone into the church when the party began to gather, and Cadfael, following at a discreet distance, found him on his knees by a transept altar, shunning notice in his private devotions before departure. It was the stiff unhappiness of the boy's face that caused Cadfael to discard discretion and draw closer. Yves heard him come, and turned on him a brief, pale smile, and hurriedly raised himself. 'I'm ready.'

The hand he leaned upon the prie-dieu wore a ring Cadfael had never seen before. A narrow, twisted gold band, no way spectacular, and so small that it had to be worn on the boy's little finger. The sort of thing a woman might give to a page as reward for some special service. Yves saw how Cadfael's eyes rested upon it, and began an instinctive movement to withdraw it from sight, but then thought better of it, and let it lie. He veiled his eyes, himself staring down at the thin band with a motionless face.

'She gave you this?' Cadfael asked, perceiving that he was permitted, even expected, to question.

Half resigned, half grateful, Yves said simply: 'Yes.' And then added: 'I tried to refuse it.'

'You were not wearing it last night,' said Cadfael.

'No. But now she will expect . . . I am not brave enough,' said Yves ruefully, 'to face her and discard it. Halfway to Gloucester she'll forget all about me, and then I can give it to some shrine – or a beggar along the way.'

'Why so?' said Cadfael, deliberately probing this manifest wound. 'If it was for services rendered?'

Yves turned his head with a sharp motion of pain, and started towards the door. Aside he said, choking on the utterance: 'It was unearned.' And again, more gently: 'I had not earned it.'

They were gone, the last of the glittering courtiers and the steel captains, the kings and the kingmakers, and the two visiting bishops, Nigel of Ely to his own diocese, Henry of Blois with his royal brother to Oxford, before going beyond, to his see of Winchester. Gone with nothing settled, nothing solved, peace as far away as ever. And one dead man lying in a mortuary chapel here until he could be coffined and disposed of wherever his family, if he had family, desired to bury him. In the great court it was even quieter than normally, since the common traffic between town and priory had not yet resumed after the departure of the double court of a still divided land.

'Stay yet a day or two,' Cadfael begged of Hugh. 'Give me so much grace, for if I then return with you I am keeping to terms. God knows I would observe the limits laid on me if I can. Even a day might tell me what I want to know.'

'After king and empress and all their following have denied any knowledge of where Olivier may be?' Hugh pointed out gently.

'Even then. There were some here who did know,' said Cadfael with certainty. 'But, Hugh, there is also this matter of Yves. True, the empress has spread her cloak over him and taken him hence in safety, but is that enough? He'll have no peace until it's known who did the thing he surely did not do. Give me a few more days, and let me at least give some thought to this death. I have asked the brothers here to let me know of anything they may have heard concerning the surrender of Faringdon, give me time at least to be sure the word has gone round, and to get an answer if any man here has an answer to give me.'

'I can stretch my leave by a day or two,' Hugh allowed doubtfully. 'And indeed I'd be loth to go back without you. Let us by all means put the boy's mind at rest if we can, and lay the blame where it belongs. If,' he added with a grimace, 'there should be any great measure of blame for removing de Soulis from the world. No, say nothing! I know! Murder is murder, as much a curse to the slayer as to the slain, and cannot be a matter of indifference, whoever the dead may be. Do you want to look at him again? An accurate stab wound, frontal, no ambush from behind. But it was dark there. A knowledgeable swordsman, if he had been waiting and had his night eyes, would have no difficulty.'

Cadfael considered. 'Yes, let's take another look at the man. And his belongings? Are they still here in the prior's charge? Could we ask, do you think?'

'The bishop might allow it. He's no better pleased at having a murderer active within the pale than you are.'

Brien de Soulis lay on the stone slab in the chapel, covered with a linen sheet, but not yet shrouded, and his coffin still in the hands of the carpenters. It seemed money had been left to provide a noble funeral. Was that Philip's doing?

Cadfael drew down the sheet to uncover the body as far as the wound, a mere thin blue-black slit now, with slightly ribbed edges, a stroke no more than a thumbnail long. The body, otherwise unmarked, was well muscled and comely, the face retained its disdainful good looks, but cold and hard as alabaster.

'It was no sword did that,' said Cadfael positively. 'The flow of blood hid all when he was found. But that was made by a dagger, not even a long one, but long enough. It's not so far into the heart. And fine, very fine. The hilt has not bruised him. It was plunged in and withdrawn quickly, quickly enough for the slayer to draw off clean before ever the bleeding came. No use looking for stained clothing, so fine a slit does not open and gush like a fountain. By the time it was flowing fast the assailant was gone.'

'And never stayed to be sure of his work?' wondered Hugh.

'He was sure of it. Very cool, very resolute, very competent.' Cadfael drew up the sheet again over the stone-still face. 'Nothing more here. Shall we consider once again the place where this happened?'

They passed through the south door, and emerged into the north walk of the cloister. Outside the third carrel the body had lain, its toes just trailing across the threshold. There was a faint pink stain, a hand's length, still visible, where his blood had seeped down under his right side and fouled the flags. Someone had been diligent in cleaning it away, but the shape still showed. 'Yes, here,' said Hugh. 'The stones will show no marks, even if there was a struggle, but I fancy there was none. He was taken utterly by surprise.'

They sat down together there in the carrel to consider the alignment of this scene.

'He was struck from before,' said Cadfael, 'and as the dagger was dragged out he fell forward with it, out of the carrel into the walk. Surely he was the one waiting here within. For someone. He wore sword and dagger himself, so he was not bound for Compline. If he designed to meet someone here in private, it was surely someone he trusted, someone never questioned, or how did he approach so close? Had it been Yves – as we know it was not – de Soulis would have had the sword out of the scabbard before ever the boy got within reach. The open hostility between those two was not the whole story. There must have been fifty souls within these walls who hated the man for what he did at Faringdon. Some who were there, and escaped in time, many others of the empress's following who were not there, but hold the treason bitterly against him no less. He would be wary of any man fronting him whom he did not know well, and trust, men of his own faction and his own mind.'

'And this one he mistook fatally,' said Hugh.

'How should treason be prepared for counter-treason? He turned in the empress's hand, now one of his own has turned in his. And he as wholly deceived as she was in him. So it goes.'

'I take it,' said Hugh, eyeing his friend very gravely, 'that we can and do accept all that Yves says as truth? I do so willingly only from knowledge of him. But should we not consider how the thing must have looked to others who do not know him?'

'So we may,' said Cadfael sturdily, 'and still be certain. True, no one has owned to seeing him among the last who came into the church, but that is well possible. He says he came late and spoke to no one, because the office had already begun. He was in a dark corner just within the door, and hence among the first out, to clear the way at the end. We heard him cry out, the first simply a gasp of surprise as he stumbled, then the alarm. Now if he had indeed avoided Compline, and had time to act at leisure while almost all were within, why cry out at all? Out of cunning, as Philip charged, to win the appearance of innocence? Yves is clever, but certainly has no cunning at all. And if he had the whole cloister at his back, he had time enough to slip away and leave others to find his dead man. He bore no arms, his sword was found, as he said, clean and sheathed in his quarters, and showed no sign of having been blooded. He had had, said Philip, the whole time of Compline to blood it, clean it and restore it to his lodging. But I saw the blade, and I could find no sign of blood. No, if he had had all the time of Compline at his disposal, he would never have sounded the alarm himself, but taken good care to be elsewhere when the dead man was found, and among witnesses, well away from the first outcry.'

'And if he had come forth from the church as he says, then he had no time to encounter and kill, and no sword or dagger on him.'

'Manifestly. And I think you know, as I know, that the death came earlier, though how much earlier it's hard to tell. He had had time to bleed, you still see there the extent of the pool that gathered under him. No, you need not have any doubts. What you know of our lad you know rightly.'

'And of the rest of this great household,' said Hugh reflectively, 'most were in the church. It need not be all, however. And as you say, he had enemies here, one at least more discreet than Yves, and more deadly.'

'And one,' Cadfael elaborated sombrely, 'of whom he was no way wary. One who could approach him closely and rouse no suspicion, one he was waiting for, for surely he was standing here, in this carrel, and stepped forth willingly when the other came, and was spitted on the very threshold.'

Hugh retraced in silence the angle of that fall, the way the body had lain, the ominous rim of the bloodstain, and could find no flaw in this account of that encounter. In their well-meant efforts to bring together in reconciliation all the power and force and passion of both sides in the contention, the bishops had succeeded also in bringing within these walls a great cauldron of hatred and malice, and infinite possibilities of further treachery.

'More intrigue, more plotting for advantage,' said Hugh resignedly. 'If two were meeting here in secret while the baronage was at worship, then it was surely for mischief. What more can we do here? Did you say you wanted to see what belongings de Soulis left behind him? Come, we'll have a word with the bishop.'

'The man's possessions,' said the bishop, 'such as he had here with him, are here in my charge, and I await word from his brother in Worcester as to future arrangements for his burial. I have no doubt the brother will be responsible for that. But if you think that examination of his effects can give us any indication as to how he died, yes, certainly we should at least put it to the test. We may not neglect any means of finding out the truth. You are fully convinced,' he added anxiously, 'that the young man who called us to the body bears no guilt for the death?'

'My lord,' said Hugh, 'from all I know of him, he is as

poor a hand at deceit or stealth as ever breathed. You saw him yourself on the day we entered here, how he sprang out of the saddle and made straight for his foe, brow to brow. That is more his way of going about it. Nor had he any weapon about him. You cannot know him as we do, but for my part and Brother Cadfael's, we are sure of him.'

'In any case,' agreed the bishop heavily, 'it can do no harm to see if there is anything, letter or sign of any kind, in the dead man's baggage that may shed light on his movements intended on leaving here, or any undertaking he had in hand. Very well! The saddle-bags are here in the vestment room.'

There was a horse in the stables, too, a good horse waiting to be delivered, like all the rest, to the younger de Soulis in Worcester. The bishop unbuckled the straps of the first bag with his own hands, and hoisted it to a bench. 'One of the brothers packed them and brought them here from the guesthall where he lodged. You may view them.' He stayed to observe, in duty bound, being now responsible for all that was done with these relics.

Spread out upon the bench before their eyes, handled scrupulously as another man's property, Brien de Soulis's equipment showed Spartan and orderly. Changes of shirt and hose, the compact means of a gentleman's toilet, a well-furnished purse. Plainly he travelled light, and was a man of neat habit. A leather pouch in the second saddle-bag yielded a compartmented box with flint and tinder, wax and a seal. A man of property, travelling far, would certainly not be without his personal seal. Hugh held it on his palm for the bishop's inspection. The device, sharply cut, was a swan with arched neck, facing left, and framed between two wands of willow.

'That is his,' Hugh confirmed. 'We saw it on the buckle of his sword-belt when we carried in the body. But embossed and facing the other way, of course. And that is all.'

'No,' said Cadfael, his hand groping along the seams of the empty bag. 'Some other small thing is here at the bottom.' He drew it out and held it up to the light. 'Also a seal! Now what would a man want with carrying two on a journey?'

What indeed? For to risk carrying both, if two had actually been made, was to risk theft or loss of one, with all the dire possibilities of having it fall into the hands of an enemy or a sharper, and being misused in many and profitable ways, to its owner's loss.

'It is not the same,' said Hugh sharply, and carried it to the window to examine it more carefully. 'A lizard – like a little dragon – no, a salamander, for he's in a nest of little pointed flames. No border but a single line at the rim. Engraved deep – little used. I have never seen this. Do you know it, my lord?'

The bishop studied it, and shook his head. 'No, strange to me. For what purpose could one man be carrying another man's personal seal? Unless it had been confided to him as the owner's proxy, for attachment to some document in absence?'

'Certainly not here,' said Hugh wryly, 'for here there have been no documents to seal, no agreement on any matter, the worse for us all. Cadfael, do you see any significance in this?'

'Of all his possessions,' said Cadfael, 'a man would be least likely to be parted from his seal. The thing carries his sanction, his honour, his reputation with it. If he did trust it to a known friend, it would be kept very securely, not dropped into the corner of a saddle-bag, thus disregarded. Yes, Hugh, I should very much like to know whose device this is, and how it came into de Soulis's possession. His recent history has not shown him as a man to be greatly trusted by his acquaintances, or lightly made proxy for another man's honour.'

He hesitated, turning the small artifact in his fingers. A circlet measuring as far across as the length of his first thumb joint, its handle of a dark wood polished high, fitting smoothly in the palm. The engraving was skilled and precise, the little conventional flames sharply incised. The head with its open mouth and darting tongue faced left. The positive would face right. Mirror images, the secret faces of real beings, hold terrifying significances. It seemed to Cadfael that the sharp ascending flames of the salamander's cradling fire were searing the fingers that touched them, and crying out for recognition and understanding.

'My lord bishop,' he said slowly, 'may I, on my oath to return it to you unless I find its true owner, borrow this seal? In my deepest conscience I feel the need of it. Or, if that is not permitted, may I make a drawing of it, in every detail, for credentials in its place?'

The bishop gave him a long, penetrating look, and then said with deliberation: 'At least in taking the copy there can be no harm. But you will have small opportunity of enquiring further into either this death, or the whereabouts of the prisoners you are seeking, if, as I suppose, you are going home to Shrewsbury now the conference is over.'

'I am not sure, my lord,' said Cadfael, 'that I shall be going home.'

Chapter Six

OU KNOW, do you not,' said Hugh very gravely, as they came from one more Compline together in the dusk, 'that if you go further, I cannot go with you. I have work of my own to do. If I turn my back upon Madog ap Meredudd many more days he'll be casting covetous eyes at Oswestry again. He's never stopped hankering after it. God knows I'd be loth to go back without you. And you know, none better, you'll be tearing your own life up by the roots if you fail to keep your time.'

'And if I fail to find my son,' said Cadfael, gently and reasonably, 'my life is nothing worth. No, never fret for me, Hugh, one alone on this labour can do as much as a company of armed men, and perhaps more. I have failed already to find any trace here, what remains but to go where he served, where he was betrayed and made prisoner? There someone must know what became of him. In Faringdon there will be echoes, footprints, threads to follow, and I will find them.'

He made his drawings with care, on a leaf of vellum from the scriptorium, one to size, with careful precision, one enlarged to show every detail of the salamander seal. There was no motto nor legend, only the slender lizard in its fiery nest. Surely that, too, harked back in some way to the surrender of Faringdon, and had somewhat to say concerning the death of Brien de Soulis, if only its language could be interpreted.

Hugh cast about, without overmuch comfort, for something to contribute to these vexed puzzles that drove his friend into unwilling exile, but there was little of help to be found. He did venture, for want of better: 'Have you thought, Cadfael, that of all those who may well have hated de Soulis, there's none with better reason than the empress? How if she prompted some besotted young man to do away with him? She has a string of raw admirers at her disposal. It could be so.'

'To the best of my supposing,' said Cadfael soberly, 'it was so. Do you remember she sent for Yves that first evening, after she had seen the lad show his paces against de Soulis? I fancy she had accepted the omen, and found him a work he could do for her, a trace more privately, perhaps, than at his first attempt.'

'No!' gasped Hugh, stricken, and halted in mid-stride. 'Are you telling me that *Yves* . . .'

'No, no such matter!' Cadfael assured him chidingly. 'Oh, he took her meaning, or I fear he did, though he surely damned himself for ever believing it was meant so. He did not *do* it, of course not! Even she might have had the wit to refrain, with such an innocent. But stupid he is not! He understood her!'

'Then may she not have singled out a second choice for the work?' suggested Hugh, brightening.

'No, you may forget that possibility. For she is convinced

that Yves took the nudge, and rid her of her enemy. No, there's no solution there.'

'How so?' demanded Hugh, pricked. 'How can you know so much?'

'Because she rewarded him with a gold ring. No great prize, but an acknowledgement. He tried to refuse it, but he was not brave enough, small blame to the poor lad. Oh, nothing was ever openly said, and of course he would deny it, she would avoid even having to make him say as much. The child is out of his depth with such women. He's bent on getting rid of her gift as soon as he safely may. Her gratitude is short, that he knows. But no, she never hired another murderer, she is certain she needed none.'

'That can hardly have added to his happiness,' said Hugh with a sour grimace. 'And no help to us in lifting the weight from him, either.'

They had reached the door of their lodging. Overhead the sky was clear and cold, the stars legion but infinitesimal in the early dark. The last night here, for Hugh had duties at home that could not be shelved.

'Cadfael, think well what you are doing. I know what you stake, as well as you know it. This is not simple going and returning. Where you will be meddling a man can vanish, and not return ever. Come back with me, and I will ask Robert Bossu to follow this quest to its ending.'

'There's no time,' said Cadfael. 'I have it in my mind, Hugh, that there are more souls than one, and more lives than my son's, to be salvaged here, and the time is very short, and the danger very close. And if I turn back now there will be no one to be the pivot at the centre, on whom the wheel of all those fortunes turns, the demon or the angel. But yes, I'll think well before you leave me. We shall see what the morning will bring.'

What the morning brought, just as the household emerged from Mass, was a dust-stained rider on a lathered horse, cantering wearily in from the street and sliding stiffly and untidily to a clattering stop on the cobbles of the court. The horse stood with drooping head and heaving sides, steaming into the air sharpened with frost, and dripping foam between rolled-back lips into the stones. The rider doubled cramped fists on the pommel, and half clambered, half fell out of the saddle to stiffen collapsing knees and hold himself upright by his mount.

'My lord bishop, pardon . . .' He could not release his hold to make due reverence, but clung to his prop, bending his head as deep and respectfully as he might. 'My mistress sends me to bring you word – the empress – she is safe in Gloucester with all her company, all but one. My lord, there was foul work along the road . . .'

'Take breath, even evil news can wait,' said Roger de Clinton, and waved an order at whoever chose to obey it. 'Bring drink – have wine mulled for him, but bring a draught now. And some of you, help him within, and see to his poor beast, before he founders.'

There was a hand at the dangling bridle in an instant. Someone ran for wine. The bishop himself lent a solid shoulder under the messenger's right arm, and braced him erect. 'Come, let's have you within, and at rest.'

In the nearest carrel of the cloister the courier leaned back against the wall and drew in breath long and gratefully. Hugh, lissome and young, and mindful of some long, hard rides of his own after Lincoln, dropped to his knees and braced experienced hands to ease off the heavy riding boots.

'My lord, we had remounts at Evesham, and made good

time until fairly close to Gloucester, riding well into the dusk to be there by nightfall. Near Deerhurst, in woodland, with the length of our company past – for I was with the rearguard – an armed band rode out at our tail, and cut out one man from among us before ever we were aware, and off with him at speed into the dark.'

'What man was that?' demanded Cadfael, stiffening. 'Name him!'

'One of her squires, Yves Hugonin. He that had hard words with de Soulis, who is dead. My lord, there's nothing surer than some of FitzRobert's men have seized him, for suspicion of killing de Soulis. They hold him guilty, for all the empress would have him away untouched.'

'And you did not pursue?' asked the bishop, frowning.

'Some little way we did, but they were fresh, and in forest they knew well. We saw no more of them. And when we sent ahead to let our lady know, she would have one of us ride back to bring you word. We were under safe conduct, this was foul work, after such a meeting.'

'We'll send to the king,' said the bishop firmly. 'He will order this man's release as he did before when FitzRobert seized the Earl of Cornwall. He obeyed then, he will obey again, whatever his own grudge.'

But would he, Cadfael wondered? Would Stephen lift a finger in this case, for a man as to whose guilt he had said neither yea nor nay, but only allowed him to leave under safe conduct at the empress's insistence. No valuable ally, but an untried boy of the opposing side. No, Yves would be left for the empress to retrieve. He had left here under her wing, it was for her to protect him. And how far would she go on Yves' behalf? Not so far as to inconvenience herself by the loss of time or advantage. His supposed infamous service to her had been acknowledged and rewarded, she owed him nothing. And he had withdrawn deliberately to the tail end of her cortège, to be out of sight and out of mind.

'I think they had a rider alongside us for some way, in cover,' said the courier, 'making sure of their man, before they struck. It was all over in a moment, at a bend in the path where the trees grow close.'

'And close to Deerhurst?' said Cadfael. 'Is that already in FitzRobert's own country? How close are his castles? He left here early, in time to have his ambush ready. He had this in mind from the first, if he was thwarted here.'

'It might be twenty miles or so to Cricklade, more to Faringdon. But closer still there's his new castle at Green-hamsted, the one he took from Robert Musard a few weeks back. Not ten miles from Gloucester.'

'You are sure,' said Hugh, a little hesitantly and with an anxious eye on Cadfael, 'that they did carry him off prisoner?'

'No question,' said the messenger with weary bluntness, 'they wanted him whole, it was done very briskly. No, they're more wary what blood they spill, these days. Men on one side have kin on the other who could still take offence and make trouble. No, be easy for that, there was no killing.'

The courier was gone into the prior's lodging to eat and rest, the bishop to his own palace to prepare letters to carry the news, notably to Oxford and Malmesbury, in the region where this raid had taken place. Whether Stephen would bestir himself to intervene in this case was doubtful, but someone would surely pass the news on to the boy's uncle in Devizes, who carried some weight with the empress. At least everything must be tried.

'Now,' said Cadfael, left contemplating Hugh's bleak and frustrated face through a long silence, 'I have two hostages to buy back. If I asked for a sign, I have it. And now there is no doubt in my mind what I must do.'

'And I cannot come with you,' said Hugh.

'You have a shire to keep. Enough for one of us to break faith. But may I keep your good horse, Hugh?'

'If you'll pledge me to bring him safely back, and yourself in the saddle,' said Hugh.

They said their farewells just within the priory gate, Hugh to return north-west along the same roads by which they had come, with his three men-at-arms at his back, Cadfael bearing south. They embraced briefly before mounting, but when they issued from the gate into the street, and separated, they went briskly, and did not look back. With every yard the fine thread that held them together stretched and thinned, attenuated to breaking point, became a fibre, a hair, a cobweb filament, but did not break.

For the first stages of that journey Cadfael rode steadily, hardly aware of his surroundings, fully absorbed in the effort to come to terms with the breaking of another cord, which had parted as soon as he turned south instead of towards home. It was like the breaking of a tight constriction which had bound his life safely within him, though at the cost of pain; and the abrupt removal of the restriction was mingled relief and terror, both intense. The ease of being loose in the world came first, and only gradually did the horror of the release enter and overwhelm him. For he was recreant, he had exiled himself, knowing well what he was doing. And now his only justification must be the redemption of both Yves and Olivier. If he failed in that he had squandered even his apostasy. Your own man, Radulfus had said, no longer any man of mine. Vows abandoned, brothers forsaken, heaven discarded.

The first need was to recognize that it had happened,

the second to accept it. After that he could ride on composedly, and be his own man, as for the former half of his life he had been, and only rarely felt a need beyond, until he found community and completion in surrendering himself. Life could and must be lived on those same terms for this while, perhaps for all the while remaining.

So by that time he could look about him again, pay attention to the way, and turn his mind to the task that lay before him.

Close to Deerhurst they had closed in and cut out Yves from his fellows. And strictly speaking, there was no proof as to who had so abducted him; but Philip FitzRobert, who alone was known to bear a great grudge against the boy, and who was patently a man bent on revenge, had three castles and a strong following in those parts, and could venture such a raid with impunity, secure of his power. Then they would not risk being abroad with their captive, even by night, longer than they must, but have him away into hold in one of the castles, out of sight and out of mind, as quickly and privately as possible. Greenhamsted, said the empress's courier, was the nearest. Cadfael did not know the region well, but he had questioned the messenger concerning the lie of the land. Deerhurst, a few miles north of Gloucester, Greenhamsted about as far to the southeast. La Musarderie, the courier had called the castle, after the family that had held it since Domesday. At Deerhurst there was an alien priory belonging to St Denis in Paris, and if he lodged there overnight he might be able to elicit some local information. Country people keep a sharp eye on the devious doings of their local lords, especially in time of civil war. For their own preservation they must.

By all accounts there had been a castle there at La Musarderie ever since King William gave the village to Hascoit Musard some time before the Domesday survey was taken. That argued enough time to have built in stone, after the first hurried timber erection to secure a foothold. Faringdon had been thrown up in a few weeks of the summer, and laid under siege almost before it was finished. Earthwork and wood, no other possibility in the time, though evidently care had been taken to make it as strong as possible. And Cricklade, whatever its defensive state might be, was not as close as Greenhamsted to the spot where Yves had been abducted. Well, he could see if anyone at Deerhurst could enlighten him on any of these matters.

He rode steadily, intending to ride late and be well on his way before night. He took no food, and said the office at tierce and sext in the saddle. Once he fell in with a mounted merchant and his packman on the way, and they rode together some miles, to a flow of talk that went in at Cadfael's left ear and out at the right, punctuated by his amicable but random murmurs of acknowledgement, while all the while his mind was on those as yet unknown fields of enterprise that awaited him in the valley of the Thames, where the lines of battle were drawn. At the approach to Stratford the merchant and his man turned off to make for the town, and Cadfael rode on alone once again, exchanging preoccupied greetings here and there with other travellers on a well-used and relatively safe highway.

In the dusk he came to Evesham, and it fell upon him suddenly with chilling shock that he had been taking for granted his welcome as a brother of the Order, he who now had no right to any privilege here, he who had with deliberation broken his vow of obedience, knowing well what he did. Recreant and self-exiled, he had no right even to the habit he wore, except of charity to cover his nakedness.

He bespoke for himself a pallet in the common hall, on the plea that his journey was penitential, and he was not deserving of entering among the choir monks until it was fully accomplished, which was as near to the truth as he cared to come. The hospitaller, gravely courteous, would not press him beyond what he cared to confide, but let him have his way, offered a confessor should he be in need, and left him to lead his horse to the stables and tend him before taking his own rest. At Vespers and at Compline Cadfael chose for himself an obscure corner of the nave, but one from which he could see the high altar. He was not excommunicate, except by his own judgement. Not yet.

But all through the office he felt within himself an impossible paradox, a void that weighed heavier than stone.

He came through the woodlands flanking the vale of Gloucester during the next afternoon. All these midland shires of England seemed to him richly treed and full of game, one great, lavish hunting chase. And in these particular glades Philip FitzRobert had hunted a man. One more desperate loss to that gallant girl now solitary in Gloucester, and with child.

He had left Tewkesbury aside on his right hand, following the most direct road for Gloucester, as the empress and her train would have done. The forest stretches were on good, broad rides that narrowed only in a few short stretches, making use of level ground. At a bend in the path where the trees grew close, the messenger had said. Nearing her journey's end, the empress would have quickened her pace to be in before dark, and they had taken fresh horses at Evesham. The rearguard had straggled somewhat; easy enough to close in from both sides and cut out a single man. Somewhere here, and two nights past now, and even the traces left by several riders in haste would be fading.

The thicker woodland opened out on the southern side

100

of the track, letting light through the trees to enrich the grasses and wild ground plants below, and someone had chosen this favourable spot to cut out an assart for himself. The hut lay some yards aside, among the trees, with a low wooden fence round it, and a byre beyond. Cadfael heard a cow lowing, very contentedly, and marked how a small space to one side had been cleared of what larger timber it had carried, to allow of modest coppicing. The man of the house was digging within his enclosure, and straightened his back to stare alertly when he heard the soft thudding of hooves along the ride. Beholding a Benedictine brother, he perceptibly relaxed his braced shoulders, slackened his grip on the spade, and called a greeting across the dozen yards or so between.

'Good day to you, brother!'

'God bless the work!' said Cadfael, and checked his horse, turning in between the trees to draw nearer. The man put down his spade and dusted his hands, willing to interrupt his labours for a gossip with a harmless passerby. A square, compact fellow with a creased brown face like a walnut, and sharp blue eyes, well established in his woodland holding, and apparently solitary, for there was no sound or sign of any other creature about the garden or within the hut. 'A right hermitage you have here,' said Cadfael. 'Do you not want for company sometimes?'

'Oh, I've a mind for quietness. And if I tire of it, I have a son married and settled in Hardwicke, barely a mile off, that way, and the children come round on holy days. I get my times for company, but I like the forest life. Whither bound, brother? You'll be in the dusk soon.'

'I'll bide the night over at Deerhurst,' said Cadfael placidly. 'So you never have troubles yourself, friend, with wild men also liking the forest life, but for no good reasons like yours?'

'I'm a man of my hands,' said the cottar confidently. 'And it's not modest prey like me the outlaws are after. Richer pickings ride along here often enough. Not that we see much trouble of that kind. Cover here is good, but narrow. There are better hunting-grounds.'

'That depends on the quarry,' said Cadfael, and studied him consideringly. 'Two nights back, I think you had a great company through here, on their way to Gloucester. About this time of day, perhaps an hour further into the dark. Did you hear them pass?'

The man had stiffened, and stood regarding Cadfael with narrowed thoughtful eyes, already wary but not, Cadfael thought, of either this enquiry or the enquirer.

'I saw them pass,' he said evenly. 'Such a stir a wise man does not miss. I did not know then who came. I know now. The empress, she that was all but queen, she came with her men from the bishops' court at Coventry, back into Gloucester. Nothing good ever comes to men like me from her skirts brushing by, nor from the edge of King Stephen's mantle, either. We watch them go by, and thank God when they're gone.'

'And did they go by in peace?' asked Cadfael. 'Or were there others abroad, lying in ambush for them? Was there fighting? Or any manner of alarm that night?'

'Brother,' said the man slowly, 'what's your interest in these matters? I stay within doors when armed men pass by, and let alone all who let me alone. Yes, there was some sort of outcry – not here, a piece back along the way, heard, not seen. Shouting, and sudden crashing about among the trees, but all was over in minutes. And then one man came riding at a gallop after the company, crying news, and later another set off back along the route in haste. Brother, if you know more of all this than I do who heard it, why question me?'

'And next morning, by daylight,' said Cadfael, 'did you go to view that place where the attack was made? And what signs did you find there? How many men, would you judge? And which way did they go, afterwards?'

'They had been waiting in hiding,' said the man, 'very patiently, most on the southern side of the track, but a few to the north. Their horses had trampled the sward among the trees. I would say at least a dozen in all. And when it was done, whatever was done, they massed and rode at speed, southward. There is a path there. Bushes broken and torn as they crashed through.'

'Due south?' said Cadfael.

'And in a hurry. Men who knew their way well enough to hurry, even in the dark. And now that I've told you what I heard and saw – and but for your cloth I would have kept my mouth shut – do you tell me what business you have with such night surprises.'

'To the best of my understanding,' said Cadfael, consenting to a curiosity as practical and urgent as his own, 'those who struck at the empress's rearguard and rode away in haste southward have seized and taken with them into captivity a young man of my close acquaintance, who has done nothing wrong but for incurring the hatred of Philip FitzRobert. And my business is to find where they have taken him, and win him free.'

'Gloucester's son, is it? In these parts it's he calls the tune, true enough, and has boltholes everywhere. But, brother,' urged the cottar, appalled, 'you'd as well beard the devil himself as walk into La Musarderie and confront Philip FitzRobert.'

'La Musarderie? Is that where he is?' echoed Cadfael.

'So they're saying. And has a hostage or two in there already, and if there's one more since that tussle here, you have as much chance of winning him free as of being taken

103

up to heaven living. Think twice and again before you venture.'

'Friend, I will. And do you live safe here from all armed men, and say a prayer now and then for all prisoners and captives, and you'll be doing your share.'

Here among the trees the light was perceptibly fading. He had best be moving on to Deerhurst. At least he had gleaned a crumb of evidence to help him on his way. A hostage or two in there already. And Philip himself installed there. And where he was, surely he would bring with him his perverse treasure of bitterness and hatred, and hoard up his revenges.

Cadfael was about to turn his horse to the track once more, when he thought of one more thing he most needed to know, and brought out the rolled leaf of vellum from the breast of his habit, and spread it open on his thigh to show the drawings of the salamander seal.

'Have you ever seen this badge, on pennant, or harness, or seal? I am trying to find its owner.'

The man viewed it attentively, but shook his head. 'I know nothing of these badges and devices of the gentles, barring the few close hereabouts. No, I never saw it. But if you're bound for Deerhurst, there's a brother of the house studies such things, and prides himself on knowing the devices of every earl and baron in the land. He can surely give this one a name.'

He emerged from the dusk of the woodland into the full daylight of the wide water-meadows flanking that same Severn he had left behind at Shrewsbury, but here twice the width and flowing with a heavy dark power. And there gleaming through trees no great way inland from the water was the creamy silver stone of the church tower, solid Saxon work, squat and strong as a castle keep. As he approached, the long line of the nave roof came into view, and an apse at the east end, with a semicircular base and a faceted upper part. An old, old house, centuries old, and refounded and endowed by the Confessor, and bestowed by him upon Saint Denis. The Confessor was always more Norman in his sympathies than English.

Once again Cadfael found himself approaching almost with reluctance the Benedictine ambience that had been home to him for so many years, and feeling that he came unworthily and without rights. But here his conscience must endure its own deception if he was to enquire freely after the knowledge he needed. When all was done, if he survived the doing, he would make amends.

The porter who admitted him into the court was a round and amiable soul in his healthy middle years, proud of his house, and happy to show off the beauties of his church. There was work going on south of the choir, a masons' lodge shelved out against the wall of the apse, and ashlar stacked for building. Two masons and their labourers were just covering the banker and laying by their tools as the light faded. The porter indicated fondly the foundations of walls outlining the additions to be made to the fabric.

'Here we are building another south-east chapel, and the like to balance it on the northern side. Our master mason is a local man, and the works of the Church are his pride. A good man! He gives work to some unfortunates other masters might find unprofitable. You see the labourer who goes lame of one leg there, from an injury. A man-at-arms until recently, but useless to his lord now, and Master Bernard took him on, and has had no cause to regret it, for the man works hard and well.'

The labourer, who went heavily on the left leg, surely after some very ill-knit fracture, was otherwise a fine, sturdy fellow, and very agile for all his disability. Probably about thirty years old, with large, able hands, and a long reach. He stood back civilly to give them passage, and then completed the covering of the stacked timber under the wall, and followed the master-mason towards the outer gate.

As yet there had been nothing harder than mild ground frosts, or building would have ceased already for the winter, and the growing walls been bedded down in turf and heather and straw to sleep until spring.

'There'll be work within for them when the winter closes in,' said the porter. 'Come and see.'

Within Deerhurst's priory church there was as yet no mark of the Norman style, all was Saxon, and the first walls of the nave centuries old. Not until the porter had shown forth all the curiosities and beauties of his church to the visitor did he hand Cadfael over to the hospitaller, to be furnished with a bed, and welcomed into the community at supper in the frater.

Before Compline he asked after the learned brother who was knowledgeable about the devices and liveries of the noble houses of England, and showed the drawings he had made in Coventry. Brother Eadwin studied them and shook his head. 'No, this I have not seen. There are among the baronage some families who use several personal variations among their many members and branches. This is certainly none of the most prominent. I have never seen it before.'

Neither, it seemed, had the prior, or any of the brethren. They studied the drawings, but could not give the badge a family name or a location.

'If it belongs in these parts,' said Brother Eadwin, willing to be helpful, 'you may find an answer in the village rather than within here. There are some good but minor families holding manors in this shire, besides those of high rank. How did it come into your hands, brother?'

'It was in the baggage of a dead man,' said Cadfael, 'but

106

not his. And the original is in the hands of the bishop of Coventry now, until we can discover its owner and restore it.' He rolled up the leaf of vellum, and retied the cord that bound it. 'No matter. The lord bishop will pursue it.'

He went to Compline with the brothers, preoccupied rather with the pain and guilt of his own self-exile from this monastic world than with the responsibility he had voluntarily taken upon himself in the secular world. The office comforted him, and the silence afterwards came gratefully. He put away all thought until the morrow, and rested in the quietness until he fell asleep.

Nevertheless, after Mass next morning, when the builders had again uncovered their stores to make use of one more working day, he remembered the porter's description of Master Bernard as a local man, and thought it worth the trial to unroll his drawings upon the stacked ashlar and call the mason to study them and give judgement. Masons may be called upon to work upon manors and barns and farmsteads as well as churches, and use brands and signs in their own mysteries, and so may well respect and take note of them elsewhere.

The mason came, gazed briefly, and said at once: 'No, I do not know it.' He studied it with detached interest, but shook his head decidedly. 'No, this I've never seen.'

Two of his workmen, bearing a laden hand-barrow, had checked for a moment in passing to peer in natural curiosity at the leaf which was engaging their master's interest. The lame man, braced on his good right leg, looked up from the vellum to Cadfael's face for a long moment, before they moved on, and smiled and shrugged when Cadfael returned the glance directly.

'No local house, then,' said Cadfael resignedly.

'None that's known to me, and I've done work for most

manors round here.' The mason shook his head again, as Cadfael re-rolled the leaf and put it back securely within his habit. 'Is it of importance?'

'It may be. Somewhere it will be known.'

It seemed he had done all that could be done here. What his next move should be he had not considered yet, let alone decided. By all the signs Philip must be in La Musarderie, where most probably his men had taken Yves into captivity, and where, according to the woodsman, he already had another hostage, or more than one, in hold. Even more convincing it seemed to Cadfael, was the argument that a man of such powerful passions would be where his hatreds anchored him. Beyond doubt Philip believed Yves guilty. Therefore if he could be convinced he was wronging the boy, his intent could and would be changed. He was an intelligent man, not beyond reason.

Cadfael took his problem with him into the church at the hour of tierce, and said the office privately in a quiet corner. He was just opening his eyes and turning to withdraw when a hand was laid softly on his sleeve from behind.

'Brother . . .'

The lame man, for all his ungainliness, could move silently in his scuffed felt shoes on the floor tiles. His weathered face, under a thatch of thick brown hair, was intent and sombre. 'Brother, you are seeking the man who uses a certain seal to his dealings. I saw your picture.' He had a low, constrained voice, well suited to confidences.

'I was so seeking,' agreed Cadfael ruefully, 'but it seems no one here can help me. Your master does not recognize it as belonging to any man he knows.'

'No,' said the lame man simply. '*But I do.*'

Chapter Seven

ADFAEL HAD opened his mouth to question eagerly, seizing upon this unforeseen chance, but he recalled that the man was at work, and already dependent on his master's goodwill, and lucky to have found such a patron. 'You'll be missed,' he said quickly. 'I can't bring you into reproof. When are you free?'

'At sext we rest and eat our bit of dinner. Long enough,' said the lame man, and briefly smiled. 'I feared you might be for leaving before I could tell you what I know.'

'I would not stir,' said Cadfael fervently. 'Where? Here? You name the place, I'll be waiting.'

'The last carrel of the walk, next to where we're building.' With the stacked ashlar and all the timber at their backs, Cadfael reflected, and a clear view of anyone who should appear in the cloister. This one, whatever the reason, natural suspicion or well-grounded caution, kept a close watch on his back, and a lock on his tongue.

'No word to any other?' said Cadfael, holding the level grey eyes that met him fairly.

'In these parts too much has happened to make a man loose-mouthed. A word in the wrong ear may be a knife in the wrong back. No offence to your habit, brother. Praise God, there are still good men.' And he turned, and went limping back to the outer world and his labours on God's work.

In the comparative warmth of noon they sat together in the end carrel of the north walk of the cloister, where they could see down the full length of the walk across the garth. The grass was dry and bleached after an almost rainless autumn, but the sky was overcast and heavy with the fore-showing of change.

'My name,' said the lame man, 'is Forthred. I come from Todenham, which is an outlier of this manor of Deerhurst. I took service for the empress under Brien de Soulis, and I was in Faringdon with his force, the few weeks the castle stood for the cause. It's there I've seen the seal you have there in the drawings. Twice I've seen it set to documents he witnessed. No mistaking it. The third time I saw it was on the agreement they drew up and sealed when they handed over Faringdon to the king.'

'It was done so solemnly?' said Cadfael, surprised. 'I thought they simply let in the besiegers by night.'

'So they did, but they had their agreement ready to show to us, the men of the garrison, proving that all six captains with followings among us had accepted the change, and committed us with them. I doubt they would have carried the day but for that. A nay word from one or two of the best, and their men would have fought, and King Stephen would have paid a stiff price for Faringdon. No, it was planned and connived at beforehand.'

'Six captains with their own companies,' said Cadfael, brooding, 'and all under de Soulis's command?'

'So it was. And some thirty or so new knights or squires without personal following, only their own arms.'

'Of those we know. Most refused to turn their coats, and are prisoners now among the king's men. But all these six who had companies of their own men were agreed, and set their seals to the surrender?'

'Every one. It would not have been done so easily else. Fealty among the common soldiery is to their own leaders. They go where their captains go. One seal missing from that vellum, and there would have been trouble. One in particular, and there would have been a battle. One who carried the most weight with us, and was the best liked and trusted.'

There was something in his voice as he spoke of this man, elect and valued, that conveyed much more than had been said. Cadfael touched the rolled leaf of vellum.

'This one?'

'The same,' said Forthred, and for a moment volunteered nothing more, but sat mute, gazing along the grass of the garth with eyes that looked inward rather than outward.

'And he, like the rest, set his seal to the surrender?'

'His seal – this seal – was certainly there to be seen. With my own eyes I saw it. I would not have believed it else.'

'And his name?'

'His name is Geoffrey FitzClare, and the Clare whose son he is is Richard de Clare, who was earl of Hertford, and the present earl, Gilbert, is his half-brother. A by-blow of the house of Clare. Sometimes these sons come by astray are better than the true coin. Though Gilbert, for all I know, is a good man, too. At least he and his half-brother have always respected and liked each other, seemingly,

111

although all the Clares are absolute for Stephen, and this chance brother chose the empress. They were raised together, for Earl Richard brought his bastard home almost newborn, and the grandam took him in care, and they did well by him, and set him up in life when he was grown. That is the man whose seal you're carrying with you, or the picture of it, at least.' He had not asked how Cadfael had come by it, to make the copy.

'And where,' wondered Cadfael, 'is this Geoffrey to be found now? If he pledged himself and his men to Stephen along with the rest, is he still with the garrison at Faringdon?'

'At Faringdon he surely is,' said the lame man, his low voice edged like steel, 'but not with the garrison. The day after the surrender they brought him into the castle in a litter, after a fall from his horse. He died before night. He is buried in the churchyard at Faringdon. He has no more need now of his seal.'

The silence that fell between them hung suspended, like a held breath, upon Cadfael's senses, before the echoes began, echoes not of the words which had been spoken, but of those which had not been spoken, and never need be. There was an understanding between them that needed no ritual form. A man certainly had need to keep a lock on his tongue, a man who had perilous things to tell, was already crippled, and had to live all too close, still, to men of power who had things to hide. Forthred had gone far in trusting even the Benedictine habit, and must not be made to utter openly what he had already conveyed clearly enough by implication.

And as yet he did not even know how Cadfael had come by the salamander seal.

'Tell me,' said Cadfael carefully, 'about those few days, how events fell out. The timing is all.'

'Why, we were pressed, that was true, and hot summer, and none too well provided with water, seeing we had a strong garrison. And Philip from Cricklade had been sending to his father for relief, time and time again, and no reply. And come that one morning, there were the king's officers let in by night, and Brien de Soulis calls on us not to resist, and brings before us this sealed agreement, to be seen by all of us, his own seal and all five of the others, the command of the entire garrison but for the young men who brought only their own proficiency in arms to the defence. And those who would not countenance the change of allegiance were made prisoner, as all men know. And the men-at-arms – small choice, seeing our masters had committed us.'

'And Geoffrey's seal was there with the rest?'

'*It* was there,' said Forthred simply. '*He* was not.'

No, that had begun to be apparent. But no doubt it had been adequately accounted for.

'They told us he had ridden to Cricklade in the night, to report to Philip FitzRobert what had been done. But before leaving he had set his seal to the agreement. First among equals he had set it there, with his own hand.'

And without it there would have been no such easy passage from empress to king. Lacking his consent, his own men and others would have taken station at his back, and there would have been a battle.

'And the next day?' said Cadfael.

'The next day he did not come back. And they began to seem anxious – as were we all,' said Forthred with level and expressionless voice, 'and de Soulis and two who were nearest to him rode out to follow the way he would have ridden. And in the dusk they brought him back in a litter,

113

wrapped in a cloak. Found in the woodland, they said, thrown from his horse and badly hurt, and the beast led back riderless. And in the night he died.'

In the night he died. But which night, thought Cadfael, and felt the same conviction burning and bitter in the man who sat beside him. A dead man can easily be removed to some private place in one night, the night of the betrayal in which he refused to take part, and brought back publicly the next night, lost by tragic accident.

'And he is buried,' said Forthred, 'there in Faringdon. They did not show us the body.'

'Had he wife or child?' asked Cadfael.

'No, none. De Soulis sent a courier to tell the Clares of his death, Faringdon being now of their party. They have had Masses said for him in all good faith.' With the house of Clare he had no quarrel.

'I have an uneasy thought,' said Cadfael tentatively, 'that there is more to tell. So soon thereafter – how did you come by your injuries?'

A dark smile crossed the composed face of the lame man. 'A fall. I had a perilous fall. From the keep into the ditch. I did not like my new service as well as the old, but it was not wisdom to show it. How did they know? How do they always know? There was always someone between me and the gate. I was letting myself down from the wall when someone cut the rope.'

'And left you there broken and unaided?'

'Why not? Another accident, they come in twos and threes. But I could crawl as far as cover, and there decent poor men found me. It has knit awry, but I am alive.'

There were monstrous debts here to be repaid some day, the worth of a life, the price of a body deliberately and coldly maimed. Cadfael suddenly felt burdened by a debt of his own, since this man had so resolutely trusted and confided in him for no return. One piece of knowledge he had, that after its perverse and inadequate fashion might at least provide proof that justice, however indirect or delayed, is certain in the end.

'I have a thing to tell you, Forthred, that you have not asked me. This seal, that was so used to confirm a betrayal, is now in the hands of my bishop in Coventry. And as to how it came there, it was among the baggage of a man who attended the conference there, and there was killed, no one knows by whose hand. His own seal he had on him, that was nothing strange. But he also had this other, from which I made these drawings. The seal of Geoffrey FitzRichard of Clare travelled from Faringdon to Coventry in the saddle-bags of Brien de Soulis, and Brien de Soulis is dead in Coventry with a dagger through his heart.'

At the end of the cloister walk the master-mason passed by returning to his work. Forthred rose slowly to follow, and his smile, bleak but assuaged, shone exultantly for an instant, and then was suppressed and veiled in his normal stony indifference. 'God is neither blind nor deaf,' he said, low-voiced, 'no, nor forgetful. Praise be!' And he stepped out into the empty walk and crossed the turf of the garth, limping heavily, and Cadfael was left gazing after him.

And now there was no cause to remain here another hour, and no doubt whither he must go. He sought out the hospitaller, and made his farewells, and went to saddle up in the stable yard. As yet he had not given a thought to how he should proceed when he came to Greenhamsted. But there are more ways than one of breaking into a castle, and sometimes the simplest is the best. Especially for a man who has forsworn arms, and taken vows that bar him from both violence and duplicity. Truth is a hard master, and costly to serve, but it simplifies all problems. And even an apostate may find it honourable to keep such vows as are not already broken.

Hugh's handsome young chestnut roan was glad to be on the move again, and came forth from his stall dancing, the light silvering into lustre the white bloom tempering the brightness of his coat. They set forth from Deerhurst southward. They had some fifteen miles to go, Cadfael judged, and would do well to give Gloucester a wide berth, leaving it on the right hand. There was heavy cloud closing in on the afternoon; it would be a pleasure to ride briskly.

They came up from the broad valley meadows into the edges of the hill country, among the high sheep villages where the wool merchants found some of their finest fleeces. They were already in the fringes of the most active battle-ground, and local farming had not gone quite unscathed, but most of the fighting was a matter of sporadic raiding by the garrisons of the castles, each faction plaguing the other, in a series of damaging exchanges in which Faringdon had been designed to play the central part for the empress, and now balanced King Stephen's line and held open communications between Malmesbury and Oxford. Somewhat tired warfare now, Cadfael realized, though still venomous. Earl Robert Bossu was right, in the end they must come to terms, because neither side was capable of inflicting defeat upon the other.

Could that, he wondered, once grasped, be a sound reason for changing sides, and transferring all one's powers and weapons to the other faction? On the consideration, for instance: I have fought for the empress nine years now, and I know we are not one step nearer winning a victory that can bring back order and government to this land. I wonder if the other party, should I transfer to them and take others with me, could do what we have failed to do, settle the whole score, and put the weapons away. Anything

116

to put an end to this endless waste. Yes, it might even seem worth the trial. But partisanship must have ebbed wholly and horribly away into exhaustion in order to reach the despairing knowledge that any end to the anarchy would be better than none.

Then what could there be beyond that stage, when the new alliance proved as wasteful, incompetent and infuriating as the old? Only total disgust with both factions, and withdrawal to spend the last remaining energies on something better worth.

The road Cadfael was travelling had levelled on the uplands, and stretched before him arrow-straight into distance. Villages here were prosperous from the wool trade, but far between, and tended to lie aside from the highway. He was forced to turn off in order to find a house at which to ask guidance, and the cottar who came out to greet him eyed him with sharp attention when he asked for La Musarderie.

'You're not from these parts, brother? Likely you don't know the place has fallen into fresh hands. If your business is with the Musards, you'll not find them. Robert Musard was taken in an ambush weeks, months back now, and had to give up his castle to the Earl of Gloucester's son, he that's declared for King Stephen recently.'

'So I had heard,' said Cadfael. 'But I have an errand there I have undertaken and must fulfill. I take it the change is not well thought of hereabouts.'

The man shrugged. 'Church and village he lets alone, provided neither priest nor reeve gets in his way. But Musards have been there ever since the first King William gave the manor to this one's great-grandsire, and no man now expects change to be for the better. So go softly, brother, if you must go. He'll be ware of any stranger before ever you get close to his walls.'

'He'll hardly fear any feats of arms from me,' said Cadfael. 'And what I have to fear from him I'll be prepared for. And thanks, friend, for the warning. Now, how must I go?'

'Go back to the road,' he was advised, with a shrug for his probably ill-fated persistence, 'and ride on for a mile or more, and there's a track on the right will bring you to Winstone. Cross the river beyond by the ford, and up through the woodland the other side, and when you come clear of the trees you'll see the castle ahead of you, it stands high. The village stands higher still, up on the crest beyond,' he said. 'Go gently, and come again safely.'

'By God's favour I hope for it,' said Cadfael, and thanked him, and turned his horse to return to the highroad.

There are more ways than one of getting into a castle, he reasoned as he rode through the village of Winstone. The simplest of all, for a lone man without an army or any means of compulsion, is to ride up to the gate and ask to be let in. I am manifestly not in arms, the day is drawing towards an early and chilly evening, and hospitality is a sacred duty. Especially is it incumbent on the nobility to open roof and board to clerics and monastics in need. Let us see, then, how far Philip FitzRobert's nobility extends.

And following the same sequence of thought: if you want to have speech with the castellan, the most obvious means is to ask; and the most unshakable story to get you into his presence is the truth. He holds two men – surely by now that is as good as certain! – two men to whom he means no good. You want them released unharmed, and have good reasons to advance why he should reconsider his intent towards them. Nothing could be simpler. Why complicate matters by going roundabout?

Beyond Winstone the road proceeded virtually due west,

and gradually dwindled into a track, though a well-made and well-used one. From open, scattered woodland and heath it plunged almost suddenly into thick forest, and began to descend steeply by winding traverses among trees into a deep valley. He heard water flowing below, no great flood but the purling sound of a little river with a stony bed; and presently he came out on a narrow slope of grass on its banks, and a narrower tongue of gravel led out into the water, marking the passage of the ford. On the further side the track rose again almost as steeply as on the side where he had descended, and old, long-established trees hid all that awaited him beyond.

He crossed, and began to climb out of the valley. Light and air showed suddenly between the trees, and he emerged from forest into cleared land, bare even of bushes; and there before and above him, at perhaps a half-mile distance, on a level promontory, stood the castle of La Musarderie.

He had been right, four generations of the same family in unchallenged possession had afforded time to build in local stone, to enlarge and to strengthen. The first hasty palisades thrown up in timber seventy-five years ago, to establish and assure ownership, had vanished long since. This was a massive bulk, a battlemented curtain wall, twin gate-towers, squat and strong, fronting this eastward approach, and the serrated crests of other flanking towers circling a tall keep within. Beyond, the ground continued to rise steeply in complex folds and levels to a long crest above, where Cadfael could just distinguish above the trees the top of a church tower, and the occasional slope of a roof, marking the village of Greenhamsted. A rising causeway, stripped of all cover and dead straight, led up to the castle gates. No one was allowed to approach La Musarderie unseen. All round it the ground had been cleared of cover.

Cadfael embarked on that climb with deliberation,

willing to be seen, waiting to be challenged. Philip Fitz-Robert would not tolerate any inefficient service. They were already alerted, long before he came within hailing distance. He heard a horn call briefly within. The great double doors were closed. It was sufficiently late in the day to have everything secured, but there was a wicket left open, lofty enough and wide enough to let in a mounted man, even a galloping man if he came pursued, and easy and light enough to slam shut after him and bar once he was within. In the twin short towers that flanked the gate there were arrow-slits that could bring to bear a dual field of fire on any pursuers. Cadfael approved, his instincts harking back to encounters long past but not forgotten.

Such a gateway, however innocently open, a man approaches with discretion, keeping both hands in clear view, and neither hastening nor hesitating. Cadfael ambled the last few yards and halted outside, though no one had appeared either to welcome or obstruct. He called through the open wicket: 'Peace on all within!' and moved on gently through the opening and into the bailey, without waiting for an answer.

In the dark, vaulted archway of the gate there were men on either side of him, and when he emerged into the ward two more were ready for him, prompt to bridle and stirrup, unhurried and unthreatening, but watchful.

'And on whoever comes in peace,' said the officer of the guard, coming out from the guardroom smiling, if a little narrowly. 'As doubtless you do, brother. Your habit speaks for you.'

'It speaks truly,' said Cadfael.

'And what's your will in these parts?' asked the sergeant. 'And where are you bound?'

'Here, to La Musarderie,' said Cadfael directly, 'if you'll afford me houseroom a while, till I speak with your lord.

My business is nothing beyond that. I come to beg audience with Philip FitzRobert, and they tell me he's here within. At your disposal and his, whenever he sees fit. I'll wait his pleasure as long as need be.'

'You're messenger for another?' the sergeant questioned, no more than mildly curious. 'He's come back from a clutch of bishops, are you here to speak for yours?'

'After a fashion, yes,' Cadfael conceded. 'But for myself also. If you'll be so good as to carry him my request, no doubt he'll also speak his mind.'

They surrounded him, but at a tolerant distance, curious and alert, faintly grinning, while their sergeant considered at leisure what to think of him and what to do with him. The bailey was not very large, but the wide clearance of cover all round the castle walls compensated for that. From the guardwalk along the wall the view would be broad enough to give ample warning of any force coming in arms, and provide a murderous field for archers, who almost certainly figured large in the garrison. The encrustation of sheds, stores, armouries and cramped living quarters all round the wall within consisted mainly of timber. Fire, Cadfael considered, might be a threat, but even so a limited one. Hall and keep and towers and curtain wall were all of stone. He wondered why he was studying the place as an objective in battle, a stronghold to be taken. So it might prove to him, but not that way.

'Light down and be welcome, brother,' said the sergeant amiably. 'We never turn away men of your cloth. As for our lord, you'll need to wait a while, for he's out riding this moment, but he shall hear your asking, never fear. Let Peter here take your horse, and he'll bring your saddle-bags into the lodging for you.'

'I tend my own horse,' said Cadfael placidly, mindful of the precaution of knowing where to find him at need;

though the sergeant was so assured of having only a simple monastic courier on his hands that there was no need to suspect him of any deception. 'I was a man-at-arms myself, long years ago. Once learned, you never lose the habit.'

'True enough,' said the sergeant indulgently, humouring this old ex-warrior. 'Then Peter will show you, and when you're done, you'll find someone in hall to see to your needs. If you've borne arms yourself you'll be used to a soldier's keep.'

'And content with it,' agreed Cadfael heartily, and led his horse away after the groom, well satisfied to be within the wards. Nor did he miss any of the evidences that Philip kept an alert and well-run household here. Recalling the dark and courteous presence encountered so briefly and privately in the priory church at Coventry, he would have expected nothing less. Every castle ward has a multifarious life of its own, that goes on without fuss, in wellhouse, bakery, armoury, store and workshops, in two parallel disciplines, one military, one domestic. Here in a region of warfare, however desultory the dangers might be, the domestic side of castle life in La Musarderie seemed to have been scaled down to a minimum, and almost womanless. Possibly Philip's steward had a wife somewhere, in charge of such women servants as might be kept here, but the economy within was starkly military and austerely male, and functioned with a ruthless efficiency that surely stemmed from its lord. Philip was unmarried and without children, wholly absorbed into the demonic conflict that no one seemed able to end. His castle reflected his obsession.

There was human activity enough about the ward and in the stables, men came and went about their proper businesses, without haste but briskly, and the babel of voices was as constant as the buzzing about a beehive. The groom Peter was easy and talkative about helping Cadfael to unsaddle and unload, groom and water the horse and settle him in a stall, and pointed him amiably to the hall when that was done. The steward's clerk who received him there with no more than momentary surprise and an acquiescent shrug, as though accepting a visitor of an unexpected but harmless kind, offered him a bed as of right, and told him where to find the chapel, for the proper hour of Vespers was past, and he had need of a pause to give thanks for present blessings and invoke help in future contentions. An elderly Benedictine wanting shelter for the night, what was there in that to enlist any man's interest for more than a moment, even where voluntary guests were few and far between?

The chapel was in the heart of the keep, and he wondered a little that they should let him into it unwatched and solitary. Philip's garrison had no hesitation in allowing a monastic access to the central defences of the castle, they had even housed him within the keep, and there could be no other reason for such confidence than simple trust in his integrity and reverence for his habit. That caused him to look more closely into his own motives and methods, and confirmed him in the directness of his approach. There was no other way but straight forward, whether to success or ruin.

He paid his belated devotions very gravely, in the chill, stony chapel, on his knees before an altar austerely draped and lit only by one small, steady lamp. The vault above withdrew into darkness, and the cold honed his mind as it stiffened his flesh. Lord God, how must I approach, how can I match, such a man? One who in casting off one coat has stripped himself naked to reproach and condemnation, and in donning another has merely covered his wounds, not healed them. I do not know what to make of this Philip.

He was rising from his knees when he heard, distantly

from the outer ward, the brisk clatter of hooves on the cobbles, a small, sharp sound. One horse only; one man only, like himself, not afraid to ride out from a castle or into a castle alone, in a region where castles were prizes to be seized at the least opportunity, and prisons to be avoided at all costs. After a moment Cadfael heard the horse being led away to the stable yard, treading out sober walking paces across the stones, ebbing into silence. He turned to leave the chapel, and went out between the guardrooms and gates of the keep, where the twilight hung pale against the black pillars of the portal. He emerged into what seemed by contrast almost daylight, and found himself crossing the path of Philip FitzRobert, just dismounted after his ride and striding across the ward to his hall, shrugging off his cloak on to one arm as he went. They met and halted, two or three yards between them, mutually at gaze.

The rising wind of evening had ruffled Philip's black hair, for he had ridden with head uncovered. The short, blown strands laced his high forehead, and caused him to frown as he stared. He went in the plainest of dark gear, independent of any manner of ornament or finery. His own bearing was his distinction. Physically, in motion or in stillness, he had an elongated elegance, and a tension like a strung bow.

'They told me I had a guest,' he said, and narrowed his full, dark brown eyes. 'Brother, I think I have seen you before.'

'I was in Coventry,' said Cadfael, 'among many others. Though whether you ever noticed me is more than I can say.'

There was a brief silence, and neither of them moved. 'You were present,' Philip said then, 'close by, but you did not speak. I do remember, you were by when we found de Soulis dead.'

124

'I was,' said Cadfael.

'And now you come to me. To have speech with me. So they have said. On whose behalf?'

'On behalf of justice and truth,' said Cadfael, 'at least in my view. On behalf of myself, and of some for whom I am advocate. And ultimately, perhaps, my lord, even on yours.'

The eyes narrowed to sharpen vision through the fading light studied him in silence for a moment, without, apparently, finding any fault with the boldness of this address.

'I shall have time to listen,' said Philip then, the courteous level of his voice unshaken even by curiosity, 'after supper. Come to me after I leave the hall. Any man of the household will show you where to find me. And if you wish, you may assist my chaplain at Compline. I respect your habit.'

'That I cannot,' said Cadfael bluntly. 'I am not a priest. Even the full right of this habit I cannot now claim. I am absent without leave from my abbot. I have broken the cord. I am apostate.'

'For cause!' said Philip, and stared upon him steadily for a long moment, his interest both caught and contained within measure. Then he said abruptly: 'Nevertheless, come!' and turned and walked away into his hall.

Chapter Eight

N PHILIP FitzRobert's hall the service was Spartan, and the company exclusively male. He presided at the high table among his knights, and the young men of his following used him with confident candour, not in awe, but to all appearances in willing duty. He ate sparingly and drank little, talked freely with his equals and courteously with his servants. And Cadfael, from his place beside the chaplain at a lower table, watched him and wondered what went on behind the lofty forehead and the deep brown eyes like slow-burning fires, and all that was mysterious in him, if not ominous.

He rose from the table early, leaving the men of his garrison to continue at their leisure, and after his going there was an easing of manners and further circling of ale and wine, and some who could make music fetched their instruments to enliven the evening. Small doubt there was a strong guard set, and all gates closed and barred. Musard, so the chaplain had reported, had foolishly gone forth hunting, and ridden straight into Philip's ambush, and been forced to surrender his castle in order to regain his freedom, and possibly also to keep himself alive; though threats against life in order to gain possession of a fortress were more likely to remain threats than to be put into action, and often met with obstinate defiance even with necks noosed and hangmen ready, in the assurance that they dared not be carried out. Family loyalties and complex intermarriages had baulked a great many such attempts. But Musard, not having a powerful relative on Stephen's side, of greater importance to the king than Philip himself, had been less confident of his safety, and given in. That was hardly likely ever to happen to Philip. He showed no fear of any man, but neither would he leave gates unbarred, or fail to set good sentries on the walls.

'I am bidden to your lord's presence,' said Cadfael, 'after he withdraws from the hall. Will you point me the way? I think he is not a man to be kept waiting when he has named the time.'

The chaplain was old and experienced, beyond surprise. In any case nothing that their castellan did, nothing he denied, nothing he granted, no princeling he rejected, no humble travelling monastic he welcomed, seemed to occasion surprise here. There would be sufficient reason for all, and whether that reason proved comprehensible or not, it would not be questioned.

The old priest shrugged, and rose obligingly from table to lead the way out from the hall. 'He keeps early hours as a rule. So he set you a time, did he? You're favoured. But he's hospitable to any who wear your habit, or come in the Church's name.'

Cadfael forbore from following that lead. It was known here that he came from the conference at Coventry, and probably assumed that he bore some further exhortation from his bishop to insinuate into Philip's ear. Let them by all means think so; it accounted for him very satisfactorily. As between himself and Philip there could be no pretences.

'In here. He lives almost priestly,' commented the chaplain, 'here in the cold of the keep, close to his chapel, none of your cushioned solars.' They were in a narrow stone passage, lit only by a small, smoky torch in a bracket on the wall. The door they approached was narrow, and stood ajar. At the chaplain's knock a voice from within called: 'Come!'

Cadfael entered a small, austere room, high-windowed on a single lancet of naked sky, in which a faint dusting of starlight showed. They were on a lofty floor raised, high enough to clear the curtain wall on this sheltered side. Below the window a large, shaded candle burned on a heavy table, and behind the table Philip sat on a broad stool buttressed with massive carved arms, his back against the dark hangings on the wall. He looked up from the book that lay open before him. It was no surprise that he was lettered. Every faculty he had he would push to the limit.

'Come in, brother, and close the door.'

His voice was quiet, and his face, lit sidelong by the candle at his left elbow, showed sharply defined in planes of light and ravines of shadow, deep hollows beneath the high cheekbones and in the ivory settings of dark, thoughtful eyes. Cadfael marvelled again how young he was, Olivier's own age. Something of Olivier, even, in his clear, fastidious face, fixed at this moment in a searching gravity, that hung upon Cadfael in continued speculation.

'You had something to say to me. Sit, brother, and say it freely. I am listening.'

A motion of his hand indicated the wooden bench against the wall at his right hand, draped with sheepskin. Cadfael would rather have remained standing, facing him directly, but he obeyed the gesture, and the contact of eyes was not broken; Philip had turned with him, maintaining his unwavering regard.

'Now, what is it you want of me?'

'I want,' said Cadfael, 'the freedom of two men, two whom, as I believe, you have in close hold.'

'Name them,' said Philip, 'and I will tell you if you believe rightly.'

'The name of the first is Olivier de Bretagne. And the name of the second is Yves Hugonin.'

'Yes', said Philip without hesitation, and without any change in the quiet level of his voice. 'I hold them both.'

'Here, in La Musarderie?'

'Yes. They are here. Now tell me why I should release them.'

'There are reasons,' said Cadfael, 'why a fairminded man should take my request seriously. Olivier de Bretagne, I judge from all I know of him, would not consider turning his coat with you when you handed over Faringdon to the king. There were several who held with him, and would not go with you. All were overpowered and made prisoner, to be held for ransom by whoever should be given them as largesse by the king. That is known openly. Why, then, has Olivier de Bretagne not been offered for ransom? Why has it not been made known who holds him?'

'I have made it known now to you,' said Philip, with a small, dry smile. 'Proceed from there.'

'Very well! It is true I had not asked you until now, and now you have not denied. But it was never published where he was, as it was for the others. Is it fair that his case should be different? There are those who would be glad to buy him free.'

'However high the price asked?' said Philip.

'Name it, and I will see it raised and paid to you.'

There was a long pause, while Philip looked at him with

eyes wide and clear, and yet unreadable, so still that not a single hair on his head quivered. 'A life, perhaps,' he said then, very softly. 'Another life in place of his to rot here solitary as he will rot.'

'Take mine,' said Cadfael.

In the arched lancet of the high window clouds had blotted out the faint starlight, the stones of the wall were now paler than the night without.

'Yours,' said Philip with soft deliberation, not questioning, not exclaiming, only saying over the single word to himself as if to incise it on the steely metal of his mind. 'What satisfaction would your life be to me? What grudge have I against you, to give me any pleasure in destroying you?'

'What grudge had you against him? What bitter pleasure will you experience in destroying him? What did he ever do to you, except hold fast to his cause when you deserted yours? Or when he so thought of what you did,' Cadfael corrected himself stoutly, 'for I tell you, I do not know how to interpret all that you have done, and he, as I well know, would be less ready to look not once, but twice, thrice and again, before judging.'

No, the protest was pointless. Olivier's fiery scorn would be enough offence. A match for Philip in his towering pride, blazing forth in unrestrained reproach, as if Philip's own mirror image cried out against him. Perhaps the only way to put that mortal wound out of mind had been to bury the accuser out of sight and out of memory.

'You valued him!' said Cadfael, enlightened and unwary.

'I valued him,' Philip repeated, and found no fault with the statement. 'It is not the first time I have been denied, rejected, misprized, left out of the reckoning, by some I most valued. There is nothing new in that. It takes time to

reach the point of cutting off the last of them, and proceed-
ing alone. But now, since you have made me an offer, why
should you, why do you, offer me your old bones to moulder
in his place? What is Olivier de Bretagne to you?'

'He is my son,' said Cadfael.

In the long, profound silence that followed, Philip released
held breath at last in a prolonged soft sigh. The chord that
had been sounded between them was complex and painful,
and echoed eerily in the mind. For Philip also had a father,
severed from him now in mutual rejection, irreconcilable.
There was, of course, the elder brother, William, Robert's
heir. Was that where the breakage began? Always close,
always loved, always sufficient, and this one passed over,
his needs and wants as casually attended to as his pleas for
Faringdon had been? That might be a part of Philip's
passion of anger, but surely not the whole. It was not so
simple.

'Do fathers owe such regard to their sons?' he said dryly.
'Would mine, do you suppose, lift a hand to release me
from a prison?'

'For ought that I know or you know,' said Cadfael sturdily, 'so he would. You are not in need. Olivier is, and
deserves better from you.'

'You are in the common error,' said Philip indifferently.
'I did not first abandon him. He abandoned me, and I
have accepted the judgement. If that was the measure of
resolution on one side, to bring this abominable waste to
an end, what is left for a man but to turn and throw his
whole weight into the other scale? And if that prove as
ineffective, and fail us as bitterly? How much more can this
poor land endure?'

He was speaking almost in the same terms as the Earl
of Leicester, and yet his remedy was very different. Robert

Bossu was trying to bring together all the wisest and most moderate minds from both factions, to force a compromise which would stop the fighting by agreement. Philip saw no possibility but to end the contention with a total victory, and after eight wasteful years cared very little which faction triumphed, provided the triumph brought back some semblance of law and normality to England. And as Philip was branded traitor and turncoat, so, some day, when he withheld his powers from battle to force his king's hand, would Robert Bossu be branded. But he and his kind might be the saviours of a tormented land, none the less.

'You are speaking now of king and empress,' said Cadfael, 'and what you say I understand, better than I did until this moment. But I am speaking of my son Olivier. I am offering you a price for him, the price you named. If you meant it, accept it. I do not think, whatever else I might think of you, that you go back on your bargains, bad or good.'

'Wait!' said Philip, and raised a hand, but very tolerantly. 'I said: perhaps a life. I am not committed by so qualified a declaration. And – forgive me, brother! – would you consider yourself fair exchange, old as you are, against his youth and strength? You appealed to me as a fairminded man, so do I turn to you.'

'I see the imbalance,' said Cadfael. Not in age and beauty and vigour, however glaring that discrepancy might be, but in the passion of confident trust and affection that could never be adequately paid by the mild passing liking this man felt now for his challenger. When it came to the extreme of testing, surely those two friends had failed to match minds, and that was a disintegration that could never be forgiven, so absolute had been the expectation of understanding. 'Nevertheless, I have offered you what you asked, and it is all that is mine to offer you. I cannot raise

132

my stake. There is no more to give. Now be as honest, and admit to me, it is more than you expected.'

'It is more,' said Philip. 'I think, brother, you must allow me time. You come as a surprise to me. How could I know that Olivier had such a father? And if I asked you concerning this so strangely fathered son of yours, I doubt you would not tell me.'

'I think,' said Cadfael, 'that I would.'

The dark eyes flared into amused interest. 'Do you confide so easily?'

'Not to every man,' said Cadfael, and saw the sparks burn down into a steady glow. And again there was a silence, that lay more lightly on the senses than the previous silences.

'Let us leave this,' said Philip abruptly. 'Unresolved, not abandoned. You came on behalf of two men. Speak of the second. You have things to argue for Yves Hugonin.'

'What I have to argue for Yves Hugonin,' said Cadfael, 'is that he had no part in the death of Brien de Soulis. Him you have altogether mistaken. First, for I know him, have known him from a child, as arrow-straight for his aim as any living man. I saw him, as you did not, not that time, I saw him when first he rode into the priory gate at Coventry, and saw de Soulis in his boldness, armed, and cried out on him for a turncoat and traitor, and laid hand to hilt against him, yes, but face to face before many witnesses. If he had killed, that would have been his way, not lurking in dark places, in ambush with a bared blade. Now consider the night of the man's death. Yves Hugonin says that he came late to Compline, when the office had begun, and remained crowded into the last dark corner within the door, and so was first out to clear the way for the princes. He says that he stumbled in the dark over de Soulis's body, and kneeled to see how bad was the man's case, and called out to us to bring lights. And so was taken in all men's sight with bloody hands. All which is patently true, whatever else you attribute to him. For you say he never was in the church, but had killed de Soulis, cleaned his sword and bestowed it safely and innocently in his lodging, where it should be, and returned in good time to cry the alarm in person over a dead man. But if that were true, why call to us at all? Why be there by the body? Why not elsewhere, in full communion with his fellows, surrounded by witnesses to his innocence and ignorance of evil?'

'Yet it could be so,' said Philip relentlessly. 'Men with limited time to cover their traces do not always choose the most infallible way. What do you object to my most bitter belief?'

'A number of things. First, that same evening I examined Yves' sword, which was sheathed and laid by as he had said. It is not easy to cleanse the last traces of blood from a grooved blade, and of such quests I have had experience. I found no blemish there. Second, after you were gone, with the bishop's leave I examined de Soulis's body. It was no sword that made that wound, no sword ever was made so lean and fine. A thin, sharp dagger, long enough to reach the heart. And a firm stroke, in deep and out clean before he could bleed. The flow of blood came later as he lay, he left the mark outlined on the flagstones under him. And now, third, tell me how his open enemy can have approached him so close, and de Soulis with sword and poniard ready to hand. He would have had his blade out as soon as he saw his adversary nearing, long before ever he came within dagger range. Is that good sense, or no?'

'Good sense enough,' Philip allowed, 'so far as it goes.'

'It goes to the heart of the matter. Brien de Soulis bore arms, he had no mind to be present at Compline, he had another assignation that night. He waited in a carrel of the cloister, and came forth into the walk when he heard and saw his man approaching. A quiet time, with everyone else in the church, a time for private conference with no witnesses. Not with an avowed enemy, but with a friend, someone trusted, someone who could walk up to him confidently, never suspected of any evil intent, and stab him to the heart. And walked away and left him lying, for a foolish young man to stumble over, and yell his discovery to the night, and put his neck in a noose.'

'His neck,' said Philip dryly, 'is still unwrung. I have not yet determined what to do with him.'

'And I am making your decision no easier, I trust. For what I tell you is truth, and you cannot but recognize it, whether you will or no. And there is more yet to tell, and though it does not remove from Yves Hugonin all cause for hating Brien de Soulis, it does open the door to many another who may have better cause to hate him even more. Even among some he may formerly have counted his friends.'

'Go on,' said Philip equably. 'I am still listening.'

'After you were gone, under the bishop's supervision we put together all that belonged to de Soulis, to deliver to his brother. He had with him his personal seal, as was to be expected. You know the badge?'

'I know it. The swan and willow wands.'

'But we found also another seal, and another device. Do you also know this badge?' He had drawn the rolled leaf out of the breast of his habit, and leaned to flatten it upon the table, between Philip's long muscular hands. 'The original is with the bishop. Do you know it?'

'Yes, I have seen it,' said Philip with careful detachment. 'One of de Soulis's captains in the Faringdon garrison used it. I knew the man, though not well. His own raising, a good company he had. Geoffrey FitzClare, a half-brother to Gilbert de Clare of Hertford, the wrong side the sheets.'

'And you must have heard, I think, that Geoffrey Fitz-Clare was thrown from his horse, and died of it, the day Faringdon was surrendered. He was said to have ridden for Cricklade during the night, after he had affixed his seal, like all the other captains who had their own followings within, to the surrender. He did not return. De Soulis and a few with him went out next day to look for him, and brought him home in a litter. Before night they told the garrison he was dead.'

'I do know of this,' said Philip, his voice for the first time tight and wary. 'A very ill chance. He never reached me. I heard of it only afterwards.'

'And you were not expecting him? You had not sent for him?'

Philip was frowning now, his level black brows knotted tightly above the deep eyes. 'No. There was no need. De Soulis had full powers. There is more to this. What is it you are saying?'

'I am saying that it was convenient he should die by accident so aptly, the day after his seal was added to the agreement that handed over Faringdon to King Stephen. If, indeed, he did not die in the night, before some other hand impressed his seal there. For there are those, and I have spoken with one of them, who will swear that Geoffrey FitzClare never would have consented to that surrender, had he still had voice to cry out or hand to lift and prevent. And if voice and hand had been raised against it, his men within, and maybe more than his would have fought on his side, and Faringdon would never have been taken.'

'You are saying,' said Philip, brooding, 'that his death

136

was no accident. And that it was another, not he, who affixed that seal to the surrender with all the rest. After the man was dead.'

'That is what I am saying. Since he would never have set it there himself, nor let it go into other hands while he lived. And his consent was essential, to convince the garrison. I think he died as soon as the thing was broached to him, and he condemned it. There was no time to lose.'

'Yet they rode out next day, to look for him, and brought him back to Faringdon openly, before the garrison.'

'Wrapped in cloaks, in a litter. No doubt his men saw him pass, saw the recognizable face plainly. But they never saw him close. They were never shown the body after they were told that he had died. A dead man in the night can very easily be carried out to lie somewhere in hiding, against his open return next day. The postern that was opened to let the king's negotiators in could as well let FitzClare's dead body out, to some hiding-place in the woods. And how else, for what purpose,' said Cadfael heavily, 'should FitzClare's seal go with Brien de Soulis to Coventry, and be found in his saddle-bag there.'

Philip rose abruptly from his seat, and rounded the table sharply to pace across the room. He moved in silence, with a kind of contained violence, as if his mind was forcing his body into motion as the only means of relief from the smouldering turmoil within. He quartered the room like a prowling cat, and came to rest at length with clenched fists braced on the heavy chest in the darkest corner, his back turned to Cadfael and the source of light. His stillness was as tense as his pacing, and he was silent for long moments. When he turned, it was clear from the bright composure of his face that he had come to a reconciliation with everything he had heard.

'I knew nothing of all this. If it is truth, as my blood in me says it is truth, I had no hand in it, nor never would have allowed it.'

'I never thought it,' said Cadfael. 'Whether the surrender was at your wish – no, at your decree! – I neither know nor ask, but no, you were not there, whatever was done was done at de Soulis's orders. Perhaps by de Soulis's hand. It would not be easy to get four other captains, with followings to be risked, to connive at murder. Better to draw him aside, man to man, and give out that he had been sent to confer with you at Cricklade, while one or two who had no objection to murder secretly conveyed away a dead man and the horse he was said to be riding on his midnight mission. And his seal was first on the vellum. No, you I never thought of as conniving at murder, whatever else I may have found within your scope. But FitzClare is dead, and de Soulis is dead, and you have not, I think, the reason you believed you had to mourn or avenge him. Nor any remaining cause to lay his death at the charge of a young man openly and honestly his enemy. There were many men in Faringdon who would be glad enough to avenge the murder of FitzClare. Who knows if some of them were also present at Coventry? He was well liked, and well served. And not every man of his following believed what he was told of that death.'

'De Soulis would have been as ready for such as for Hugonin,' said Philip.

'You think they would betray themselves as enemies? No, whoever set out to get close to him would take good care not to give any warning. But Yves had already cried out loud before the world his anger and enmity. No, yourself you know it, he would never have got within a sword's reach, let alone a slender little knife. Set Yves Hugonin free,' said Cadfael, 'and take me in my son's stead.'

Philip came back slowly to his place at the table, and sat down, and finding his book left open and unregarded, quietly closed it. He leaned his head between long hands, and fixed his unnerving eyes again on Cadfael's face. 'Yes,' he said, rather to himself than to Cadfael, 'yes, there is the matter of your son Olivier. Let us not forget Olivier.' But his voice was not reassuring. 'Let us see if the man I have known, I thought well, is the same as the son you have known. Never has he spoken of a father to me.'

'He knows no more than his mother told him, when he was a child. I have told him nothing. Of his father he knows only a too kindly legend, coloured too brightly by affection.'

'If I question too close, refuse me answers. But I feel a need to know. A son of the cloister?'

'No,' said Cadfael, 'a son of the Crusade. His mother lived and died in Antioch. I never knew I had left her a son until I met with him here in England, and he named her, mentioned times, left me in no doubt at all. The cloister came later.'

'The Crusade!' Philip echoed. His eyes burned up into gold. He narrowed their brightness curiously upon Cadfael's grizzled tonsure and lined and weathered face. 'The Crusade that made a Christian kingdom in Jerusalem? You were there? Of all battles, surely the worthiest.'

'The easiest to justify, perhaps,' Cadfael agreed ruefully. 'I would not say more than that.'

The bright, piercing gaze continued to weigh and measure and wonder, with a sudden personal passion, staring through Cadfael into far distances, beyond the fabled Midland Sea, into the legendary Frankish kingdoms of Outremer. Ever since the fall of Edessa Christendom had been uneasy in its hopes and fears for Jerusalem, and popes and abbots were stirring in their sleep to consider their beleaguered capital, and raise their voices like clarions calling to the defence of the Church. Philip was not yet so old but he could quicken to the sound of the trumpet.

'How did it come that you encountered him here, all unknown? And once only?'

'Twice, and by God's grace there will be a third time,' said Cadfael stoutly. He told, very briefly, of the circumstances of both those meetings.

'And still he does not know you for his sire? You never told him?'

'There is no need for him to know. No shame there, but no pride, either. His course is nobly set, why cause any tremor to deflect or shake it?'

'You ask nothing, want nothing of him?' The perilous bitterness was back in Philip's voice, husky with the pain of all he had hoped for from his own father, and failed to receive. Too fierce a love, perverted into too fierce a hate, corroded all his reflections on the anguished relationship between fathers and sons, too close and too separate, and never in balance.

'He owes me nothing,' said Cadfael. 'Nothing but such friendship and liking as we have deserved of each other by free will and earned trust, not by blood.'

'And yet it is by blood,' said Philip softly, 'that you conceive you owe him so much, even to a life. Brother, I think you are telling me something I have learned to know all too well, though it took me years to master it. We are born of the fathers we deserve, and they engender the sons they deserve. We are our own penance and theirs. The first murderous warfare in the world, we are told, was between two brothers, but the longest and the bitterest is between fathers and sons. Now you offer me the father for the son, and you are offering me nothing that I want or need, in a currency I cannot spend. How could I ease my anger on you? I respect you, I like you, there are even things you might ask of me that I would give you with goodwill. But I will not give you Olivier.'

It was a dismissal. There was no more speech between them that night. From the chapel, hollowly echoing along the corridors of stone, the bell chimed for Compline.

Chapter Nine

ADFAEL ROSE at midnight, waking by long habit even without the matins bell, and being awake, recalled that he was lodged in a tiny cell close to the chapel. That gave him further matter for thought, though he had not considered earlier that it might have profound implications. He had declared himself honestly enough in his apostasy to Philip, and Philip, none the less, had lodged him here, where a visiting cleric might have expected such a courtesy. And being so close, and having been so considerately housed there, why should he not at least say Matins and Lauds before the altar? He had not surrendered or compromised his faith, however he had forfeited his rights and privileges.

The very act of kneeling in solitude, in the chill and austerity of stone, and saying the familiar words almost silently, brought him more of comfort and reassurance than he had dared to expect. If grace was not close to him, why should he rise from his knees so cleansed of the doubts

142

and anxieties of the day, and clouded by no least shadow of the morrow's uncertainties?

He was in the act of withdrawing, and a pace or two from the open door, which he had refrained from closing in case it should creak loudly enough to wake others, when one who was awake, and as silent as he, looked in upon him. The faint light showed them to each other clearly enough.

'For an apostate,' said Philip softly, 'you keep the hours very strictly, brother.' He wore a heavy furred gown over his nakedness, and walked barefooted on the stone. 'Oh, no, you did not disturb me. I sat late tonight. For that you may take the blame if you wish.'

'Even a recusant,' said Cadfael, 'may cling by the hems of grace. But I am sorry if I have kept you from sleep.'

'There may be better than sorrow in it for you,' said Philip. 'We will speak again tomorrow. I trust you have all you need here, and lie at least as softly as in the dortoir at home? There is no great difference between the soldier's bed and the monk's, or so they tell me. I have tried only the one, since I came to manhood.'

Truth, indeed, since he had taken up arms in this endless contention in support of his father before he reached twenty.

'I have known both,' said Cadfael, 'and complain of neither.'

'So they told me, I recall, at Coventry. Some who knew of you. As I did not – not then,' said Philip, and drew his gown closer about him. 'I, too, had a word to say to God,' he said, and passed Cadfael and entered his chapel. 'Come to me after Mass.'

'Not behind a closed door this time,' said Philip, taking Cadfael by the arm as they came out from Mass, 'but

143

publicly in hall. No, you need not speak at all, your part is done. I have considered all that has emerged concerning Brien de Soulis and Yves Hugonin, and if the one matter is still unproven, guilty or no, the other cries out too loud to be passed over. Let Brien de Soulis rest as well as he may, it is too late to accuse him, at least here. But Hugonin – no, there is too great a doubt. I no longer accuse him, I dare not. Come, see him released to ride and rejoin his own faction, wherever he pleases.'

In the hall of La Musarderie trestle tables and benches were all cleared away, leaving the great space stark and bare, the central fire roused and well tended, for winter was beginning to bite with night frosts, and for all the shelter of the deep river valley the winds found their bitter way in by every shutter and every arrow-slit. Philip's officers gathered there turned impartial faces as he entered, and a cluster of men-at-arms held off and watched, awaiting his will.

'Master of arms,' said Philip, 'go and bring up Yves Hugonin from his cell. Take the smith with you, and strike off his chains. It has been shown me that in all probability I have done him wrong in thinking him guilty of de Soulis's death. At least I have doubt enough in me to turn him loose and clear him of all offence against me. Go and fetch him here.'

They went without hesitation, with a kind of indifferent briskness that came naturally to these men who served him. Fear had no part in their unquestioning promptness. Any who feared him would have fallen off from him and taken themselves elsewhere.

'You have given me no chance to be grateful,' said Cadfael in Philip's ear.

'There is no occasion for gratitude here. If you have told me truth, this is due. I make too much haste, sometimes,

144

but I do not of intent spit in the face of truth.' And to some of the men who hovered in the doorway: 'See his horse saddled, and his saddle-roll well provided. No, wait a while for that. His own grooming may take a while, and we must send our guests forth fed and presentable.'

They went to do his bidding, to heat water and carry it to an empty apartment, and install there the saddle-roll that had been hoisted from the horse when Yves had been brought in prisoner. So it was more than half an hour later when the boy was brought into the hall before his captor, and baulked and stared at the sight of Brother Cadfael standing at Philip's side.

'Here is one says I have grossly mistaken you,' said Philip directly, 'and I have begun to be of his opinion. I make known now that you are free to go, no enemy henceforth of mine, and not to be meddled with where my writ runs.'

Yves looked from one to the other, and was at a loss, so suddenly hailed out of his prison and brought forth into the light. He had been captive for so short a time that the signs hardly showed on him at all. His wrists were bruised from the irons, but there was no more than a thin blue line to be seen, and either he had been housed somewhere clean and dry, or he had changed into fresh clothes. His hair, still damp, curled about his head, drying fluffy as a child's. But there were the dark shadows of anger and suspicion in the stiffness of his face when he looked at Philip.

'You won him fairly,' said Philip indifferently, smiling a little at the boy's black stare. 'Embrace him!'

Bewildered and wary, Yves tensed at the very touch of Cadfael's hands on his shoulders, but as suddenly melted, and inclined a flushed and still half-reluctant cheek for the kiss, quivering. In a stumbling breath he demanded helplessly: 'What have you done? What brings you here? You should never have followed.'

'Question nothing!' said Cadfael, putting him off firmly to the length of his arms. 'No need! Take what is offered you, and be glad. There is no deceit.'

'He said you had won me.' Yves turned upon Philip, frowning, ready to blaze. 'What has he done? How did he get you to let go of me? I do not believe you do it for nothing. What has he pledged for me?'

'It is true,' said Philip coolly, 'that Brother Cadfael came offering a life. Not, however, for you. He has reasoned me out of you, my friend, no price has been paid. Nor asked.'

'That is truth,' said Cadfael.

Yves looked from one to the other, swayed between belief in the one and disbelief in the other. 'Not for me,' he said slowly. 'It's true, then, it must be true. Olivier is here! Who else?'

'Olivier is here,' agreed Philip equably, and added with finality: 'And stays here.'

'You have no right.' Yves was too intent and solemn now to have room for anger. 'What you held against me was at least credible. Against him you have no justification. Let him go now. Keep me if you will, but let Olivier go free.'

'I will be the judge,' said Philip, his brows drawn formidably, but his voice as level as before, 'whether I have ground of bitter complaint against Olivier de Bretagne. As for you, your horse is saddled and provided, and you may ride where you will, back to your empress without hindrance from any man of mine. The gate will open for you. Be on your way.'

The curtness of the dismissal raised a flush in Yves' smooth, scrubbed cheeks, and for a moment Cadfael feared for the young man's newly achieved maturity. Where would be the sense in protesting further when the situation put all but dignified compliance out of his reach? A few months back, and he might have blazed in ineffective rage, in the perilous confusion of the transition from boy to man. But somewhere beneath one of the curtain towers of La Musarderie Yves had completed his growing up. He confronted his antagonist with mastered face and civil bearing.

'Let me at least ask,' he said, 'what is your intent with Brother Cadfael. Is he also prisoner?'

'Brother Cadfael is safe enough with me. You need not fear for him. But for the present I desire to retain his company, and I think he will not deny me. He is free to go when he will, or stay as long as he will. He can keep the hours as faithfully in my chapel as in Shrewsbury. And so he does,' said Philip with a brief smile, remembering the night encounter, 'even the midnight matin. Leave Brother Cadfael to his own choice.'

'I have still business here,' said Cadfael, meeting the boy's earnest eyes, that widened to take in more meanings than the mere words conveyed.

'I go, then,' he said. 'But I give you to know, Philip FitzRobert, that I shall come back for Olivier de Bretagne in arms.'

'Do so,' said Philip, 'but do not complain then of your welcome.'

He was gone, without looking back. A hand to the bridle, a foot in the stirrup, and a light spring into the saddle, and the reins were gathered in one hand, and his spurless heels drove into the horse's dappled flanks. The ranks of curious soldiers, servants and retainers parted to let him through, and he was out at the gate and on the descending causeway, towards the rim of the trees in the river valley below. There he would cross, and climb out again through the thick belt of woodland that everywhere surrounded Greenhamsted. By the same way that Cadfael had come, Yves departed, out to the great, straight road the Romans had made long ago, arrow-straight across the plateau of the Cotswolds, and when he reached it he would turn left, towards Gloucester and back to his duty.

Cadfael did not go towards the gate to watch him depart. The last he saw of him that day was clear against a sullen sky in the gateway, his back as straight as a lance, before the gates were closed and barred behind him.

'He means it,' said Cadfael by way of warning. For there are young men who say things they do not really mean, and those who fail to understand how to distinguish between the two may live to regret it. 'He will come back.'

'I know it,' said Philip. 'I would not grudge him his flourish even if it was no more than a flourish.'

'It is more. Do not disdain him.'

'God forbid! He will come, and we shall see. It depends how great a force she has now in Gloucester, and whether my father is with her.' He spoke of his father quite coldly, simply estimating in his competent mind the possible forces arrayed against him.

The men of the garrison had dispersed to their various duties. A wind from the courtyard brought in the scent of fresh, warm bread carried in trays from the bakery, sweet as clover, and the sharp, metallic chirping of hammers from the armoury.

'Why,' asked Cadfael, 'should you wish to retain my company? It is I who had business unfinished with you, not you with me.'

Philip stirred out of his pondering to consider question and questioner with sharp attention. 'Why did you choose to remain? I told you you might go whenever you wished.'

'The answer to that you know,' said Cadfael patiently. 'The answer to my question I do not know. What is it you want of me?'

'I am not sure myself,' Philip owned with a wry smile.

'Some signpost into your mind, perhaps. You interest me more than most people.'

That, if it was a compliment, was one which Cadfael could have returned with fervent truth. Some signpost into this man's mind, indeed, might be a revelation. To get some grasp of the son might even illuminate the father. If Yves found Robert of Gloucester with the empress in the city, would he urge her to the attack against Philip with a bitterness the match of Philip's own, or try to temper her animosity and spare his son?

'I trust,' said Philip, 'you will use my house as your own, brother, while you are here. If there is anything lacking to you, ask.'

'There is a thing lacking.' He stepped directly into Philip's path, to be clearly seen and heard, and if need be, denied, eye to eye. 'My son is withheld from me. Give me leave to see him.'

Philip said simply: 'No.' Without emphasis or need of emphasis.

'Use your house as my own, you said. Do you now place any restriction on where I may go within these walls?'

'No, none. Go where you will, open any unlocked door, wherever you please. You may find him, but you will not be able to get in to him,' said Philip dispassionately, 'and he will not be able to get out.'

In the early twilight before Vespers, Philip made the rounds of his fortress, saw every guard set, and all defences secured. On the western side, where the ground rose steeply towards the village on the ridge, the wall was bratticed with a broad timber gallery braced out from its crest, since this was the side which could more easily be approached closely to attack the walls with rams or mining. Philip paced the length of the gallery to satisfy himself that all the traps

149

built into its floor to allow attack from above on any besiegers who reached the wall, without exposing the defenders to archery, were clear of all obstacles and looked down stark stone to the ground, uncluttered by outside growth of bush or sapling. True, the brattice itself could be fired. He would have preferred to replace the timber with stone, but was grateful that Musard had at least provided this temporary asset. The great vine that climbed the wall on the eastern side had been permitted to remain, clothing a corner where a tower projected, but approach from that direction, climbing steeply over ground cleared of cover, was no great threat.

On this loftier side, too, he had stripped a great swathe of the hillside bare, so that siege engines deployed along the ridge must stay at a distance to remain in cover, and unless heavy engines were brought up for the attack, the walls of La Musarderie would be safely out of range.

His watchmen on the towers were easy with him, sure of his competence and their own, respected and respecting. Many of his garrison had served him for years, and come here with him from Cricklade. Faringdon had been a different matter, a new garrison patched together from several bases, so that he had had less cause to expect absolute trust and understanding from them. Yet it was the man deepest in his affection and confidence, the one on whom he had most relied for understanding, who had turned upon him with uncomprehending contempt, and led the recusants against him. A failure of language? A failure somewhere in the contact of minds? Of vision? Of reading of the stages in the descent to despair? A failure of love. That, certainly.

Philip looked down from the wall into his own castle wards, where torches began to flare, resinous fires in the deepening dusk. Overhanging the towers on this western side the clouds were heavy, perhaps with snow, and the watchmen on the wall swathed themselves in their cloaks and gathered themselves stolidly against a biting wind. That gallant, silly boy must have reached Gloucester by now, if indeed Gloucester was where he was bound.

Philip recalled Yves' stiffnecked simplicity with a faint, appreciative smile. No, the Benedictine was almost certainly right about him. Folly to suppose such a creature could kill by stealth. He showed as a minor copy of that other, all valour and fealty; no room there for the troubled mind that might look for a way through the labyrinth of destruction by less glorious ways than the sword. White on white on the one hand, black on black on the other, and nowhere room for those unspectacular shades of grey that colour most mortals. Well, if some of us mottled and maimed souls can somehow force a way to a future for the valiant and disdainful innocents, why grudge it to them? But why, having achieved that effort of the mind, is it so hard to come by the tough resignation that should go with it? Burning is never easy to bear.

The activity in the ward below, customary and efficient, sealed in La Musarderie for the night, small, foreshortened figures going about from the buildings under the wall to hall and keep, a tiny hearth of reflected light from the smith's furnace red on the cobbles outside the forge. Two gowned figures swept their dark skirts in at the door of the keep. Chaplain and Benedictine monk together, heading for Vespers. An interesting man, this Benedictine from Shrewsbury, a brother but deprecating his own brotherhood, no priest and yet a father, and having experienced a son's confrontation with a father of his own in youth, since doubtless he was engendered like the rest of humankind. And now himself a father for more than twenty years without knowing it, until he was suddenly presented with the revelation of his offspring in the fullness of manhood, with none of the labours, frustrations and anxieties that go to the making of a mature man. And such a man, perfect and entire, but for the saving leaven of self-doubt which keeps a man humble. And I have not shown much of that myself, thought Philip wryly.

Well, it was time. He descended the narrow stone staircase that led down from the guardwalk, and went to join them at Vespers.

They were a reduced company at the office that night, the guard having been strengthened, and the smiths still at work in forge and armoury. Philip listened with an open mind as the Benedictine brother from Shrewsbury read the psalm. It was the feast day of Saint Nicholas, the sixth day of December.

'I am numbered among such as go down into the pit; I am made as one having no more strength:

'Thou hast committed me to the lowest pit, in darkness, in the depths . . .'

Even here he reminds me, thought Philip, accepting the omen. Yet the psalm was set for this day, and not by Cadfael.

'Thou hast put away my acquaintance, far distant from me; thou hast made me an abomination to them. I am shut up, and I cannot come forth.'

How easy it is to be persuaded into believing that God puts words into the office of the day of intent, for the appropriate mouth to utter them. The *sortes* by another way. But I, thought Philip, between regret and defiance, do not believe it. All this chaotic world fumbles along by chance.

'Wilt thou show forth thy marvels to men entombed? Shall the dead arise and praise thee?'

Well? Philip challenged in silence: Shall they?

After the evening meal in hall Philip withdrew alone to his own quarters, took the most private of his keys, and went out from the keep to the tower at the north-western corner of the curtain wall. A thin sleet was falling, not yet snow, though it made a faint and fleeting white powdering upon the cobbles. By morning it would be gone. The watchman on the tower marked the passage of the tall figure across the ward, and was motionless, knowing the man and his errand. It had not happened now for a matter of weeks. There was a name which had been banished from mention, but not from mind. What could have recalled it on this particular night the guard speculated, but without over-much curiosity.

The door at the foot of the tower, which opened to the first key, was narrow and tall. One swordsman, with an archer three steps up the stair at his back and aiming above his head, could hold it against an army. There was a short brand burning in a sconce on the wall within, shedding light down the well of the continuing stair that spiralled downwards. Even the airshafts that slanted up to the light on the two levels below, through the thick stone of the walls, gave only on to the enclosed and populous ward, not the outer world. Even could a man slough off his chains and compress himself painfully into the narrowing shaft, he would emerge only to be thrust back into his prison. There was no escape there.

On the lower level Philip thrust his second key into the lock of another door, narrow and low. It functioned as smoothly and quietly as everything else that served him. Nor did he trouble to lock it behind him when he entered.

This lower cell was carved out from the rock for more than half the height of the walls, clenched together with stone above, and spacious enough for a wary captor, if he visited at all, to stay well out of reach of a prisoner in irons. The cold within was sharp but dry. The shaft that slanted up to a grid in the tower wall within the ward sent a chill draught across the cell. On a bracket in the solid rock a massive candle burned steadily, well aside from the current of air, and within reach from the levelled rock ledge on which the prisoner's bed was laid. At the edge of the bracket there was a new candle standing ready, for the present one was burning down to its ending.

And on the bed, rigidly erect at the first grate of key in lock, and eyes levelled like javelins upon the doorway, was Olivier de Bretagne.

'No greeting for me?' said Philip. The candle guttered for the first time in the counter-draught he had let in with him. He observed it, and meticulously closed the door at his back. 'And after so long? I have neglected you.'

'Oh, you are welcome,' said Olivier, coldly gracious. The tones of the two voices, a little complicated by an immediate and yet distant echo, matched and clashed. The echo made an unnerving third in the room, listener and commentator. 'I regret I have no refreshment to offer you, my lord, but no doubt you have dined already.'

'And you?' said Philip, and briefly smiled. 'I see the empty trays returning. It has been a reassurance to me that you have not lost your appetite. It would be a disappointment if ever you weakened in your will to keep all your powers intact, against the day when you kill me. No, say nothing, there is no need, I acknowledge your right, but I am not ready yet. Be still, let me look at you.'

He looked, with grave attention, for some time, and all the while the levelled eyes, wide, round, golden-irised and fierce as a hawk's, stared back unwaveringly into his. Olivier was thin, but with the restless leanness of energy confined, not with any bodily deprivation, and bright with the intolerable brightness of frustration, anger and hatred. It was, it had been from the first, a mutual loss, their rage and anguish equal, either of them bereaved and embittered. Even in this they were matched, a perfect pairing. And Olivier was neat, decently clothed, his bed well furnished, his dignity discreetly preserved by the stone vessel and leather bucket for his physical needs, and the candle that gave him light or darkness at will. For he had even the means of relighting it to hand beside his pallet, flint and steel and tinder in a wooden box. Fire is a dangerous gift, but why not? It cannot set light to stone, and no sane man cased in stone is going to set light to his own bed, or what else within will burn, and himself with it. And Olivier was almost excessively sane, so much so that he could see only by his own narrow, stainless standards, and never so far as the hopes and despairs and lame and sorry contrivances by which more vulnerable people cope with a harsh world.

Confinement, resentment and enforced patience had only burnished and perfected his beauty, the eager bones accentuated, the suave flesh polished into ivory. The black, glossy hair clasped his temples and hollow cheeks like hands loving but alien, blue-black, live with tension. Daily he had plunged into the water brought to him, like a swimmer into the sea, urgent to be immaculate whenever his enemy viewed him, never to decline, never to submit, never to plead. That above all.

There in the east, Philip thought, studying him, from that Syrian mother, he must have brought this quality in him that will not rust or rot or anyway submit to desecration. Or was it, after all, from that Welsh monk I have left outside this meeting? What a mating that must have been, to bring forth such a son.

'Am I so changed?' Olivier challenged the fixed stare.

When he moved, his chains chimed lightly. His hands were untrammelled, but thin steel bands encircled his ankles, and tethered him by a generous length of chain to a ring in the stone wall beside his pallet. Knowing his ingenuity and his mettle, Philip was taking no chances. Even if helpers could penetrate here, they would have much ado to hammer him loose from his prison. There was no will to mar or defile him, but an absolute will to keep him immured from the world, a solitary possession on which no price could ever be set.

'Not changed,' said Philip, and moved nearer, within arm's length of his captive. Fine hands Olivier had, elegant and large and sinewy; once they had established a first well-judged grip on a throat it would not be easy to break free. Perhaps the temptation and the provocation would have been even more irresistible if those hands had been chained. A fine chain round a throat would have choked out life even more efficiently.

But Olivier did not move. Philip had tempted him thus more than once since the irredeemable breakage of Faringdon; and failed to rouse him. His own death, of course, would probably have followed. But whether that in itself was what restrained him there was no guessing.

'Not changed, no.' And yet Philip watched him with a new, intense interest, searching for the subtle elements of those two disparate creatures who had brought this arrogant excellence into being. 'I have a guest in my hall, Olivier, who has come on your behalf. I am learning things about you that I think you do not know. It may be high time that you did.'

Olivier looked back at him with a fixed and hostile face, and said never a word. It was no surprise that he should be sought, he knew he had his value, and there would be those anxious to retrieve him. That any of those well disposed to him should by reason or luck have tracked him down to this place was more surprising. If Laurence d'Angers had indeed sent here to ask after his lost squire, it was a bow drawn at a venture. And the arrow would not hit the mark.

'In truth,' said Philip, 'I had here two equally concerned for your fate. One of them I have sent away empty-handed, but he says he will be back for you in arms. I have no cause to doubt he'll keep his word. A young kinsman of yours, Yves Hugonin.'

'Yves?' Olivier stiffened, bristling. 'Yves has been here? How could that be? What brought him here?'

'He was invited. Somewhat roughly, I fear. But never fret, he's away again as whole as he came, and in Gloucester by this time, raising an army to come and drag you out of hold. I thought for a time,' said Philip consideringly, 'that I had a quarrel with him, but I find I was in error. And even if I had not been, it turned out the cause was valueless.'

'You swear it? He's unharmed, and back to his own people? No, I take that back,' said Olivier fiercely. 'I know you do not lie.'

'Never, at any rate, to you. He is safe and well, and heartily hating me for your sake. And the other – I told you there were two – the other is a monk of the Benedictines of Shrewsbury, and he is still here in La Musarderie, of his own will. His name is Cadfael.'

Olivier stood utterly confounded. His lips moved, repeating the familiar but most unexpected name. When he found a voice at last, he was less than coherent.

'How can he be here? A cloistered brother – no, they go nowhere, unless ordered – his vows would not allow—And why here? For *me* . . .? No, impossible!'

'So you do know of him? His vows – yes, he declares himself recusant, he is absent and unblessed. For cause.

157

For you. Do me justice, it was you said I do not lie. I saw this brother at Coventry. He was there seeking news of you, like the young one. By what arts he traced you here I am not wholly sure, but so he did, and came to redeem you. I thought that you should know.'

'He is a man I revere,' said Olivier. 'Twice I have met with him and been thankful. But he owes me nothing, nothing at all.'

'So I thought and said,' agreed Philip. 'But he knows better. He came to me openly, asking for what he wanted. You. He said there were those who would be glad to buy you free; and when I asked, at whatever price? . . . he said, name it, and he would see it paid.'

'This is out of my grasp,' said Olivier, lost. 'I do not understand.'

'And I said to him: "A life, perhaps." And he said: "Take mine!"'

Olivier sat down slowly on the rugs of the bed, astray between the present wintry reality and memories that crowded back upon him fresh as Spring. A brother of the Benedictines, habited and cowled, who had used him like a son. They were together waiting for midnight and Matins in the priory of Bromfield, drawing plans upon the floor to show the way by which Olivier could best be sure of getting his charges safely away out of Stephen's territory and back to Gloucester. They were under the rustling, fragrant bunches of herbs hanging from the rafters of Cadfael's workshop, that last time, when, without even giving it a thought, Olivier before departing had stooped his cheek for the kiss proper between close kin, and blithely returned it.

'And then I asked him: "Why should you offer me your old bones to moulder in his place? What is Olivier de Bretagne to you?" And he said: "He is my son."'

After long silence, the dying candle suddenly sputtered

and flowed into molten wax, and the wick lolled sidewise into the pool and subsided into a last spreading, bluish flame. Philip tilted the new one to pick up the fading spark out of the enclosing darkness, and blew out the last remnant, anchoring the renewed light upon the congealing remains of the old. Olivier's face, briefly withdrawn into twilight, burned slowly bright again as the flame drew constant and tall. He was quite still, the focus of his wide, astonished eyes lengthened into infinite distance.

'Is it true?' he asked almost soundlessly, but not of Philip, who did not lie. 'He never told me. Why did he never tell me?'

'He found you already mounted and launched and riding high. A sudden father clutching at your arm might have thrust you off your course. He let well alone. As long as you remained in ignorance, you owed him nothing.' Philip had drawn back a pace or two towards the door, the key ready in his hand, but he checked a moment to correct his last utterance. 'Nothing, he says, but what is fairly earned between man and man. For until you knew, that was all you were. It will not be so easy between father and son, that I know. Debts proliferate, and the prices set come all too high.'

'Yet he comes offering all for me,' said Olivier, wrestling with this paradox almost in anger. 'Without sanction, exiled, leaving his vocation, his quietude, his peace of mind, offering his life. He has cheated me!' he said in a grievous cry.

'I leave it with you,' said Philip from the open doorway. 'You have the night for thinking, if you find it hard to sleep.'

He went out quietly, and closed and relocked the door.

159

Chapter Ten

YVES MAINTAINED his disdainful withdrawal down the open causeway only as far as he was in full view from the gateway and the guardwalk above. Once secure in cover he found himself a place where he could look back between the trees at the stony outline of the castle. From here, so far below, it looked formidably lofty and solid, yet it was not so great a stronghold. It was well garrisoned and well held, yet with force enough it could be taken. Philip had got it cheaply, by ambushing its lord well out of his own ground, and forcing him to surrender it under threats. Siege was of little use here, it takes far too long to starve out a well-provided garrison. The best hope was a total assault with all the force available, and a quick resolution.

Meantime, the surrounding forests circled the open site on all sides, and even the cleared ground did not remove the walls too far for Yves' excellent distant sight to record details, gradients, even weaknesses if Philip had left any. If he could bring any helpful observations with him to

Gloucester, so much the better, and well worth losing a couple of hours in the inspection.

He took a long look at this frontal approach, for hitherto he had seen only the interior of a cell under one of the towers, being hustled within there with a cloak swathed round his head, and his arms bound. The flanking towers of the gatehouse afforded clear ground for archers across the gate and both left and right to the next towers along the wall. Across all this face the brattice had not been continued, approach up this slope being the most difficult to sustain. Yves turned his horse in the thick cover of the trees, to circle the castle widdershins. That would bring him out at the end on the high ground near the village, with the way clear to make for the fastest route to Gloucester.

Through the edges of the woodland he had a clear view of the most northerly of the towers, and the stretch of wall beyond. In the corner between them, a great coiling growth, blackened now in its winter hibernation, stripped of leaves, clambered as high as the battlements where the brattice began. A vine, very old, stout as a tree. When it had its foliage, he thought, it might partially obscure at least one arrow-slit. No great risk to leave it there. It might admit one man, with care and by night, but it could hardly let in more than one, and even the first would be risking his life. There was a guard on the wall there, pacing between towers. He caught the gleam of light on steel. Still, bear it in mind. He wondered which of four generations of Musards had planted the vine. The Romans had had vineyards in these border shires, centuries ago.

There were four towers in all, in the circuit of the walls, besides the twin towers of the gatehouse, and a watchman on every guardwalk between. Sometimes, in that circuit, Yves had to withdraw further into the trees, but he pursued his inspection doggedly, looking for possible weak spots, but finding none. By the time he was viewing the last tower he was already on ground much higher than the castle itself, and nearing the first cottages of the village. After this last rise the ground levelled into the Cotswold plateau, wide and flat on top of its elevated world, with great, straight roads, big open fields and rich villages fat with sheep. Here, just short of the crest, would be the place to deploy mangonels. And from here would be the best place to launch a mining party or a ram, in a rapid downhill rush to reach the wall by night. At the foot of this last tower there was masonry of a differing colour, as if repairs had been done there. If it could be breached there by a ram, firing might bring down part of the weight of the tower.

At least note even the possibility. There was no more he could do here. He knew the lie of the land now, and could report it accurately. He left the houses of the village behind him and made due east by the first promising track, to reach the highroad that went striding out north-west for Gloucester, and south-east for Cirencester.

He entered the city by the Eastgate late in the afternoon. The streets seemed to him busier and more crowded than he had ever seen them, and before he reached the Cross he had picked out among the throng the badges or the livery of several of the empress's most powerful adherents, among them her younger half-brother Reginald FitzRoy, Baldwin de Redvers, earl of Devon, Patrick of Salisbury, Humphrey de Bohun, and John FitzGilbert the marshall. Her court officers he had expected to see in close attendance, but the more distant partisans he had supposed to be by now dispersed to their own lands. His heart rose to the omen. All those bound south and west must have halted and foregathered again here to take counsel after the failure of the bishops' endeavours for peace, and see how best to take advantage of the time, before their enemies forestalled them. She had an army here assembled, force enough to threaten greater strongholds than La Musarderie. And in the castle here she had assault engines, light enough to be moved quickly, heavy enough in load to breach a wall if used effectively; and most formidable weapon of all, she had the unswerving loyalty of Robert of Gloucester, his person to confront and disarm his renegade son, his blood to lay claim to Philip's blood and render him helpless.

Certainly Philip had fought for King Stephen as relentlessly as ever he had for the empress, but never yet face to face with the father he had deserted. The one enormity, the only one, that had been ruled out in this civil war, was the killing of close kinsmen, and who could be closer kin than father and son. Fratricidal war, they called it, the very thing it was not. When Robert declared himself at the gates of La Musarderie and demanded surrender, his own life in the balance, Philip must give way. Or even if he fought, for very pride's sake, it must be with no more than half his heart, always turning away from confrontation with his own progenitor. Loved or hated, that was the most sacred and indissoluble tie that bound humankind. Nothing could break it.

He must take his story straight to the earl of Gloucester, and trust to him to know how to set about the errand. At the Cross, therefore, he turned away from the abbey, and towards the castle, down a busy and populous Southgate towards the river, and the water-meadows that still grew green in the teeth of winter. The great grey bulk of the castle loomed above the streets on this townward side, above the jetties and the shore and the wide steely waters on the other. The empress preferred somewhat more comfort when she could get it, and would certainly have installed herself and her women in the guest apartments of the abbey. Earl Robert was content in the sterner quarters of the castle with his men. By the bustle and the abundance of armed men and noble liveries about the town a considerable number of other billets must have been commandeered temporarily to accommodate the assembled forces. So much the better, there was more than enough power here to make short work of storming La Musarderie.

Yves dreamed ardently of climbing up by the great vine and remaining within, in concealment, long enough to find a postern that could be opened, or a guard who could be overpowered and robbed of his keys. The less fighting the better, the less time wasted, the less destruction to be made good, and the less bitter ill will afterwards to smooth away into forgetfulness. Between faction and faction, between father and son. There might even be a reconciliation.

Before he reached the gates, Yves began to be hailed by some of his own kind, squires of this nobleman or that, astonished to see Philip FitzRobert's victim come riding in merrily, as if he had never fallen foul of that formidable enemy. He called greetings back to them gladly, but waved them off from delaying him now. Only when he entered the outer ward of the castle did he rein in beside the guardhouse, and stop to question, and to answer questions. Even then he did not dismount, but leaned from the saddle to demand, a little breathlessly from the excitement of the message he bore and the pleasure of being welcomed back among friends:

'The earl of Gloucester? Where shall I find him? I have news he should hear quickly.'

The officer of the guard had come out to view the arrival, and stared up at him in amazement. A squire in the earl of Devon's following shouted aloud from among the multifarious activities in the ward beyond, and came running in delight to catch at his bridle.

'Yves! You're free? How did you break out? We heard how you were seized, we never thought to see you back so soon.'

'Or ever?' said Yves, and laughed, able to be lighthearted about that possibility now the danger was past. 'No, I'm loosed to plague you yet a while. I'll tell you all later. Now I need to find Earl Robert quickly.'

'You'll not find him here,' said the guard. 'He's in Hereford with Earl Roger. No word yet when we can expect him back. What's so urgent?'

'Not here?' echoed Yves, dismayed.

'If it's that vital,' said the officer briskly, 'you'd better take it to her Grace the empress herself, at the abbey. She doesn't care to be passed over, even for her brother, as you should know if you've been in her service long. She won't thank you if she has to hear it from another, when you come riding in hot with it.'

That was exactly what Yves was very reluctant to do. Her favour and her disfavour were equally scarifying, and equally to be avoided. No doubt she was still under the misapprehension that he had done her, at her clear suggestion, an appalling service, but also he had been the unfortunate cause of some disruption in her passage home to Gloucester, and put her to some trouble in consequence, for which she certainly would not thank him. And if she looked for her ring on his little finger, and failed to find it, that was hardly likely to count in his favour. Yves admitted to himself that he was afraid to confront her, and shook himself indignantly at the thought.

'She's at the abbey with her women. In your shoes I'd make for there as fast as may be,' said the guard shrewdly.

'She was roused enough when you were taken, go and show your face, and set her mind at rest on one count, at least.'

'I'd advise it,' agreed the squire with a good-humoured grin, and clapped Yves heartily on the back. 'Get that over, and come and take your ease. You come as a welcome sight, we've been in a taking over you.'

'Is FitzGilbert with her?' demanded Yves. If Robert of Gloucester was not available, at least he would rather deal with the marshall than with the lady alone, and it was the marshall who would have to talk good sense into the lady as to how to deal with this opportunity.

'And Bohun, and her royal uncle of Scotland. Her close council, nobody else.'

Yves waved away the brief, inevitable delay, and turned his horse to return to the Southgate and the Cross, and so to the abbey enclave where the empress kept her court. A pity to have missed Gloucester himself. It meant delay, surely. She would not act on her own, without her brother's counsel and support, and Olivier had been in durance long enough. But make the best of it. She had the means to act, the town was bursting with troops. She could well afford to allow the raising of a voluntary force to try what could be done by stealth, if she would not move in strength. Yves had no doubts of her courage and valour, but all too many of her competence and generalship.

He rode into the great court of the abbey, and crossed to the guest apartments, through the preoccupied bustle of the court. The carrying of arms and presence of armed men was discreetly limited here, but for all that there were as many fighting men as brothers within the precinct, out of armour and not carrying steel, but unmistakably martial. The presence of a guard on the stairway to the great door of the hall indicated that the whole building had been taken over for Maud's use, and lesser mortals approached her

166

presence only after proving the validity of their business. Yves submitted to being crisply halted and questioned.

'Yves Hugonin. I serve in the empress's household. My lord and uncle is Laurence d'Angers, his force is now in Devizes. I must see her Grace. I have a report to make to her. I went first to the castle, but they told me to come to her here.'

'You, is it?' said his questioner, narrowing sharp eyes to view him more attentively. 'I remember, you're the one they cut out from her retinue, on the way from Coventry. And we'd heard never a word of you since. Seemingly it's turned out better than we feared. Well, she should be glad to see you alive and well, at any rate. Not every man is getting a welcome these days. Come in to the hall, and I'll send a page in to let her know.'

There were others waiting in the hall to be summoned to the presence, more than one minor magnate among them, besides some of the merchants of the town who had favours to ask or merchandise to offer for sale. While she kept her court here, with a substantial household about her, she was a source of profit and prosperity to Gloucester, and her resident armies a sure protection.

She kept them all waiting for some time. Half an hour had passed before the door to her apartments opened, and a girl came through it to call two names, and usher two minor lords, if not yet into the empress's presence, at least into her anteroom. Yves recognized the bold, self-assured young woman who had submitted him to such a close scrutiny at Coventry before she decided that he would do. Dark hair, with russet lights in its coils, and bright eyes, greenish hazel, that summed up men in sweeping glances and pigeon-holed them ruthlessly, discarding, it seemed, all who were past thirty. Her own age might have been nineteen, which was also Yves'. While she summoned, surveyed and dismissed the two lordlings she had been sent to bring in, she did not fail to devote one long glance to Yves, not altogether dismissively, but his mind was on other matters, and he did not observe it. She was gone with her charges almost before he had recalled where he had first encountered her. A favourite among the royal gentlewomen, probably; certainly she had adopted some of her mistress's characteristics.

Another half-hour had passed, and one or two of the townsmen had given up and departed the hall, before she returned for Yves.

'Her Grace is still in council, but come within and be seated, and she will send for you shortly.'

He followed her along a short corridor and into a large, light room where three girls were gathered in one corner with embroideries in their laps, and their chatter subdued to low tones because there was only a curtained door between them and the imperial council. Occasionally they put in a dutiful stitch or two, but very desultorily. Their attendance was required, but it need not be made laborious. They were instantly more interested in Yves, when he entered, all the more because he showed a grave, preoccupied face, and no particular interest in them. Brief silence saluted his coming, and then they resumed their soft and private conversation, with a confidential circumspection that suggested he figured in it. His guide abandoned him there, and went on alone into the inner room.

There was an older woman seated on a cushioned bench against the wall, withdrawn from the gaggle of girls. She had a book in her lap, but the light was dimming towards evening, and she had ceased to read. The empress would need a few literate ladies about her, and this one seemed to be an essential member of her retinue. Her, too, he remembered from Coventry. Aunt and niece, they had told him, the only gentlewomen Maud had brought with her into that stark male assembly. She looked up at him now, and knew him. She smiled, and made a slight gesture of her hand that was clearly an invitation to join her.

'Yves Hugonin? It *is* you? Oh, how good to see you here, alive and well. And free! I had heard you were lost to us. Most of us knew nothing of that outrage until after we reached Gloucester.'

She was perfectly composed, indeed he could not imagine her calm ever being broken; and yet he was dazzled for an instant by the widening and warming of her eyes when she had recognized him. She had the illusionless eyes of middle age, experienced, lined, proof against most surprises, and yet in that one flash of glad astonishment they had a lustre and depth that shook him to the heart. It had mattered to her deeply, that even after the empress's protection extended to him at Coventry, he should again be put in peril of his life. It mattered to her now that he came thus unexpectedly back to Gloucester, free and unharmed.

'Come, sit! You may as well, waiting for audience here is a weary business. I am so glad,' she said, 'to see you alive and well. When you left Coventry with us, and no one tried to prevent, I thought that trouble was safely over, and no one would dare accuse you of any wrong deed again. It was very ill fortune that ever you fell under such suspicion. But her Grace stood firm for your right, and I thought that would be the end of it. And then that assault . . . We never heard until next day. How did you escape him? And he so bitter against you, we feared for you.'

'I did not escape him,' said Yves honestly, and felt boyishly diminished by having to admit it. It would have been very satisfying to have broken out of La Musarderie by his own ingenuity and daring. But then he would not even have known that Brother Cadfael was there within, nor could he have been certain that Olivier was held there, and he would not have stated his resolve and laid down his challenge to return for him in arms. That was of more importance than his own self-esteem. 'I was set free by Philip FitzRobert. Dismissed, indeed! He acquits me of any part in de Soulis's death, and so has no more use for me.'

'The more credit to him,' said Jovetta de Montors. 'He has cooled and come to reason.'

Yves did not say that Philip had had some encouragement along the road to reason. Even so, it was credit to him indeed, that he had acknowledged his change of heart, and acted upon it.

'He did believe I had done murder,' said Yves, doing his enemy justice, though still with some resentment and reluctance. 'And he valued de Soulis. But I have other quarrels with him that will not be so easily settled.' He looked earnestly at the pale profile beside him, tall brow under braided silver hair, straight, fine nose and elegantly strong line of the jaw, and above all the firm, full, sensitive way her lips folded together over her silences, containing in dignified reticence whatever she had learned in her more than fifty years of life. 'You never believed me a murderer?' he asked, and himself was startled to find how he ached for the right answer.

She turned to him fully, wide-eyed and grave. 'No,' she said, 'never!'

The door to the audience chamber opened, and the girl Isabeau came out with a swirl of brocaded skirts and held it open. 'Her Grace will receive you now.' And she mouthed at him silently: 'I am dismissed. They are talking high strategy. Go in to her, and tread softly.'

170

There were four people in the room he entered, besides two clerks who were just gathering up the tools of their trade, and the scattering of leaves of vellum spread across the large table. Wherever the empress moved her dwelling there would be charters to draw up and witness, sweets of property and title to dole out to buy favour, minor rewards to be presented to the deserving, and minor bribes to those who might be most useful in future, the inevitable fruits of faction and contention. King Stephen's clerks were occupied with much the same labour. But these had finished their work for this day, and having cleared the table of all signs of their profession, went out by a further door, and quietly closed it behind them.

The empress had pushed back her large, armed stool to allow the clerks to circle the table freely. She sat silent, with her hands on the broad, carved arms of her seat, not gripping, simply laid along the brocaded tissue, for once at rest. Her rich and lustrous dark hair was plaited into two long braids over her shoulders, intertwined with cords of gold thread, and lay upon the breast of her purple bliaut stirring and quivering to her long, relaxed breathing as though it had a life of its own. She looked a little tired, and a little as though she had recently been out of temper, but was beginning to put by the vexations of business and emerge from her darker mood. Behind her sombre magnificence the wall was draped with hangings, and the benches adorned with cushions and rich coverings. She had brought her own furnishings with her to create this audience room, the largest and lightest the abbey could provide.

The three who at the moment composed her closest council had risen from the table when the last charter was ready for copying and witnessing, and moved some paces apart after a long session. Beside one darkening window King David of Scotland stood, drawing in the chilling air, half turned away from his imperial niece. He had been at her side through most of the years of this long warfare, with staunch family loyalty, but also with a shrewd eye on his own and his nation's fortunes. Contention in England was no bad news to a monarch whose chief aim was to gain a stranglehold on Northumbria, and push his own frontier as far south as the Tees. Able, elderly and taciturn, a big man and still handsome for all the grey in his hair and beard, he stood stretching his wide shoulders after too long of sitting forward over tedious parchments and challenging maps, and did not turn his head to see what further petitioner had been admitted so late in the day.

The other two hovered, one on either side of the empress; Humphrey de Bohun, her steward, and John Fitz-Gilbert, her marshall. Younger men both, the props of her personal household, while her more spectacular paladins paraded their feats of arms in the brighter light of celebrity. Yves had seen something of these two during his few weeks in the empress's entourage, and respected them both as practical men with whom their fellowmen could deal with confidence. They turned on him preoccupied but welcoming faces now. Maud, for her part, took a long moment to recall the circumstances in which he had come to absent himself, and did so with a sudden sharp frown, as though he had been to blame for causing her considerable trouble.

Yves advanced a few paces, and made her a deep reverence.

'Madam, I am returned to my duty, and not without news. May I speak freely?'

'I do remember,' she said slowly, and shook off her abstraction. 'We have known nothing of you since we lost you, late in the evening, on the road through the forest near Deerhurst. I am glad to see you alive and safe. We wrote that capture down to FitzRobert's account. Was it so? And where have you been in his hold, and how did you break free?' She grew animated, but not, he thought, greatly concerned. The misuse of one squire, even his death, would not have added very much to the score she already held against Philip FitzRobert. Her eyes had begun to burn up in small, erect flames at the mention of his name.

'Madam, I was taken to La Musarderie, in Greenhamsted, the castle he took from the Musards a few months back. I cannot claim to have broken free by any effort of mine, he has loosed me of his own will. He truly believed I had murdered his man de Soulis.' His face flamed at the recollection of what she had believed of him, and still believed, and he shrank from trying to imagine with what amused approval she was listening to this discreet reference to that death. Probably she had not expected such subtlety from him. She might even have had some uneasy moments at his reappearance, and have scored up even that embarrassment against Philip, for not making an end of his captive. 'But he has abandoned that belief,' Yves rushed on, making short work of what, after all, was of no importance now. 'He set me at liberty. For myself I have no complaint, I have not been misused, considering what he held against me.'

'You have been in chains,' said de Bohun, eyeing the boy's wrists.

'So I have. Nothing strange in that, as things were. But madam, my lords, I have discovered that he has Olivier de Bretagne, my sister's husband, in his dungeons in that same castle, and has so held him ever since Faringdon, and will listen to no plea to let him go freely, or offer him for ransom. There are many would be glad to buy him out of prison, but he will take no price for Olivier. And, madam, strong as La Musarderie is, I do believe we have the force

173

here to take it by storm, so quickly they shall not have time to send to any of his other fortresses for reinforcements.'

'For a single prisoner?' said the empress. 'That might cost a very high price indeed, and yet fail of buying him. We have larger plans in mind than the well being of one man.'

'Olivier has been a very profitable man to our cause,' urged Yves strenuously, evading provoking her with '*your* cause' just in time. It would have sounded like censure, and that was something not even those nearest to her and most regarded would have dared. 'My lords,' he appealed, 'you know his mettle, you have seen his valour. It is an injustice that he should be held in secret when all the others from Faringdon have been honourably offered for ransom, as the custom is. And there is more than one man to win, there is a good castle, and if we move quickly enough we may have it intact, almost undamaged, and a mass of arms and armour with it.'

'A fair enough prize,' agreed the marshall thoughtfully, 'if it could be done by surprise. But failing that, not worth a heavy loss to us. I do not know the ground well. Do you? You cannot have seen much of their dispositions from a cell underground.'

'My lord,' said Yves eagerly, 'I went about the whole place before I rode here. I could draw out plans for you. There's ground cleared all about it, but not beyond arrow range, and if we could move engines to the ridge above . . .'

'No!' said the empress sharply. 'I will not stir for one captive, the risk is too great, and too little to gain. It was presumptuous to ask it of me. Your sister's husband must abide his time, we have greater matters in hand, and cannot afford to turn aside for a luckless knight who happens to have made himself well hated. No, I will not move.'

'Then, madam, will you give me leave to try and raise a

174

lesser force, and make the attempt by other means? For I have told Philip FitzRobert to his face, and sworn it, that I will return for Olivier in arms. I said it, and I must and will make it good. There are some who would be glad to join me,' said Yves, flushed and vehement, 'if you permit.'

He did not know what he had said to rouse her, but she was leaning forward over the table now, gripping the curved arms of the stool, her ivory face suddenly burningly bright. 'Wait! What was that you said? To his face! You told him to his face? He was there this very morning, in person? I had not understood that. He gave his orders – that could be done from any of his castles. We heard that he was back in Cricklade, days ago.'

'No, it's not so. He is there in La Musarderie. He has no thought of moving.' Of that, for some reason, Yves was certain. Philip had chosen to keep Brother Cadfael, and Brother Cadfael, no doubt for Olivier's sake, had elected to stay. No, there was no immediate plan to leave Green-hamsted. Philip was waiting there for Yves to return in arms. And now Yves understood the working of her mind, or thought he did. She had believed her hated enemy to be in Cricklade, and to get at him there she would have had to take her armies well to the south-east, into the very ring of Stephen's fortresses, surrounded by Bampton, Faring-don, Purton, Malmesbury, all ready to detach companies to repel her, or, worse still, surround her and turn the besiegers into the besieged. But Greenhamsted was less than half the distance, and if tackled with determination could be taken and regarrisoned before Stephen's relief forces could arrive. A very different proposition, one that caused the fires in her eyes to burn up brilliantly, and the stray tresses escaping from her braids to quiver and curl with the intensity of her resolution and passion.

'He is within reach, then,' she said, vengefully glowing.

'He is within reach, and I will have him! If we must turn out every man and every siege engine we have, it is worth it.'

Worth it to take a man she hated, not worth it to redeem a man who had served her all too faithfully, and lost his liberty for her. Yves felt his blood chill in apprehension. But what could she do with Philip when she had him, but hand him over to his father, who might curb and confine him, but surely would not harm him. She would grow tired of her own hatred once she had suppressed and had the better of her traitor. Nothing worse could happen. There might even be a reconciliation, once father and son were forced to meet, and either come to terms or destroy each other.

'I will have him,' said the empress with slow and burning resolve, 'and he shall kneel to me before his own captive garrison. And then,' she said with ferocious deliberation, 'he shall hang.'

The breath went out of Yves in a muted howl of consternation and disbelief. He gulped in air to find a voice to protest, and could not utter a word. For she could not mean it seriously. Her brother's son, a revolted son perhaps, but still his own flesh and blood, her own close kin, and a king's grandson. It would be to shatter the one scruple that had kept this war from being a total bloodbath, a sanction that must not be broken. Kinsman may bully, cheat, deceive, outmanoeuvre kinsman, but not kill him. And yet her face was set in iron resolution, smouldering and gleeful, and she did mean it, and she would do it, without a qualm, without pause for relenting.

King David had turned sharply from his detached contemplation of the darkening world outside the window, to stare first at his niece, and then at the marshall and the steward, who met his eyes with flashing glances, acknowledging and confirming his alarm. Even the king hesitated to say outright what was in his mind; he had long experience of the empress's reaction to any hint of censure, and if he had no actual fear of her rages, he knew their persistency and obstinacy, and the hopelessness of curbing them, once roused. It was in the most reasonable and mild of voices that he said:

'Is that wise? Granted his offence and your undoubted right, it would be well worth it to hold your hand at this moment. It might rid you of one enemy, it would certainly raise a dozen more against you. After talk of peace this would be one way to ensure the continuance of war, with more bitterness than ever.'

'And the earl,' added the steward with emphasis, 'is not here to be consulted.'

No, thought Yves, abruptly enlightened, for that very reason she will move this same night, set forward preparations to shift such of her siege engines as can be transported quickly, take every man she can raise, leave all other plans derelict, all to smash her way into La Musarderie before the earl of Gloucester hears what is in the wind. And she will do it, she has the hardihood and the black ingratitude. She will hang Philip and present Earl Robert with a fait accompli and a dead son. She dare do it! And then what awful disintegration must follow, destroying first her own cause, for that she does not care, provided she can get a rope round the neck of this one enemy.

'Madam,' he cried, tearing King David's careful moderation to shreds, 'you cannot do it! I offered you a good castle, and the release of an honourable soldier to add to your ranks, I did not offer you a death, one Earl Robert will grieve for to his life's end. Take him, yes, give him to the earl, prisoner, let them settle what lies between them.

That is fair dealing. But this – this you must not and cannot do!'

She was on her feet by then, raging but contained, for Yves was only a minor insolence to be brushed aside rather than crushed, and at this moment she still had a use for him. He had seen her blaze up like this to flay other unfortunates, now the fire scorched him, and even in his devouring anger he shrank from it.

'Do you tell me what I can and cannot do, boy? Your part is to obey, and obey you shall, or be slung back into a worse dungeon and heavier irons than you've suffered yet. Marshall, call Salisbury and Reginald and Redvers into council at once, and have the engineers muster the man-gonels, all that can be moved quickly. They shall set forth before us, and by noon tomorrow I want the vanguard on the road, and the main army mustering. I want my traitor dead within days, I will not rest until I see him dangling. Find me men who know the roads and this Greenhamsted well, we shall need them. And you,' she turned her flashing eyes again upon Yves, 'wait in the anteroom until you are called. You say you can draw us plans of La Musarderie, now you shall prove it. Make it good! If you know of any weak spots, name them. Be thankful I leave you your liberty and a whole skin, and take note, if you fall short of deliver-ing what you have promised me, you shall lose both. Now go, get out of my sight!'

Chapter Eleven

O NOW there was nothing to be done but to go along with what had already been done and could not be undone, make the best of it, and try by whatever means offered to prevent the worst. Nothing was changed in his determination to return to La Musarderie, and do his part to the limit in the battle to release Olivier. He would do all he could to press the assault. He had spent some hours of the night drawing out plans of the castle, and the ground from the ridge to the river below, and done his best to estimate the extent of the cleared land all round the fortress, and the range the siege engines would have to tackle. He had even indicated the curtain tower where there had been damage and repair, according to his observations, and where possibly a breach might be effected. The empress was welcome to the castle, once Olivier was safely out of captivity, but she was not, if he could prevent it, entitled to kill the castellan. Challenged by others more daring and more established than himself, she had argued vehemently that

Earl Robert was as mortally affronted by Philip's treason as she herself was, and would not hesitate to approve the death. But she was in ruthless haste to be about the business before any word of her intention could get to her brother's ears, all the same. Not that she was afraid of Robert, or willing to acknowledge that she could do nothing effective without him. She had been known to humiliate him in public, on occasion, as arrogantly and ruthlessly as any other. No, what she aimed at was to present him with a death already accomplished, past argument, past redemption, her own unmistakable and absolute act, the statement of her supremacy. For surely all these years, while she had used and relied on him, she had also been jealous of him, and grudged him his pre-eminence.

Yves slept the few hours left to him after the council ended rolled in his cloak on a bench in the darkened hall, without a notion in his troubled head as to how to circumvent the empress's revenge. It was not simply that such an act would disrupt and alienate half her following, and fetch out of their scabbards every sword that was not bared and blooded already, to prolong and poison this even now envenomed warfare. It was also, though he had not the penetration to probe into motives after such a day, that he did not want Philip's death. A daunting, inward man, hard to know, but one he could have liked in other circumstances. One whom Olivier had liked, but equally did not understand.

Yves slept fitfully until an hour before dawn. And in the bleak morning hours he made ready, and rode with the main body of the empress's army, under John FitzGilbert, to the assault of La Musarderie.

The deployment of the siege force around the castle was left to the marshall, and the marshall knew his business,

180

and could get his engineers and their mangonels into position along the ridge without noise or commotion enough to reach the ears of the watchmen on the walls, and his companies strategically placed within cover all about the site, from the bank of the river round to the fringes of the village above, where the empress and her women had taken possession of the priest's house, rather than face the ardours of a camp. The operation might have been much more difficult, and the secret out before the end of the day, had not the villagers of Greenhamsted fared rather well under the Musards, and felt no inclination at all to send warning to the present castellan of La Musarderie. Their complacency with the present total occupation would stand them in good stead with one faction, the one that had appeared among them with convincing strength. They held their peace, sat circumspectly among their invading soldiery, and awaited events.

The dispersal went on into the darkness, and the first fires in the camp above, insufficiently covered and damped, alerted the guards on the wall. A round of the guardwalks discovered a number of similar sparks dispersed among the trees, all round the perimeter of the cleared ground.

'He has brought down the whole mass of her army on us,' said Philip dispassionately to Cadfael, up on the south tower, watching the minute glints that showed the ring of besiegers. 'A lad of his word! Pure chance that she seems to have mustered a council of earls about her in Gloucester, with all their companies, when I could well have done without them. Well, I invited him to the feast. I am as ready as I can be, with such odds against me. Tomorrow we shall see. At least now we're warned.' And he said to his monastic guest, very civilly: 'If you wish to withdraw, do so freely, now, while there's time. They will respect and welcome you.'

'I take that offer very kindly,' said Cadfael with equally placid formality, 'but I do not go from here without my son.'

Yves left his station among the trees to northward when it was fully dark, and with a sky muffled by low-hanging clouds that hid moon and stars. Nothing would happen this night. With such a show of force there would certainly be a demand for surrender, rather than set out from the beginning to batter a valuable asset to pieces. At dawn, then. He had this one night to make contact if he could.

Yves' memory was excellent. He could still repeat word for word what Philip had said of his unexpected guest: 'He can keep the hours as faithfully in my chapel as in Shrewsbury. And so he does, even the midnight matin.' Moreover, Yves knew where that chapel must be, for when they had plucked him out of his cell and brought him forth from the keep to the hall he had seen the chaplain emerge from a dim stone corridor with his missal in his hand. Somewhere along that passage Cadfael might, if God willed, keep his solitary office this night also, before the clash of battle. This night of all nights he would not neglect his prayers.

The darkness was great blessing. Even so, black-cloaked and silent, movement may be perceptible by a quiver in the depth of the blackness, or the mere displacement of air. And the stripped slope he had to cross seemed to him at this moment a matter of tedious miles. But even a shaven hillside can undulate, providing shallow gullies which nevertheless would be deep enough to offer a consistent path from trees to curtain wall, and the shadowy corner under the north tower where the great vine grew. Even a dip in the ground can provide some kind of shelter in the gradations of shadow. He wished he could see the head of the guard who paced the length of wall between those two towers, but the distance was too great for that. Beyond the halfway mark there might be enough variation between solid bulk and sky to show the outline of towers and crenellations, if without detail; perhaps even the movement of the head against space as the watchman patrolled his length of guardwalk. Pointless to hope for a greater degree of visibility, it would mean only that he, too, could be seen.

He wrapped the heavy black frieze about him, and moved forward clear of the trees. From within the wards a faint reflection of light from torches below made a just perceptible halo under the thick cloud cover. He fixed his eyes on that, and walked forward towards it, his feet testing the invisible ground, doing the function of eyes as they do for the blind. He went at a steady pace, and there was no wind to flap at his cloak and hair, and make itself palpable, even over distance.

The black bulk against the sky loomed nearer. His ears began to catch small sounds that emanated from within, or from the watchmen on the walls when they changed guard. And once there was a sudden torch-flare and a voice calling, as someone mounted from the ward, and Yves dropped flat to the ground, burying head and all under the cloak, and lay silent where everything round him was silent, and motionless where nothing moved, in case those two above should look over from the embrasure, and by some infinitesimal sign detect the approach of a living creature. But the man with the torch lit himself briskly down the stair again, and the moment passed.

Yves gathered himself up cautiously, and stood a moment still, to breathe freely and stare ahead, before he resumed his silent passage. And now he was close enough to be able to distinguish, as movement makes the invisible perceptible even in the dark, the passage of the guard's head, as he paced the length of wall between the towers. Here in the corner of tower and wall the brattice began; he had taken careful note of it again before darkness fell, and he had seen how the thick, overgrown branches of the vine reached crabbed arms to fasten on the timber gallery that jutted from the stone. It should be possible to climb over into the gallery while the watchman's beat took him in the other direction. And after that?

Yves came unarmed. Sword and scabbard are of little use in climbing either vines or castle walls, and he had no intention of attacking Philip's guard. All he wanted was to get in and out undetected, and leave the word of warning he had to deliver, for the sake of whatever fragile chance of reconciliation and peace remained alive after the débâcle of Coventry. And how he accomplished it, well or ill, must depend on chance and his own ingenuity.

The guard on the wall was moving away towards the further tower. Yves seized the moment and ran for it, risking the rough ground, to drop thankfully under the wall, and edge his way along it until he reached the corner, and drew himself in under the maze of branches. Here the brattice above was a protection to him instead of a threat. Midnight must still be almost an hour away, he could afford to breathe evenly for some minutes, and listen for the footsteps above, very faint even when they neared this point, fading out altogether as soon as the guard turned away.

The cloak he must leave behind, to climb in it would be awkward and possibly dangerous, but he had seen to it that the clothing he wore beneath it was equally black. He let the footsteps return over him twice, to measure the interval, for at each return he would have to freeze into stillness. The third time, as the sound faded, he felt his way to a firm grip among the branches, and began to climb.

184

Almost leafless, the vine made no great stir or rustle, and the branches were twisted and gnarled but very strong. Several times on the way he had to suspend all movement and hang motionless while the watchman above halted briefly at the turn to stare out over the cleared ground, as he must have been staring at intervals all the time Yves was making his way here to the precarious shelter of the curtain wall. And once, feeling for a hold against the rounded masonry of the tower, he put his hand deep into an arrow-slit, and caught a glimmer of light within, reflected through a half-open door, and shrank back into the corner of the stonework in dread that someone might have seen him. But all continued quiet, and when he peered cautiously within there was nothing to be seen but the edge of that inner door and the sharp rim of light. Now if there should also be an unlocked door into the tower from the guardwalk. . . . They would have been moving weapons during the day, as soon as they knew the danger, and the place for light mangonels and espringales was on the wall and the towers. And stones and iron for the mangonels, surely by now piled here in store, and the darts and javelins for the espringales. . . .

Yves waited to move again, and hoped.

The towers of La Musarderie jutted only a shallow height beyond the crenellated wall, and the vine had pushed its highest growth beyond the level of the brattice, still clinging to the stone. He reached the stout timber barrier before he realized it, and hung still to peer over it along the gallery. He was within three paces of the guard this time when the man reached the limit of his patrol, and turned again. Yves let him withdraw half the length of his charge before daring to reach out for the solid rail where the brattice began, and swing himself over into the gallery. One more interval now before he could climb over to the guardwalk. He lay down close under one of the merlons, and let the pacing feet pass by him and again return. Then he crept cautiously through the embrasure on to the solid level of stone, and turned to the tower. Here beside it the garrison had indeed been piling missiles for the defence engines, but the door was now fast closed, and would not give to his thrust. They had not needed to use the tower to bring up their loads, there was a hoist standing by over the drop into the bailey, and just astride from it the head of one of the stairways from bailey to wall. There was but one way to go, before the watchman turned at the end of his beat. Yves went down the first steps of the flight in desperate haste, and then lowered himself by his hands over the edge, and worked his way down step by step, dangling precariously over the drop.

He hung still as the guard passed and repassed, and then continued his aching descent, into this blessedly remote and dark corner of the ward. There was still light and sound in the distant armoury, and shadowy figures crossing in purposeful silence from hall to stores, and smithy to armoury. La Musarderie went about its siege business calmly and efficiently, not yet fully aware of the numbers ranged against them. Yves dropped the last steps of the stairway, and flattened himself back against the wall to take stock of his ground.

It was not far to the keep, but too far to risk taking at a suspect run. He schooled himself to come out of his hiding-place and cross at a rapid, preoccupied walk, as the few other figures out thus late in the night were doing. They were sparing of torches where everything was familiar, all he had to do was keep his face averted from any source of light, and seem to be headed somewhere on garrison business of sharp importance. Had he encountered someone closely he would have had to pass by with a muttered word, so intent on his errand that he had no attention to spare for anything else. And that would have been no lie. But he reached the open door and went in without challenge, and heaved a great sigh to have got so far in safety.

He was creeping warily along the narrow, stone-flagged passage when the chaplain emerged suddenly from a door ahead, and came towards him, with a small oil flask in his hand, fresh from feeding and trimming the altar lamp. There was no time to evade, and to have attempted it would have penetrated even the tired old man's preoccupation. Yves drew to the wall respectfully to let him pass, and made him a deep reverence as he went by. Short-sighted eyes went over him gently, and a resigned but tranquil voice blessed him. He was left trembling, almost shamed, but he took it for a good omen. The old man had even shown him where the chapel was to be found, and pointed him to the altar. He went there humbly and gratefully, and kneeled to give thanks for a dozen undeserved mercies that had brought him thus far. He forgot even to be careful, to be ready to take alarm at a sound, to regard his own life or take thought for how he should ever find his way out again. He was where he had set out to be. And Cadfael would not fail him.

The chapel was lofty, cramped and stonily cold, but its austerity had been tempered a little by draping the walls with thick woollen hangings, and curtaining the inner side of the door. In the dim light of the corner behind the door, where the folds of curtain and wall hanging met amply, a man could stand concealed. Only if someone entering closed the door fully behind him would the alien presence risk detection. Yves took his stand there, shook the folds into order to cover him, and settled down to wait.

In the several days that he had been a guest in La

Musarderie Cadfael had awakened and risen at midnight largely from habit, but also from the need to cling at least to the memory of his vocation, and of the place where his heart belonged. If he did not live to see it again, it mattered all the more that while he lived that link should not be broken. It was also a solemn part of his consolation in keeping the monastic observances that he could do it in solitude. The chaplain observed every part of the daily worship due from a secular priest, but did not keep the Benedictine hours. Only once, on that one occasion when Philip had also had a word to say to God, had Cadfael had to share the chapel at Matins with anyone.

On this night he came a little early, without the necessity of waking from sleep. There would be little sleep for most of the garrison of La Musarderie. He said the office, and continued on his knees in sombre thought rather than private prayer. All the prayers he could make for Olivier had already been uttered and heard, and repeated in the mind over and over, reminders to God. And all that he might have pleaded for himself was seen to be irrelevant in this hour, when the day is put away, with all its unresolved anxieties, and the morrow's troubles are not yet, and need not be anticipated.

When he rose from his knees and turned towards the door, he saw the folds of the curtain behind it quiver. A hand emerged at the edge, putting the heavy cloth aside. Cadfael made no sound and no movement, as Yves stepped forth before his eyes, soiled and dishevelled from his climb, with urgent gesture and dilated eyes enjoining caution and silence. For a moment they both hung still, staring at each other. Then Cadfael flattened a hand against Yves' breast, pressing him back gently into hiding, and himself leaned out from the doorway to look both ways along the stone corridor. Philip's own chamber was close, but it was questionable whether he would be in it this night. Here nothing stirred, and Cadfael's narrow cell was not ten yards distant. He reached back to grip Yves' wrist, and pluck him hastily along the passage into sanctuary there, and close the door against the world. For a moment they embraced and stood tense, listening, but all was still.

'Keep your voice low,' said Cadfael then, 'and we are safe enough. The chaplain sleeps nearby.' The walls, even these interior walls, were very thick. 'Now, what are you doing here? And how did you get in?' He was still gripping the boy's wrist, so tightly as to bruise. He eased his grip, and sat his unexpected visitor down on the bed, holding him by both shoulders, as if to touch was to hold inviolable. 'This was madness! What can you do here? And I was glad to know that you were out of it, whatever comes.'

'I climbed up by the vine,' said Yves, whispering. 'And I must go back the same way, unless you know of a better.' He was shivering a little in reaction; Cadfael felt him vibrating between his hands like a bowstring gradually stilling after the shot. 'No great feat – if the guard can be distracted while I reach the gallery. But let that wait. Cadfael, I had to get word in here to you somehow. He must be told what she intends . . .'

'He?' said Cadfael sharply. 'Philip?'

'Philip, who else? He has to know what he may have to deal with. She – the empress – she has half a dozen of her barons with her, they were all gathered in Gloucester, and all their levies with them. Salisbury, Redvers of Devon, FitzRoy, Bohun, the king of Scots and all, the greatest army she has had to hand for a year or more. And she means to use everything against this place. It may cost her high, but she will have it, and quickly, before Gloucester can get word what's in the wind.'

'Gloucester?' said Cadfael incredulously. 'But she needs

him, she can do nothing without him. All the more as this is his son, revolted or not.'

'No!' said Yves vehemently. 'For that very reason she wants him left ignorant in Hereford until all's over. Cadfael, she means to hang Philip and be done with him. She has sworn it, and she'll do it. By the time Robert knows of it, there'll be nothing for him but a body to bury.'

'She would not dare!' said Cadfael on a hissing breath.

'She will dare. I saw her, I heard her! She is hellbent on killing, and this is her chance. Her teeth are in his throat already, I doubt if Robert himself could break her death-grip, but she has no mind to give him the opportunity. It will all be over before ever he knows of it.'

'She is mad!' said Cadfael. He dropped his hands from the boy's shoulders, and sat staring down the long procession of excesses and atrocities that would follow that death: every remaining loyalty torn apart, every kinship disrupted, the last shreds of hope for conciliation and sanity ripped loose to the winds. 'He would abandon her. He might even turn his hand against her.' And that, indeed, might have ended it, and brought about by force the settlement they could not achieve by agreement. But no, he would not be able to bring himself to touch her, he would only withdraw from the field with his bereavement and grief, and let others bring her down. A longer business, and a longer and more profound agony for the country fought over, back and forth to the last despair.

'I know it,' said Yves. 'She is destroying her own cause, and damning to this continued chaos every man of us, on either side, and God knows, all the poor souls who want nothing but to sow and reap their fields and go about their buying and selling, and raising their children in peace. I tried to tell her so, to her face, and she flayed me for it. She listens to no one. So I had to come.'

And not only to try and avert a disastrous policy, Cadfael thought, but also because that imminent death was an offence to him, and must be prevented solely as the barbaric act it was. Yves did not want Philip FitzRobert dead. He had come back in arms for Olivier, certainly, and he would stand by that to his last breath, but he would not connive at his liege lady's ferocious revenge.

'To me,' said Cadfael. 'You come to me. So what is it you want of me, now you are here?'

'Warn him,' said Yves simply. 'Tell him what she has in mind for him, make him believe it, for she'll never relent. At least let him know the whole truth, before he has to deal with her demands. She would rather keep the castle and occupy it intact than raze it, but she'll raze it if she must. It may be he can make a deal that will keep him man alive, if he gives up La Musarderie.' But even the boy did not really believe in that ever happening, and Cadfael knew it never would. 'At least tell him the truth. Then it is his decision.'

'I will see to it,' said Cadfael very gravely, 'that he is in no doubt what is at stake.'

'He will believe you,' said Yves, sounding curiously content. And he stretched and sighed, leaning his head back against the wall. 'Now I had better be thinking how best to get out of here.'

They were quite used to Cadfael by that time, he was accepted in La Musarderie as harmless, tolerated by the castellan, and respectably what his habit represented him as being. He mixed freely, went about the castle as he pleased, and talked with whom he pleased. It stood Yves in good stead in the matter of getting out by the same route by which he had entered.

The best way to escape notice, said Cadfael, was to go

about as one having every right and a legitimate reason for going wherever he was seen to be going, with nothing furtive about him. Risky by daylight, of course, even among a large garrison of reasonably similar young men, but perfectly valid now in darkness, crossing wards even less illuminated than normally, to avoid affording even estimates of provision for defence to the assembled enemy.

Yves crossed the ward to the foot of the staircase up to the guardwalk by Cadfael's side, quite casually and slowly, obeying orders trustfully, and melted into the dark corner to flatten himself against the wall, while Cadfael climbed the steps to lean into an embrasure between the merlons of the wall and peer out towards the scattered sparkle of fires, out there among the trees. The watchman, reaching this end of his patrol, lingered to lean beside him and share his speculations for a moment, and when he resumed his march back to the distant tower, Cadfael went with him. Yves, listening below, heard their two low voices recede gradually. As soon as he felt they should be sufficiently distant, he crept hastily up the steps and flung himself through the embrasure, to flatten himself on the floor of the brattice under a merlon. He was at the end of the gallery, the gnarled black branches and twisted tendrils of the vine leaned inward over him, but he did not dare to rise and haul himself in among them until the guard had made one more turn, and again departed, leaving Cadfael to descend to the ward and seek his bed for what remained of the night.

Above Yves' head the familiar voice said very softly: 'He's away. Go now!'

Yves rose and heaved himself over the parapet and into the sinewy coils of the vine, and began to let himself down cautiously towards the ground far below. And Cadfael, when the boy had vanished, and the first shaking and rustling of the branches had subsided, descended the steps to the ward, and went to look for Philip.

Philip had made the rounds of his defences alone, and found them as complete as he had the means to make them. This assault came early, young Hugonin must have been uncommonly persuasive, and the empress unusually well provided with men and arms, or he would have had more time to prepare. No matter, it would be decided the sooner.

He was on the walk above the gate when Cadfael found him, looking down upon the open causeway by which, in the early morning, the first challenger would approach under flag of truce.

'You, brother?' he said, turning a mildly surprised face. 'I thought you would have been sleeping hours ago.'

'This is no night for sleeping,' said Cadfael, 'until all's done that needs to be done. And there is yet something needed, and I am here to see it done. My lord Philip, I have to tell you, and take it in earnest, for so it is, that the empress's mind against you is deadly. Yves Hugonin has brought all this host down upon you to deliver his friend and kinsman. But not she! She is here, not even to take a castle, though she must do that first. She is here to take a man. And when she has you, she means to hang you.'

There was a silence. Philip stood gazing eastward, where the first grey blanching of the day would come, before dawn. At length he said quietly: 'Her mind I never doubted. Tell me, if you know so much, brother, is that also my father's mind towards me?'

'Your father,' said Cadfael, 'is not here in arms. He does not know her army has moved, and she will take good care he does not find out, not until all is over. Your father is in Hereford with Earl Roger. For once she has moved without him. For good reason. She sees her chief enemy within her

193

grasp. She is here to destroy you. And since she goes to such pains to keep this from him,' said Cadfael, his voice detached and mild, 'it would seem that she, at any rate, is by no means certain of his mind towards you.'

A second silence fell between them. Then Philip said, without turning his head: 'I knew her well enough to be out of reach now of surprise. I looked for nothing better, should it ever come to this. I made her of none account when I turned to the king, that is true, though less true, or only partial truth, that I turned against her. She was of none effect, that was the heart of it. And here, if not in Normandy, Stephen was and is in the ascendant. If he can win, as she could not, and put an end to this chaos and waste, let as many coats turn as may be needed to bring it about. Any end that will let men live, and till their fields, and ride the roads and ply their trades in safety, is to be desired above any monarch's right and triumph. My father,' he said, 'determined the way I went. As lief Stephen as Maud, to me, if he can enforce order. But I understand her rage. I grant her every fibre of her grudge against me. She has a right to hate me, and I'll abide her hate.'

It was the first time he had spoken thus freely, temperately, without regret or penitence.

'If you have believed me,' said Cadfael, 'that she means your shameful death, that is my mission done. If you know the whole truth, you can dispose yourself to meet it. She has an eye to gain, as well as to revenge. If you choose, you could bargain.'

'There are things I will not trade,' said Philip, and turned his head, and smiled.

'Then hear me yet a moment,' said Cadfael. 'You have spoken of the empress. Now speak to me of Olivier.'

The dark head turned sharply away again. Philip stood

mute, staring eastward, where there was nothing to see, unless his own mind peopled the darkness.

'Then I will speak of him,' said Cadfael. 'I know my son. He is of a simpler mode than you, you asked too much of him. I think you had shared many dangerous moments with him, that you had come to rely on each other and value each other. And when you changed course, and he could not go with you, the severance was doubly bitter, for each of you felt that the other had failed him. All he saw was treason, and what you saw was a failure of understanding that was equally a betrayal.'

'It is your story, brother,' said Philip with recovered serenity, 'not mine.'

'There is as sharp a point to it as to a dagger,' said Cadfael. 'You do not grudge the empress her resentment. Why can you not extend the same justice to my son?'

He got no answer from Philip, but he needed none; he already knew. Olivier had been dearly loved. The empress never had.

Chapter Twelve

HE EXPECTED embassage came with the dawn, and it was the marshall who brought it. The party appeared out of the woods, taking to the open causeway to be seen as soon as they left cover: a knight with a white pennant before, then FitzGilbert with three attendant officers at his back, not in mail or showing weapons, to indicate clearly that at this moment they intended no threat and expected none. Philip, roused from his brief sleep as soon as they were sighted, came out to the guardwalk over the gate, between the two towers, to receive them.

Cadfael, below in the ward, listened to the exchange from the doorway of the hall. The stillness within the walls was like the hush before storm, as every man halted and froze to hear the more clearly; not from fear, rather with a piercing tremor of excitement, many times experienced and by now customary and almost welcome.

'FitzRobert,' called the marshall, halted some yards from the closed gates, the better to look up at the man he challenged, 'open your gates to her Grace the empress, and receive her envoy.'

'Do your errand from there,' said Philip. 'I hear you very well.'

'Then I give you to know,' said FitzGilbert forcefully, 'that this castle of yours is surrounded, and strongly. No relief can get in to your aid, and no man of you can get out unless by agreement with her Grace. Make no mistake, you are in no case to withstand the assault we can make upon you, can and will, if you are obdurate.'

'Make your offer,' said Philip, unmoved. 'I have work to do, if you have none.'

FitzGilbert was too old a hand at the manoeuvrings of civil war to be shaken or diverted by whatever tone was used to him. 'Very well,' he said. 'Your liege lady the empress summons you to surrender this castle forthwith, or she will take it by storm. Give it up intact, or fall with it.'

'And on what conditions?' said Philip shortly. 'Name the terms.'

'Unconditional surrender! You must submit yourself and all you hold here to her Grace's will.'

'I would not hand over a dog that had once barked at her to her Grace's will,' said Philip. 'On reasonable terms I might consider. But even then, John, I should require your warranty to back hers.'

'There'll be no bargaining,' said the marshall flatly. 'Surrender or pay the price.'

'Tell the empress,' said Philip, 'that her own costs may come high. We are not to be bought cheaply.'

The marshall shrugged largely, and wheeled his horse to descend the slope. 'Never say you were not warned!' he called back over his shoulder, and cantered towards the trees with his herald before him and his officers at his back.

After that they had not long to wait. The assault began with a volley of arrows from all the fringes of cover round the castle. For a good bowman the walls were within range, and whoever showed himself unwisely in an embrasure was a fair mark; but it seemed to Cadfael, himself up on the south-western tower, which came nearest to the village on the crest, that the attackers were being lavish of shafts partly to intimidate, having no fear of being left short of arrows. The defenders were more chary of waste, and shot only when they detected a possible target unwarily breaking cover. If they ran down their stock of shafts there was no way of replenishing it. They were reserving the espringales, and the darts and javelins they shot, to repel a massed attack. Against a company they could scarcely fail to find targets, but against one man on the move their bolts would be wasted, and waste was something they could not afford. The squat engines, like large crossbows, were braced in the embrasures, four of them on this south-westerly side, from which attack in numbers was most likely, two more disposed east and west.

Of mangonels they had only two, and no target for them, unless the marshall should be unwise enough to despatch a massed assault. They were the ones who had to fear the battering of siege engines, but at need heavy stones flung into a body of men making a dash to reach the walls could cut disastrous swathes in the ranks, and render the method too expensive to be persisted in.

The activity was almost desultory for the first hours, but one or two of the attacking archers had found a mark. Only minor grazes as yet, where some unwary youngster had shown himself for a moment between the merlons. No doubt some of these practised bowmen on the walls had also drawn blood among the fringes of the trees on the ridge. They were no more than feeling their way as yet.

Then the first stone crashed short against the curtain wall below the brattice, and rebounded without more damage than a few flying chips of masonry, and the siege engines were rolled out to the edge of cover, and began to batter insistently at the defences. They had found their range, stone after heavy stone howled through the air and thudded against the wall, low down, concentrating on this one tower, where Yves had detected signs of previous damage and repair. This, thought Cadfael, would continue through the day, and by night they might try to get a ram to the walls, and complete the work of battering a way through. In the meantime they had lost at any rate one of their engineers, who had ventured into view too clearly in his enthusiasm. Cadfael had seen him dragged back into the trees.

He looked out over the high ground that hid the village of Greenhamsted, probing for movement among the trees, or glimpses of the hidden machines. This was a battle-ground in which he should have had no part. Nothing bound him to either the besiegers or the besieged, except that both were humankind like himself, and could bleed. And he had better by far be making himself useful in the one way he could justify here. But even as he made his way along the guardwalk, sensibly from merlon to merlon like an experienced soldier with a proper regard for his own skin, he found himself approving Philip's deployment of his bowmen and his espringales, and the practical way his garrison went about their defence.

Below in the hall the chaplain and an elderly steward were attending to such minor injuries as had so far been suffered, bruises and cuts from flying splinters of stone

199

spattered high by the battering of the wall, and one or two gashes from arrows, where an arm or a shoulder had been exposed at the edge of the protecting merlons. No graver harm; not yet. Cadfael was all too well aware that before long there would be. He added himself to the relieving force here, and took comfort in the discovery that for some hours he had little enough to do. But before noon had passed it became clear that FitzGilbert had his orders to bring to bear upon La Musarderie every means of assault he had at his disposal, to assure a quick ending.

One frontal attack upon the gatehouse had been made early, under cover of the continued impact of stone upon stone under the tower to westward, but the espringales mounted above the gate cut a swathe with their javelins through the ranks of the attackers, and they were forced to draw off again and drag their wounded with them. But the alarm had distracted some degree of attention from the main onslaught, and diverted a number of the defenders to strengthen the gate-towers. The besiegers on the ridge took the opportunity to run their heaviest mangonel forward clear of the trees, and let loose all the heaviest stones and cases of iron rubble at the defences, raising their aim to pound incessantly at the timber brattice, more vulnerable by far than the solid masonry of the wall. From within, Cadfael felt the hall shaken at every impact, and the air vibrating like impending thunder. If the attackers raised their range yet again, and began lobbing missiles over among the buildings within the ward, they might soon have to transfer their activities and their few wounded into the rocklike solidity of the keep.

A young archer came down dangling a torn arm in a bloody sleeve, and sat sweating and heaving at breath while the cloth was cut away from his wound, and the gash cleaned and dressed.

'My drawing arm,' he said, and grimaced. 'I can still loose the espringale, though, if another man winds it down. A great length of the brattice is in splinters, we nearly lost a mangonel over the edge when the parapet went, but we managed to haul it in over the embrasure. I leaned out too far, and got this. There's nothing amiss with Bohun's bowmen.'

The next thing, Cadfael thought, smoothing his bandage about the gashed arm, will be fire arrows into the splintered timbers of the gallery. The range, as this lad has proved to his cost, is well within their capabilities, there is hardly any deflecting wind, indeed by this stillness and the feel of the air there will be heavy frost, and all that wood will be dry as tinder.

'They have not tried to reach the wall under there?' he asked.

'Not yet.' The young man flexed his bandaged arm gingerly, winced, and shrugged off the twinge, rising to return to his duty. 'They're in haste, surely, but not such haste as all that. By night they may try it.'

In the dusk, under a moonless sky with heavy low cloud, Cadfael went out into the ward and climbed to the guard-walk on the wall, and peered out from cover at the splintered length of gallery that sagged outward drunkenly in the angle between tower and curtain wall. Within the encircling woodland above there were glimmerings of fires, and now and then as they flared they showed the outlines of monstrous black shapes that were the engines of assault. Distance diminished them into elusive toys, but did not diminish their menace. But for the moment there was a lull, almost a silence. Along the wall the defenders emerged cautiously from the shelter of the merlons to stare towards the ridge and the village beyond. The light was too far gone for archery, unless someone offered an irresistible target by stepping full into the light of a torch.

They had their first dead by then, laid in the stony cold of the chapel and the corridors of the keep. There could be no burying.

Cadfael walked the length of the wall between the towers, among the men braced and still in the twilight, and saw Philip there at the end of the walk, where the wreckage of the brattice swung loose from the angle of the tower. Dark against the dark, still in mail, he stood sweeping the rim of the trees for the gleams of fire and the location of the mangonels the empress had brought against him.

'You have not forgotten,' said Cadfael, close beside him, 'what I told you? For I told you absolute truth.'

'No,' said Philip, without turning his head, 'I have not forgotten.'

'Nor disbelieved it?'

'No,' he said, and smiled. 'I never doubted it. I am bearing it in mind now. Should God forestall the empress, there will be provision to make for those who will be left.' And then he did turn his head, and looked full at Cadfael, still smiling. 'You do not want me dead?'

'No,' said Cadfael, 'I do not want you dead.'

One of the tiny fires in the distance, no bigger than a first spark from the flint, burned up suddenly into a bright red glow, and flung up around it shadows of violent movement, a little swirl of just perceptible chaos in the night and the woodland, where the branches flared in a tracery like fine lace, and again vanished. Something soared into the darkness hissing and blazing, a fearful comet trailing a tail of flames. One of the young archers, ten yards from where Cadfael stood, was staring up in helpless fascination, a mere boy, unused to siegecraft. Philip uttered a bellow of alarm and warning, and launched himself like a flung lance, to grasp the boy round the body and haul him back with him into the shelter of the tower. The three of them dropped together, as men were dropping under every merlon along the wall, pressed into the angle of wall and flagged walk. The comet, spitting sparks and flashes of flaming liquid, struck the centre of the length of damaged gallery, and burst, hurling burning tar from end to end of the sagging timbers, and splashing the guardwalk through every embrasure. And instantly the battered wood caught and blazed, the flames leaping from broken planks and splintered parapet all along the wall.

Philip was on his feet, hauling the winded boy up with him.

'Are you fit? Can you go? Down with you, never mind fighting it. Go get axes!'

There would be burns and worse to deal with afterwards, but this was more urgent now. The young man went scrambling down into the ward in frantic haste, and Philip, stooping under the shelter of the wall, went running the length of the blaze, hoisting his men up, despatching those worst damaged down to take refuge below and find help. Here the brattice would have to be hacked free, before it spread the fire within, flashed into the woodwork of the towers, spat molten tar over the ward. Cadfael went down the steps with a moaning youth in his arms, nursing him down stair by stair, his own scapular swathed round the boy's body to quench the lingering smouldering of cloth and the smell of scorched flesh. There were others below waiting to receive him, and more like him, and hoist them away into cover. Cadfael hesitated, almost wishing to go back. On the guardwalk Philip was hacking away the blazing timbers among his remaining guards, wading through lingering puddles of flaming tar to reach the beams that still clung to their shattered hold upon the wall.

No, he was not of the garrison, he had no right to take a hand in this quarrel upon either side. Better go and see what could be done for the burned.

Perhaps half an hour later, from among the pallets in the hall, with the stench of burned woollens and flesh in his nostrils, he heard the timbers of the gallery break free and fall, creaking as the last fibres parted, flaring with a windy roar as they fell, fanned by their flight, to crash under the tower and settle, in a series of spitting collapses, against the stones.

Philip came down some time later, blackened to the brow and parched from breathing smoke, and stayed only to see how his wounded fared. He had burns of his own, but paid them little attention.

'They will try and breach the wall there before morning,' he said.

'It will still be too hot,' objected Cadfael, without pausing in anointing a badly burned arm.

'They'll venture. Nothing but wood, a few hours of the night's cold. And they want a quick ending. They'll venture.'

'Without a sow?' They could hardly have hauled a whole stout wooden shelter, long enough to house and cover a team of men and a heavy ram, all the way from Gloucester, Cadfael surmised.

'They'll have spent most of the day building one. They have plenty of wood. And with half the brattice on that side down, we'll be vulnerable.' Philip settled his mail over a bruised and scorched shoulder, and went back to his guardwalk to watch out the night. And Cadfael, drawing breath at length among the injured, guessed at the approach of midnight, and made a brief but fervent office of Matins.

Before first light the assault came, without the precaution

of the shelter a sow would have afforded, but with the added impetus of speed to balance that disadvantage. A large party issued from the woods and made a dash downhill for the wall, and though the mounted espringales cut some furrows in their ranks, they reached the foot of the tower, just aside from the glowing remnants of the fire. Cadfael heard from the hall the thudding of their ram against the stone, and felt the ground shake to the blows. And now, for the want of that length of gallery, the defenders were forced to expose themselves in order to hoist stones over the embrasures, and toss down oil and flares to renew the blaze. Cadfael had no knowledge of how that battle must be going; he had more than enough to do where he was. Towards morning Philip's second in command, a border knight from near Berkeley named Guy Camville, touched him on the shoulder, rousing him out of a half-doze of exhaustion, and told him to get away into comparative quiet in the keep, and snatch a couple of hours of honest sleep, while it was possible.

'You've done enough, brother,' he said heartily, 'in a quarrel that's been none of your making.'

'None of us,' said Cadfael ruefully, clambering dazedly to his feet, 'has ever done enough – or never in the right direction.'

The ram was withdrawn, and the assault party with it, before full light, but by then they had made a breach, not through the curtain wall, but into the base of the tower. A fresh approach by full daylight was too costly to contemplate without cover, but the besiegers were certainly hard at work by now building a sow to shelter the next onslaught, and if they contrived to get branches and brushwood inside they might be able to burn their way through into the ward. Not, however, without delaying their own entry in any numbers until the passage was cool enough to risk. Time was the only thing of which they lacked enough. Philip massed his own mangonels along the threatened south-western wall, and set them to a steady battering of the edge of the woodland, to hamper the building of the sow, and reduce the number of his enemies, or confine them strictly to cover until nightfall.

Cadfael observed all, tended the injured along with every other man who could be spared for the duty, and foresaw an ending very soon. The odds were too great. Weapons spent here within, every javelin, every stone, could not be replaced. The empress had open roads and plenteous wagons to keep her supplied. No one knew it better than Philip. In the common run of this desultory war she would not have concentrated all this fury, costly in men and means, upon one solitary castle like La Musarderie. In just one particular she justified the expenditure, without regard to those she expended: her most hated enemy was here within. No cost was too great to provide her his death. That also he knew, none better. It had hardly needed telling; yet Cadfael was glad that Yves had risked his liberty, and possibly his own life, to bring the warning, and that it had been faithfully delivered.

While the attackers waited for night to complete the breach, and the defenders laboured to seal it, all the siege engines on the ridge resumed their monotonous assault, this time dividing their missiles between the foot of the tower and a new diversion, raising their trajectory to send stones and butts of iron fragments and tar casks over the wall into the ward. Twice roofs were fired within, but the fires were put out without great damage. The archers on the walls had begun selecting their quarries with care, to avoid profitless expense in shafts from a dwindling store. The engineers managing the siege machines were their main target, and now and again a good shot procured a moment's respite, but there were so many practised men up there that every loss was soon supplied.

They set to work damping down all the roofs within the curtain wall, and moved their wounded into the greater safety of the keep. There were the horses to be thought of, as well as the men. If the stables caught they would have to house the beasts in the hall. The ward was full of purposeful activity, unavoidably in the open, though the missiles kept flying over the wall, and to be in the open there was one way of dying.

It was in the dark that Philip emerged from the breached tower, with all done there that could be done against the inevitable night assault; the breach again barricaded, the tower itself sealed, locked and barred. If the enemy broke in there, for hours at least they would be in possession of nothing beyond. Philip came forth last, with the armourer's boy beside him, fetcher and carrier for the work of bolting iron across the gap in the wall. The armourer and one of his smiths had climbed to the guardwalk, to ensure there should be no easy way through at that level. The boy came out on Philip's arm, and was restrained from bolting at once for the door of the keep. They waited close under the wall a moment, and then crossed at a brisk walk.

They were halfway across when Philip heard, as every man heard, the howling, whistling flight as perhaps the last missile of the day hurtled over the wall, black, clumsy and murderous, and crashed on the cobbles a few feet before them. Even before it had struck he had caught the boy in his arms, whirled about with no time to run, and flung them both down on the ground, the boy face-down beneath him.

The great, ramshackle wooden crate crashed at the same moment, and burst, flinging bolts and twisted lumps of iron, furnace cinder, torn lengths of chain-mail, for thirty yards around in all directions. The weary men of the garrison shrank into the walls on every side, hugging their cowering flesh until the last impact had passed in shuddering vibration round the shell of the ward, and died into silence.

Philip FitzRobert lay unmoving, spread along the cobbles, head and body distorted by two misshapen lumps of iron of the empress's gift. Under him the terrified boy panted and hugged the ground, heaving at breath, undamaged.

They took him up, the trembling boy hovering in tears, and carried him into the keep and into his own austere chamber, and there laid him on his bed, and with difficulty eased him of his mail and stripped him naked to examine his injuries. Cadfael, who came late to the assembly, was let in to the bedside without question. They were accustomed to him now, and to the freedom with which their lord had accepted him, and they knew something of his skills, and had been glad of his willingness to use them on any of the household who came by injury. He stood with the garrison physician, looking down at the lean, muscular body, defaced now by a torn wound in the left side, and the incisive dark face just washed clean of blood. A lump of waste iron from a furnace had struck him in the side and surely broken at least two ribs, and a twisted, discarded lance-head had sliced deep through his dark hair and stuck fast in the left side of his head, its point at the temple. Easing it free without doing worse damage took them a grim while, and even when it was out, there was no knowing whether his skull was broken or not. They swathed his body closely but not too tightly, wincing at the short-drawn breaths that signalled the damage within. Throughout, he was deep beneath the pain. The head wound they cleansed carefully, and dressed. His closed eyelids never quivered, and not a muscle of his face twitched.

'Can he live?' whispered the boy, shivering in the doorway.

'If God wills,' said the chaplain, and shooed the boy away, not unkindly, going with him the first paces with a hand on his shoulder, and dropping hopeful words into his ear. But in such circumstances, thought Cadfael grievously, remembering the fate that awaited this erect and stubborn man if God did please to have him survive this injury, which of us would care to be in God's shoes, and how could any man of us bear to dispose his will to either course, life or death?

Guy Camville came, the burden of leadership heavy on him, made brief enquiry, stared down at Philip's impervious repose, shook his head, and went away to do his best with the task left to him. For this night might well be the crisis.

'Send me word if he comes to his senses,' said Camville, and departed to defend the damaged tower and fend off the inevitable assault. With a number of men out of the battle now, it was left to the elders and those with only minor grazes to care for the worst wounded. Cadfael sat by Philip's bed, listening to the short, stabbing breaths he drew, painful and hard, that yet could not break his swoon and recall him to the world. They had wrapped him well against the cold, for fear fever should follow. Cadfael moistened the closed lips and the bruised forehead under the bandages. Even thus in helplessness the thin, fastidious face looked severe and composed, as the dead sometimes look.

Close to midnight, Philip's eyelids fluttered, and his brows knotted in a tightly drawn line. He drew in deeper breaths, and suddenly hissed with pain returning. Cadfael moistened the parted lips with wine, and they stirred and accepted the service thirstily. In a little while Philip opened his eyes, and looked up vaguely, taking in the shapes of his own chamber, and the man sitting beside him. He had his senses and his wits again, and by the steady intelligence of his eyes as they cleared, memory also.

He opened his lips and asked first, low but clearly: 'The boy – was he hurt?'

'Safe and well,' said Cadfael, stooping close to hear and be heard.

He acknowledged that with the faintest motion of his head, and lay silent for a moment. Then: 'Bring Camville. I have affairs to settle.'

He was using speech sparingly, to say much in few words; and while he waited he closed lips and eyes, and hoarded the clarity of his mind and the strength left to his body. Cadfael felt the force with which he contained and nursed his powers, and feared the fall that might follow. But not yet, not until everything had been set in order.

Guy Camville came in haste, to find his lord awake and aware, and made rapid report of what he might most want to hear. 'The tower is holding. No break through yet, but they're under the wall, and have rigged cover for the ram.'

Philip perceptibly gathered his forces, and drew his deputy down by the wrist beside his bed. 'Guy, I give you charge here. There'll be no relief. It is not La Musarderie she wants. She wants me. Let her have me, and she'll come to terms. At first light – flag FitzGilbert and call him to parley. Get what terms you best can, and surrender to her. If she has me, she'll let the garrison march out with honour. Get them safe to Cricklade. She'll not pursue. She'll have what she wants.'

Camville cried in strong protest: 'No!'

'But I say yes, and my writ still runs here. Do it, Guy!

210

Get my men out of her hands, before she kills them all to get her hands on me.'

'But it means your life—' Camville began, shaken and dismayed.

'Talk sense, man! My life is not worth one death of those within here, let alone all. I am within a hair's breadth of my death already, I have no complaint. I have been the cause of deaths here among men I valued, spare me any more blood on my head in departing. Call truce, and get what you can for me! At first light, Guy! As soon as a white banner can be seen.'

And now there was no denying him. He spoke as he meant, sanely and forcefully, and Camville was silenced. Only after he had departed, shocked but convinced, did Philip seem suddenly to shrink in his bed, as if air and sinew had gone out of him with the urgency. He broke into a heavy sweat, and Cadfael wiped it away from forehead and lip, and trickled drops of wine into his mouth. For a while there was silence, but for the husky breaths that seemed to have grown both easier and shallower. Then a mere thread of a voice said, with eerie clarity: 'Brother Cadfael?'

'Yes, I am here.'

'One more thing, and I have done. The press yonder . . . open it.'

Cadfael obeyed without question, though without understanding. What was urgent was already done. Philip had delivered his garrison free from any association with his own fate. But whatever still lay heavy on his mind must be lifted away.

'Three keys . . . hanging under the lock within. Take them.'

Three on one ring, dwindling in size from large and

ornate to small, crude and plain. Cadfael took them, and closed the press.

'And now?' He brought them to the bedside, and waited. 'Tell me what it is you want, and I will get it.'

'The north-west tower,' said the spectral voice clearly. 'Two flights below ground, the second key. The third unlocks his irons.' Philip's black, burningly intelligent eyes hung unwaveringly upon Cadfael's face. 'It might be well to leave him where he is until she makes her entry. I would not have him charged with any part of what she holds against me. But go to him now, as soon as you will. Go and find your son.'

Chapter Thirteen

ADFAEL DID not stir until the chaplain came to take his place by the bedside. Twice the sick man had opened his eyes, that now lay sunken in bluish pits in the gaunt face, and watched him sitting there unmoving with the keys in his hand, but given no sign of wonder or disapproval, and uttered no more words. His part was done. Cadfael's part could be left to Cadfael. And gradually Philip sank again beneath the surface of consciousness, having no more affairs to set in order. None, at least, that it was in his power to better. What remained awry must be left to God.

Cadfael watched him anxiously, marking the sunken hollows beneath the cheekbones, the blanching of the brow, the tension of drawn lips, and later the heavy sweat. A strong, tenacious life, not easy to quench. These wounds he had might well put an end to it, but it would not be yet. And surely by noon tomorrow FitzGilbert would be in La Musarderie, and Philip his prisoner. Even if the empress delayed her entry a day or two more, to have proper apartments prepared for her reception, the respite could last no longer. She would be implacable. He had made her of none account, and she would requite the injury in full. Even a man who cannot stand and is barely alive can be hoisted the extra yard or two in a noose, for an example to all others.

So there were still vital affairs to be set in order, as is proper before an imminent death. And under the prompting of God, who was to make provision?

When the chaplain came to relieve his watch, Cadfael took his keys, and went out from the comparative quiet of the keep into the din of battle in the ward. Inevitably the besiegers had pursued their assault upon the same spot they had already weakened, and this time with a hastily constructed sow to shield the ram and the men who wielded it. The hollow, purposeful rhythm of the ram shook the ground underfoot, and was perforated constantly by the irregular thudding of stones and iron flung down on the sow's wooden roof from the damaged brattice above, and the embrasures along the guardwalk. The soft, sudden vibration of bowstrings and hiss of arrows came only very rarely from the air above. Archers were of less use now.

From wall to wall the clash and roar of steel and voices washed in echoing waves from the foot of the damaged tower, round the bulk of the keep, to die in the almost-silence under the other tower, that north-western tower under which Olivier lay in chains. But here where the hand-to-hand battle was joined the mass of men-at-arms, lancers, swordsmen, pikemen, heaved round and within the base of the breached tower. Above their heads, framed in the grotesque shapes left standing in the shattered outer wall, Cadfael could see fractured spaces of sky, paler than the opaque black of masonry, and tinted with the surviving glow of fire. The inner wall was pierced, the door and the

214

stonework that surrounded it battered into the ward, lying here and there among the massed defenders. Not a great gap, and it seemed that the onslaught had been repelled, and the breach successfully filled up with men and steel; but a gap none the less. Not worth repairing, if tomorrow the castle was to be surrendered, but still worth holding to prevent further dying. Philip had dealt in accordance with his office; from the situation he had created he was extricating as many lives as he could, at the expense merely of his own.

It was still good policy to hug the walls when moving about the ward, though in the night the rain of missiles had ceased, and only the occasional fire-arrow was launched over the wall to attempt the diversion of a roof in flames. Cadfael circled the mass of the keep and came to the almost deserted north-western corner of the ward, where only the wall and the brattice were manned, and even much of the noise from the turmoil at the breach was strangely withdrawn into distance. The keys had grown warm in his hand, and the air this night was not frosty. Tomorrow, after the surrender, they might be able to bury their dead, and rest their many wounded.

The narrow door at the foot of the tower opened to the first key without so much as a creak. Two flights down, Philip had said. Cadfael descended. There was a flare in a sconce halfway down the winding staircase; nothing had been forgotten here, even in the stresses of siege. At the cell door he hesitated, breathing deeply and long. There was no sound from within, the walls were too thick; and here no sound from without, only the dim light pulsating silently as the flare flickered.

With the key in the lock, his hand trembled, and suddenly he was afraid. Not of finding some emaciated wreck within the cell; any such fear had long since left his mind.

215

He was afraid of having achieved the goal of his journey, and being left with only the sickening fall after achievement, and the way home an endless, laborious descent into a long darkness, ending in nothing better than loss.

It was the nearest he had ever come to despair, but it lasted only a moment. At the metal kiss of key in lock it was gone, and his heart rose in him to fill his throat like a breaking wave. He thrust open the door, and came face to face with Olivier across the bare cell.

The captive had sprung erect at the first inward movement of his prison door, and stood braced, expecting to be confronted by the only visitor he ever had now, apart from the gaoler who attended him, and confounded by this unexpected apparition. He must have heard, funnelled downwards through the slanting shaft from the ward to his cell, the clamour of battle, and fretted at his own helplessness, wondering what was happening above. The glare he had fixed upon the doorway was suddenly softened and shaken by bewilderment; then his face was still, intent and wary. He believed what he saw; he had his warning. But he did not understand. His wide, wild, golden stare neither welcomed nor repelled; not yet. The chains at his ankles had clashed one sharp peal, and lay still.

He was harder, leaner, unnervingly bright, bright to incandescence with energy frustrated and restrained. The candle on its shelf of rock cast its light sidelong over him, honing every sharp line of his face into a quivering razor-edge, and flaming in the dazzling irises of his eyes, dilated with doubt and wonder. Neat, shaven clean, no way defaced, only the fetters marking him as a prisoner. He had been lying on his bed when the key turned in the lock; his burnished black hair clasped his olive cheeks with ruffled wings, casting blue shadows into the hollows there beneath the smooth, salient bones. Cadfael had never seen him more beautiful, not even on that first day when he had glimpsed this face through the open gate at the priory of Bromfield, stooping suave cheek to cheek with the girl who was now his wife. Philip had not failed to respect, value and preserve this elegance of body and mind, even though it had turned irrevocably against him.

Cadfael took a long step forward towards the light, uncertain whether he was clearly seen. The cell was spacious beyond what he had expected, with a low chest in a dark corner, and items of clothing or harness folded upon it. 'Olivier?' he said hesitantly. 'You know me?'

'I know you,' said Oliver, low-voiced. 'I have been taught to know you. You are my father.' He looked from Cadfael's face to the open door, and then to the keys in Cadfael's hand. 'There's been fighting,' he said, struggling to make sense of all these chaotic factors that crowded in on him together. 'What has happened? Is he dead?'

He. Philip. Who else could have told him? And now he asked instantly after his sometime friend, supposing, Cadfael divined, that only after that death could these keys have come into other hands. But there was no eagerness, no satisfaction in the voice that questioned, only a flat finality, as one accepting what could not be changed. How strange it was, thought Cadfael, watching his son with aching intensity, that this complex creature should from the first have been crystal to the sire who engendered him.

'No,' he said gently, 'he is not dead. He gave them to me.'

He advanced, almost cautiously, as though afraid to startle a bird into flight, and as warily opened his arms to embrace his son, and at the first touch the braced body warmed and melted, and embraced him ardently in return.

'It is true!' said Olivier, amazed. 'But of course, true! He never lies. And you knew? Why did you never tell me?'

217

'Why break into another man's life, midway, when he is already in noble transit and on his way to glory? One breath of a contrary wind might have driven you off course.' Cadfael stood him off between his hands to look closely, and kissed the hollow oval cheek that leaned to him dutifully. 'All the father you needed you had from your mother's telling, better than truth. But now it's out, and I am glad. Come, sit down here and let me get you out of these fetters.'

He kneeled beside the bed to fit the last key into the anklets, and the chains rang again their sharp, discordant peal as he opened the gyves and hoisted the irons aside, dropping the coil against the rock wall. And all the time the golden eyes hung upon his face, with passionate concentration, searching for glimpses that would confirm the continuity of the blood that bound them together. And after a moment Olivier began to question, not the truth of this bewildering discovery, but the circumstances that surrounded it, and the dazzling range of possibilities it presented.

'How did you know? What can I ever have said or done to make you know me?'

'You named your mother,' said Cadfael, 'and time and place were all as they should be. And then you turned your head, and I saw her in you.'

'And never said word! I said once, to Hugh Beringar I said it, that you had used me like a son. And never trembled when I said it, so blind I was. When he told me you were here, I said it could not be true, for you would not leave your abbey unless ordered. Recusant, apostate, unblessed, he said, he is here to redeem you. I was *angry*!' said Olivier, wrenching at memory and acknowledging its illogical pain. 'I said you had cheated me! You should not so have thrown away all you valued, for me, made yourself exile and sinner, offered your life. Was it fair to load me with such a terrible burden of debt? Lifelong I could not repay it. All I felt was the sting of my own injury. I am sorry! Truly I am sorry! I know better now.'

'There is no debt,' said Cadfael, rising from his knees. 'All manner of reckoning or bargaining is for ever impossible between us two.'

'I know it! I do know it! I felt so far outdone, it scalded my pride. But that's gone.' Olivier rose, stretched his long legs, and stalked his cell back and forth. 'There is nothing I will not take from you, and be grateful, even if there never comes the day when I can do whatever needs to be done in your worship and for your sake. But I trust it may come, and soon.'

'Who knows?' said Cadfael. 'There is a thing I want now, if I could see how to come by it.'

'Yes?' Olivier shook off his own preoccupations in penitent haste. 'Tell me!' He came back to his bed, and drew Cadfael down beside him. 'Tell me what is happening here. You say he is not dead – Philip. He *gave* you the keys?' It seemed to him a thing only possible from a deathbed. 'And who is it laying siege to this place? He made enemies enough, that I know, but this must be an army battering the walls.'

'The army of your liege lady the empress,' said Cadfael ruefully. 'And stronger than commonly, since she was accompanied home into Gloucester by several of her earls and barons. Yves, when he was loosed, rode for Gloucester to rouse her to come and rescue you, and come she most surely has, but not for your sake. The lad told her Philip was here in person. She has vowed, too publicly to withdraw even if she wished, and I doubt she does, to take his castle and his body, and hang him from his own towers, and before his own men. No, she won't withdraw. She is determined to take, humiliate and hang him. And I am equally resolute,' said Cadfael roundly, 'that she shall not, though how it's to be prevented is more than I yet know.'

'She cannot do it,' said Olivier, aghast. 'It would be wicked folly. Surely she knows it? Such an act would have every able man in the land, if he had laid down his weapons, rushing to pick them up again and get into the field. The worst of us, on either side, would hesitate to kill a man he had bested and captured. How do you know this is truth, that she has so sworn?'

'I know it from Yves, who was there to hear it, and is in no doubt at all. She is in earnest. Of all men she hates Philip for what she holds to be his treason—'

'It was treason,' said Olivier, but more temperately than Cadfael had expected.

'By all the rules, so it was. But also it was more than simply treason, however extreme the act. Before long,' said Cadfael heavily, 'some of the greatest among us, on both sides of the argument, and yes, the best, will be accused of treason on the same grounds. They may not turn to fight upon the other side, but to leave their swords in the sheath and decline to continue killing will just as surely be denounced as treachery. Whatever his crime may be called, she wants him in her grasp, and means to be his death. And I am determined she shall not have him.'

Olivier thought for a moment, gnawing his knuckles and frowning. Then he said: 'It would be well, for her more than any, that someone should prevent.' He turned the intensity of his troubled stare upon Cadfael. 'You have not told me all. There is something more. How far has this attack gone? They have not broken through?' The use of 'they' might simply have been because he was enforcedly out of this battle, instead of fighting for his chosen cause with the rest, but it seemed to set him at an even greater distance from the besiegers. Cadfael had almost heard the partisan 'we' springing to mind to confront the 'they'.

'Not yet. They have breached one tower, but have not got in, or had not when I came down to you,' he amended scrupulously. 'Philip refused surrender, but he knows what she intends to do with him . . .'

'How does he know?' demanded Olivier alertly.

'He knows because I told him. Yves brought the message at his own risk. At no risk to me I delivered it. But I think he knew. He said then that if God, by chance, should choose to forestall the empress, he must take thought for the men of his garrison. He has done so. He has handed over the charge of La Musarderie to his deputy Camville, and given him leave – no, orders! – to get the best terms he can for the garrison, and surrender the castle. And tomorrow that will be done.'

'But he would not . . .' began Olivier, and cried out abruptly: 'You said he is not dead!'

'No, he is not dead, but he is badly hurt. I don't say he will die of his wounds, though he may. I do say he will not die of his wounds in time to escape being dragged aloft, whatever his condition, in the empress's noose, once she gets into La Musarderie. He has consented in his own shameful death to procure the release of his men. She cares nothing for any of them, if she has Philip. She'll keep the castle and the arms, and let the men depart alive.'

'He has consented to this?' asked Olivier, low-voiced.

'He has ordered it.'

'And his condition? His injuries?'

'He has badly broken ribs, and I fear some lacerations inside from the broken bones. And head injuries. They tossed in a crate of lumps of iron, broken lance-heads, cinder from the furnaces. He was close when it struck and burst. A bad head wound from a piece of a lance, and maybe

221

foul at that. He came to his senses long enough to make his dispositions, and that he did clearly, and will be obeyed. When they enter, tomorrow, he will be her prisoner. Her only prisoner, for if FitzGilbert agrees to terms he'll keep his word.'

'And it is bad? He cannot ride? He cannot even stand and walk? But what use,' said Olivier helplessly, 'even if he could? Having bought their freedom he would not make off and leave the price unpaid. Never of his own will. I know him! But a man so sick, and at her mercy. . . . She would not!' said Olivier strenuously, and looked along his shoulder at Cadfael's face, and ended dubiously: 'Would she?'

'He struck her to the heart, where her pride is. Yes, I fear she would. But when I left him to come to you, Philip was again out of his senses, and I think may well remain so for many hours, even days. The head wound is his danger.'

'You think we might move him, and he not know? But they are all round us, no easy way out. I do not know this castle well. Is there a postern that might serve? And then, it would need a cart. There are those in the village that I do know,' said Olivier, 'but they may be no friends to Philip. But at the mill by Winstone I'm known, and they have carts. Now, while the night is black, is there anywhere a man could get out? For if they get their truce, by morning they'll cease their close watch. Something might yet be done.'

'There's a clear way out where they've breached the tower,' said Cadfael, 'I saw sky through it. But they're still outside there with the ram, and only held outside by force of arms. If a man of the garrison tried to slip out there, it would be one way of dying quickly. Even if they draw off, he could hardly go along with them.'

222

'But I can!' Olivier was on his feet, glowing. 'Why not? I'm one of them. I'm known to have kept my fealty. I have her badge on my sword-belt, and her colours on my surcoat and my cloak. There may be some there who know me.' He crossed to the chest, and swept the covering cloak from sword and scabbard and light chainmail coat, the links ringing.

'You see? All my harness, everything that came with me when I was dragged out of Faringdon, and the lions of Anjou, that the old king gave to Geoffrey when he married his daughter to him, clear to be seen, marking me for hers. He would not so much as displace the least of another man's possessions, though he might kill the man. In chainmail and armed, and in the dark, who's to pick me out from any of the other besiegers outside the walls? If I'm challenged I can openly answer that I've broken out in the turmoil. If not, I can keep my own counsel, and make for the mill. Reinold will help me to the loan of a cart. But it would be daylight before I could get it here.' He checked, frowning. 'How can we account for it then?'

'If you are in earnest,' said Cadfael, carried away in this gale, 'something might be attempted. Once there's truce, there can be movement in and out, and traffic with the village. For all I know, there may be local men within here, and some wounded or even among the dead, and their kin will be wanting to get news of them, once the way's open.'

Olivier paced, hugged his body in embracing arms, and considered. 'Where is the empress now?'

'She set up her court in the village, so they say. I doubt if she'll make her appearance here for a day or so, she'll need a degree of state, and a grand entrance. But even so,' said Cadfael, 'all the time we have is the rest of this night, and the first few hours of truce, while there's still confusion, and no such close watch.'

'Then we must make it enough,' said Olivier. 'And say we do begin well . . . Where would you have him taken? To have the care he needs?'

Cadfael had given thought to that, though then without much hope of ever being able to pursue it. 'There is a house of the Augustinians in Cirencester. I remember the prior at Haughmond has regular correspondence with one of the canons there, and they have a good name as physicians. And with them sanctuary would be inviolable. But it is a matter of ten miles or more.'

'But the best and fastest road,' said Olivier, gleaming brightly in this fury of planning, 'and would not take us near the village. Once through Winstone we should be on the straight run to Cirencester. Now, how are we to get him out of the castle and keep him man alive?'

'Perhaps,' said Cadfael slowly, 'as a man already dead. The first task, when the gates are open, will be to carry out the dead and lay them ready for burial. We know how many there should be, but FitzGilbert does not. And should there be a man from Winstone shrouded among them, his kin might very well come with a cart, to fetch him home.'

With his eyes burning steadily upon Cadfael's face, Olivier voiced the final question and the final fear: 'And if he is in his senses then, and forbids – as he might – what then?'

'Then' said Cadfael, 'I will remove him at least into the chapel, and we'll put her and any other under the ban of the Church if they dare break his sanctuary. But there is no more I can do. I have no medicines here that could put a man to sleep for hours. And even if I had – you said that I had cheated you by laying you in my debt without your knowledge. He might accuse me of forcing him to default on a debt, to his dishonour. I have not the hardihood to do that to Philip.'

'No,' agreed Olivier, and suddenly smiled. 'So we had better make a success of it while he is still senseless. Even that may be straining our rights, but we'll argue that afterwards. And if I am going, as well go quickly. This once, my father, will you be my squire and help me to arm?'

He put on the mail hauberk, to make one more among the besiegers who were massed outside the walls, drawn off for a few minutes to regroup and attack yet again, and over it the surcoat of linen that bore the lions of Anjou plain to be seen. Cadfael buckled the sword-belt round his son's loins, and for a moment had the world in his arms.

The cloak was necessary cover here within the walls, to hide Geoffrey's blazon, for no one but Cadfael yet knew that Philip had set his prisoner free, and some zealous man-at-arms might strike first and question afterwards. True, it bore on the shoulder the imperial eagle which the empress had never consented to relinquish after her first husband's death, but the badge was dark and unobtrusive on the dark cloth, and would not be noticed. If Olivier could inveigle himself successfully in among the defenders in the obscurity and confusion within the tower, he must discard the cloak before attempting to break out and venture among the attackers, so that the lions might show clear on the pallor of the linen, even by night, and be recognized.

'Though I would rather pass unrecognized,' admitted Olivier, stretching his broad shoulders under the weight of the mail, and settling the belt about his hips. 'Every moment of this night I need, without wasting any in questioning and accounting. Well, my father, shall we go and make the assay?'

Cadfael locked the door after them, and they climbed the spiral stair. At the outer door Cadfael laid a hand on Olivier's arm, and peered out cautiously into the ward, but in the shelter of the keep all was still, only the movements of the guards on the wall came down to them almost eerily.

'Stay by me. We'll make our way close along the wall until we're among them. Then take your moment when you see it. Best when the next thrust comes, and they crowd into the tower to fend it off. And no goodbyes! Go, and God go with you!'

'It will not be goodbye,' said Olivier. Cadfael felt him tensed and quivering at his back, confident, almost joyous. After long confinement his frustrated energy ached for release. 'You will see me tomorrow, whether in my own or another shape. I have kept his back many a time, and he mine. This one more time, with God's help and yours, I'll do him that same service, whether he will or no.'

The door of the tower Cadfael also locked, leaving all here as it should be. They crossed the open ward to the keep, and circled in its shadow to reach the threatened tower on the other side. Even here the clamour of battle had subsided into the shifting murmur of recoil between onsets, and even that subdued, to keep the hearing sharp and ready for the next alarm. They stirred restlessly, like the sea in motion, spoke to one another briefly and in lowered voices, and kept their eyes fixed upon the foremost ranks, filling the jagged gap in the base of the tower. Fragments of masonry and rubble littered the ground, but the torn hole was not yet so big as to threaten the tower's collapse. The fitful light of torches, such as still burned, and the dull glow in the sky outside the wall, where fire had burned out half the roof of the sow, left the ward almost in darkness.

A sudden warning outcry from within the tower, taken up and echoed back over the ranks within the ward, foretold the next assault. The mass drove in, tightening in support, to seal the breach with their bodies. Cadfael, on the fringe of the throng, felt the instant when Olivier slipped away from him like the tearing of his own flesh. He was gone, in among the men of the garrison, lithe and rapid and silent, lost to view in a moment.

Nevertheless, Cadfael drew back only far enough to be out of the way of the fighting men, and waited patiently for this assault, like the last, to be driven back. It never reached the ward. Certainly there was bitter fighting within the shell of the tower, but never a man of the attackers got beyond. It took more than half an hour to expel them completely, and drive them to a safe distance away from the walls, but after that the strange, tense quietness came back and with it a number of those who had fought the foremost came back to draw breath in safety until the next bout. But not Olivier. Either he was lurking somewhere in the broken shell, or else he was out into the turmoil of the night with the repelled invaders, and on his way, God grant, to cover in the woodland, and thence to some place where he could cross the river, and emerge on the road to the mill at Winstone.

Cadfael went back to the chamber where Philip lay, the chaplain nodding gently beside him. Philip's breathing scarcely lifted the sheet over his breast, and then in a short, rapid rhythm. His face was livid as clay, but impenetrably calm, no lines of pain tightening his forehead or lips. He was deep beyond awareness of any such trivial matters as peril, anger or fear. God keep him so a while yet, and prevent impending evil.

There would be need of help in carrying this body towards its peace along with the rest, but it must be in innocence. For a moment Cadfael considered asking the priest, but discarded the idea almost as soon as it was conceived. There could be no embroiling this tired old man in an enterprise which could incur the empress's deadly disfavour, and place him in reach of her immediate and implacable rage. What was to be done must be done in such a way that no one else could be blamed, or feel any betraying uneasiness.

But now there was nothing to be done but be still and pray, and wait for the summons to action. Cadfael sat in a corner of the room, and watched the old man drowse, and the wounded man's withdrawal into something far more profound than sleep. He was still sitting there motionless when he heard the sound of the blown trumpets, calling the attention of the investing forces to the white banners fluttering from the towers of La Musarderie in the first dim light of predawn.

FitzGilbert rode down from the village, ceremoniously attended, and talked with Guy Camville before the gate. Brother Cadfael had come out into the ward to hear the terms of the exchange, and was not surprised when the first words the marshall uttered were: 'Where is Philip FitzRobert?' Blunt and urgent: patently he had his orders.

'My lord,' said Camville from the walk above the gate, 'is wounded, and has authorized me to make terms with you to surrender the castle. I ask that you will treat the garrison fairly and with honour. Upon reasonable conditions La Musarderie shall be yielded to the empress, but we are not so pressed as to accept shameful or ungenerous usage. We have wounded, we have dead. I ask that we may have truce from this hour, and will open the gates to you now, that you may see we are prepared to observe that truce and lay by all arms. If you are satisfied we are in good faith, give us the morning hours until noon to restore some order here within, and marshal our wounded, and carry out our dead for burial.'

'Fair asking so far,' said the marshall shortly. 'What then?'

'We were not the attackers here,' said Camville equally briskly, 'and have fought according to our sworn allegiance, as men owing fealty must. I ask that the garrison may be allowed to march out at noon and depart without hindrance, and that we take with us all our wounded who are fit to go. Those with worse injuries I ask that you will see tended as well as may be, and our dead we will bury.'

'And if I do not like your terms?' asked FitzGilbert. But it was plain from the complacency of his voice that he was well satisfied to be gaining, without further effort or waste of time, what all the empress's host had come to win. The common soldiery here within would have been only so many more mouths to feed, and a continuing risk if things went wrong. To have them depart was a satisfaction.

'Then you may go back empty-handed,' said Camville boldly, 'and we will fight you to the last man and the last arrow, and make you pay dear for a ruin you may have intact if you choose well.'

'You abandon here all your arms,' said the marshall, 'even personal arms. And leave all engines undamaged.'

Camville, encouraged by this indication of consent, made a token objection, hardly meant to be taken seriously, and withdrew it when it was rejected. 'Very well, we go disarmed.'

'So far, good! We allow your withdrawal. All but one! Philip FitzRobert stays here!'

'I believe you have agreed, my lord,' said Camville, 'that the wounded who cannot go with us shall be properly tended. I trust you make no exceptions to that? I have told you my lord is wounded.'

'In the case of FitzRobert I gave no assurances,' said the

229

marshall, goaded. 'You surrender him into the empress's hands unconditionally or there will be no agreement.'

'On that head,' said Camville, 'I am already instructed by my lord Philip, and it is at his orders, not at yours, FitzGilbert, that I leave him here at your mercy.'

There was a perilous silence for a long moment. But the marshall was long experienced in accommodating himself to these embarrassments endemic in civil warfare.

'Very well! I will confirm truce, as I have already called a halt to action. Be ready to march out by noon, and you may go unhindered. But hark, I shall leave a party here outside the gates until noon, when we enter formally, to view everything and every man you take away with you. You will have to satisfy them that you are keeping to terms.'

'The terms I make I keep,' said Camville sharply.

'Then we shall not renew the quarrel. Now open the gate to me, let me see in what state you leave all within.'

By which he meant, Cadfael judged, let him see that Philip lay wounded and helpless within, and could not slip through the empress's fingers. Cadfael took the hint, and went back hastily to the bedchamber, to be there in attendance when FitzGilbert reached it, which he did very promptly. Priest and monastic flanked the bed when Camville and the marshall entered. Philip's shallow breathing had begun to rasp hollowly in throat and breast. His eyes were still closed, the full, arched lids had an alabaster pallor.

FitzGilbert came close, and stood looking down at the drawn face for a long time, whether with satisfaction or compunction Cadfael could not determine. Then he said indifferently: 'Well . . .' and shrugged, and turned away abruptly. They heard his footsteps echoing along the stony corridors of the keep, and out into the ward. He departed assured that the empress's arch-enemy could not so much as lift a hand to ward off the noose, much less rise from his bed and ride away out of reach of her vengeance.

When the marshall was gone, and the trumpets ceased exchanging their peremptory signals across the bleached grass of the open ground between the armies, Cadfael drew breath deep, and turned to Philip's chaplain.

'There'll be no worse now. It's over. You have watched the night through. Go and get your proper rest. I'll stay with him now.'

Chapter Fourteen

LONE WITH Philip, Cadfael searched the chest and the press for woollen rugs to swathe his patient against cold and the buffeting of the roads, and wound him in a sheet, with only a single thickness of linen over his face, so that air might still reach him. One more dead man prepared for burial; and now all that remained was to get him either into the chapel with the rest, or out among the first to the turf of the meadow, where several of his men-at-arms were digging a communal grave. And which was the more hazardous course was a moot question. Cadfael had locked the door of the room while he went about his preparations, and hesitated to open it too soon, but from within he could not determine what was going on. It must be mid-morning by this time, and the garrison mustering for their withdrawal. And FitzGilbert in his rapid tour of the damage within must have taken note of the perilous state of one tower, and would be bringing masons in haste to make the stonework safe, even if proper repairs must wait.

Cadfael turned the key in the lock, and opened the door just wide enough to peer out along the passage. Two young men of the garrison passed by towards the outer door of the keep, bearing between them one of the long shutters from the inward-facing windows, with a shrouded body stretched upon it. It had begun already, as well move quickly. The bearers had no weapons now, with all arms already piled in the armoury, but at least their lives were secured. They handled these less fortunate souls they carried with rueful respect. And after this present pair came one of the officers of the marshall's guard, in conversation with a workman clearly from the village, leather-jerkined, authoritative and voluble.

'You'll need timber props under that wall as fast as I can bring them in,' he was saying as they passed. 'Stone can wait. Keep your men well away from there when you enter, and I'll have my lads here with props by the afternoon.'

The wind of his passing smelled of wood; and of wood there was plenty around Greenhamsted. The dangling stonework of the breached tower, inner wall and outer wall alike, would soon be braced into stability again, waiting for the masons. And by the sound of it, thought Cadfael, I at least had better venture in there before they come, for somewhere in the rubble there may well be a discarded cloak with the imperial eagle on the shoulder, and what I need least, at this moment, is the empress's officers asking too many questions. True, such a thing might have belonged to one of the besiegers who had managed to penetrate within, but he would hardly be manning the ram hampered by his cloak. The less any man wonders, the better.

For the moment, however, his problem was here, and he needed another pair of hands, and needed them now, before more witnesses came on the scene. The officer had accompanied the master-builder only as far as the door of the keep. Cadfael heard him returning, and emerged into the passage full in his path, thrusting the door wide open at his back. His habit gave him a kind of right, at any rate, to be dealing with the dead, and possibly a slight claim on any handy help in the work.

'Sir, of your kindness,' he said civilly, 'will you lend me a hand with this one more here? We never got him as far as the chapel.'

The officer was a man of fifty or so, old enough to be tolerant of officious Benedictine brothers, goodnatured enough to comply with casual demands on some minutes of his time, where he had little work to do but watch others at work, and already gratified at being spared any further fighting over La Musarderie. He looked at Cadfael, looked in without curiosity at the open door, and shrugged amiably. The room was bare enough and chill enough not to be taken at sight for the castellan's own apartment. In his circuit of the hall and living quarters he had seen others richer and more comfortable.

'Say a word in your prayers for a decent soldier,' he said, 'and I'm your man, brother. May someone do as much for me if ever I come to need it.'

'Amen to that!' said Cadfael. 'And I won't forget it to you at the next office.' And that was fervent truth, considering what he was asking.

So it was one of the empress's own men who advanced to the head of the bed, and stooped to take up the swathed body by the shoulders. And all the while Philip lay like one truly dead, and it was in Cadfael's mind, resist it as he would, that so he might be before ever he left these walls. The stillness when the senses are out of the body, and only a thread of breath marks the border not yet crossed, greatly resembles the stillness after the soul is out. The thought aroused in him a strangely personal grief, as if he and not Robert of Gloucester had lost a son; but he put it from him, and refused belief.

'Take up pallet and all,' he said. 'We'll reclaim it afterwards if it's fit for use, but he bled, and there's no want of straw.'

The man shifted his grip compliantly, and lifted his end of the bier as lightly as if it had been a child they carried. Cadfael took the foot, and as they emerged into the passage sustained his hold one-handed for a moment while he drew the door closed. God prevent the accidental discovery too soon! But to linger and turn the key on an empty room would have been cause for immediate suspicion.

They passed through all the activity in the ward, and out at the gatehouse into the dull grey December light, and the guard on the paved apron without passed them through indifferently. They had no interest in the dead; they were there only to ensure that no arms and accoutrements of value were taken away when the garrison departed, and perhaps to check that Philip FitzRobert should not pass as one of the wounded. A short space to the left from the causeway there was a level place where the common grave was being opened, and beside the plot the dead were laid decently side by side.

Between this mournful activity and the rim of the woodland several people from the village, and perhaps from further afield, had gathered to watch, curious but aloof. There was no great love among the commonalty for either of these factions, but the present threat was over. A Musard might yet come back to Greenhamsted. Four generations had left the family still acceptable to their neighbours.

A cart, drawn by two horses, came up the slope from the river valley, and ground steadily up the causeway towards the gatehouse. The driver was a thickset, bearded, well-fleshed man of about fifty, in dark homespun and a shoulder cape and capuchon of green, but all their colours faintly veiled and dusted over from long professional days spent in an air misty with the milling of grain. The lad at his back had sackcloth draped over his shoulders and the opened end of a sack over his head, a long young fellow in the common dun-coloured cotte and hose of the countryside. Cadfael watched them approach and gave thanks to God.

Beholding the work in progress in the meadow, the row of shrouded bodies, the last of them just brought forth and laid beside the rest, and the chaplain, drooping and disconsolate, stumbling after, the driver of the cart, blithely ignoring the guards at the gate, turned his team aside, and made straight for the place of burial. There he climbed down briskly, leaving his lad to descend after him and wait with the horses. It was to Cadfael the miller addressed himself, loudly enough to reach the chaplain's ears also.

'Brother, there was a nephew of mine serving here under Camville, and I'd be glad to know how he's fared, for his mother's sake. We heard you had dead, and a deal more wounded. Can I get news of him?'

He had lowered his voice by then as he drew close. For all it gave away his face might have been oak.

'Rid your mind of the worst before you need go further,' said Cadfael, meeting shrewd eyes of no particular colour, but bright with sharp intelligence. The chaplain was halted a little apart, talking to the officer of FitzGilbert's guard. 'Walk along the line with me, and satisfy yourself that none of these here is your man. And take it slowly,' said Cadfael quietly. Any haste would be a betrayal. They walked the length of the ranks together, talking in low tones, stooping to uncover a face here and there, very briefly, and at every assay the miller shook his head.

'It's been a while since I saw him last, but I'll know.' He talked easily, inventing a kinsman not so far from the truth, not so close as to be an irreparable loss, or long or deeply lamented, but still having the claim of blood, and not to be abandoned. 'Thirty year old, he'd be, black-avised, a good man of his hands with quarter-staff or bow. Not one for keeping out of trouble, neither. He'd be into the thick of it with the best.'

They had arrived at the straw pallet on which Philip lay, so still and mute that Cadfael's heart misdoubted for a moment, and then caught gratefully at the sudden shudder and crepitation of breath. 'He's here!'

The miller had recognized not the man, but the moment. He broke off on a word, stiffening and starting back a single step, and then as promptly stooped, with Cadfael's bulk to cover the deception, and made to draw back the linen from Philip's face, but without touching. He remained so, bending over the body, a long moment, as if making quite sure, before rising again slowly, and saying clearly: 'It is! This is our Nan's lad.'

Still adroit, sounding almost as much exasperated as grieved, and quick to resignation from long experience now of a disordered land, where death came round corners unexpectedly, and chose and took at his pleasure. 'I might have known he'd never make old bones. Never one to turn away from where the fire was hottest. Well, what can a man do? There's no bringing them back.'

The nearest of the grave-diggers had straightened his back to get a moment's relief and turned a sympathetic face.

'Hard on a man to come on his own blood kin so. You'll be wanting to have him away to lie with his forebears? They might allow it. Better than being put in the ground among all these, without even a name.'

237

Their close, half-audible conference had caught the attention of the guards. Their officer was looking that way, and in a moment, Cadfael judged, might come striding towards them. Better to forestall him by bearing down upon him with the whole tale ready.

'I'll ask,' he offered, 'if that's your will. It would be a Christian act to take the poor soul in care.' And he led the way back towards the gate at a purposeful pace, with the miller hard on his heels. Seeing this willing approach, the officer halted and stood waiting.

'Sir,' said Cadfael, 'here's the miller of Winstone, over the river there, has found his kinsman, his sister's son, among our dead, and asks that he may take the lad's body away for burial among his own people.'

'Is that it?' The guard looked the petitioner up and down, but in a very cursory examination, already losing interest in an incident nowadays so common. He considered for a moment, and shrugged.

'Why not? One more or less . . . As well if we could clear the ground of them all at one deal. Yes, let him take the fellow. Here or wherever, he's never going to let blood or shed it again.'

The miller of Winstone touched his forelock very respectfully, and gave fitting thanks. If there was an infinitesimal overtone of satire about his gratitude, it escaped notice. He went stolidly back to his cart and his charge. The long lad in sacking had drawn the cart closer. Between them they hoisted the pallet on which Philip lay, and, in full and complacent view of the marshall's guards, settled it carefully in the cart. Cadfael, holding the horses meantime, looked up just once into the shadow of the sacking hood the young man wore, and deep into profound black eyes, golden round the pupils, that opened upon him in a blaze of affection and elation, promising success. There was no word said. Olivier sat down in the body of the cart, and cushioned the head of the thin straw pallet upon his knees. And the miller of Winstone clambered aboard and turned his team back towards the river, down the bleached green slope, never looking back, never hurrying, the picture of a decent man who had just assumed an unavoidable duty, and had nothing to account for to any man.

At noon FitzGilbert appeared before the gate with a company drawn up at his back, to watch the garrison march out and quit their possession of La Musarderie. They had mounted some of their wounded, who could ride but could not maintain a march for long, and put the rest into such carts as they had in store, and set these in the middle of their muster, to have fit men upon either flank in case of need. Cadfael had thought in time to establish his ownership of the fine young chestnut roan Hugh had lent him, and stayed within the stables to maintain his claim, in case it should be questioned. Hugh would lop me of my ears, he thought, if I should let him be commandeered from under my nose. So only late in the day, when the rearguard was passing stiffly by the watching and waiting victors, did he witness the withdrawal from La Musarderie.

Every rank as it passed was sharply scrutinized from either side, and the carts halted to search for concealed bows, swords and lances, but Camville, curling a lip at their distrust, watched without comment and protested only when some of the wounded were disturbed too roughly for his liking. When all was done, he led his garrison away eastward, over the river and through Winstone to the Roman road, heading, most likely, for Cricklade, which was secure from immediate threat, and the centre of a circle of other castles held by the king, Bampton, Faringdon, Purton and Malmesbury, among which safe harbours his fighting men and his wounded could be comfortably distributed. Olivier and the miller of Winstone had set off by the same way, but had not so far to go, a matter maybe of a dozen miles.

And now Cadfael had things yet to do here. He could not leave until a few other sufferers, too frail or sick to go with their fellows, were committed to responsible care under the marshall's wardship. Nor did Cadfael feel justified in leaving until the worst of the empress's rage had passed, and no one here was in peril of death in recompense for the death of which she had been cheated.

Minutes now, and all her main companies would be riding in, to fill the almost empty stables and living quarters, view their trophy of arms, and make themselves at home here. Cadfael slipped back into the ward ahead of them, and made his way cautiously into the shell of the broken tower. Stepping warily among the fallen ashlar and rubble from the filling of the wall, he found the folded cloak wedged into a gap in the stonework, where Olivier had thrust it the moment before he slipped out into the night among the besiegers. The imperial eagle badge was still pinned into the shoulder. Cadfael rolled it within, and took his prize away with him to his own cell. Almost it seemed to him that a trace of the warmth of Olivier's body still clung to it.

They were all in before the light faded, all but the empress's personal household, and their forerunners were already busy with hangings and cushions making the least Spartan apartment fit for an imperial lady. The hall was again habitable, and looked much as it had always looked, and the cooks and servants turned to feeding and housing one garrison as philosophically as another. The damaged tower was shored up stoutly with seasoned timbers, and a watch placed on it to warn off any unwary soul from risking his head within.

And no one yet had opened the door to Philip's bed-chamber, and found it empty. Nor had anyone had time to remark that the Benedictine guest who had been the last to sit in attendance on the wounded man had been at large about the ward and at the graveside for the past three hours, and so had the chaplain. Everyone had been far too preoccupied to wonder who, then, was keeping watch by the bedside during their absence. It was a point to which Cadfael had not given full consideration, and now that what was most urgent had been accomplished, it began to dawn upon him that he would have to make the discovery himself, in fairness to all the rest of Philip's remaining household. But preferably with a witness.

He went to the kitchens, almost an hour before Vespers, and asked for a measure of wine and a leather bucket of hot water for his patient, and enlisted the help of a scullion to carry the heavy bucket for him across the ward and into the keep.

'He was in fever,' he said as they entered the corridor, 'when I left him some hours ago to go out to the burial ground. We may manage to break it, if I bathe him now and try to get a drop of wine into him. Will you spare me a few minutes to help lift him and turn him?'

The scullion, a shock-headed young giant, his mouth firmly shut and his face equally uncommunicative under this new and untested rule, slid a glance along his shoulder at Cadfael, made an intelligent estimate of what he saw there, and uttered through motionless lips but clearly: 'Best let him go, brother, if you wish him well.'

'As you do?' said Cadfael in a very similar fashion. It was a small skill, but useful on occasion.

No answer to that, but he neither expected nor needed one.

'Take heart! When the time comes, tell what you have seen.'

They reached the door of the deserted bedchamber. Cadfael opened it, the wine flask in his hand. Even in the dimming light the bed showed disordered and empty, the covers tumbled every way, the room shadowy and stark. Cadfael was tempted to drop the flask in convincing astonishment and alarm, but reflected that by and large Benedictine brothers do not respond to sudden crises by dropping things, least of all flasks of wine, and further, that he had just as good as confided in this random companion, to remove all necessity for deception. There were certainly some among Philip's domestic household who would rejoice in his deliverance.

So neither of them exclaimed. On the contrary, they stood in mute and mutual content. The look they exchanged was eloquent, but ventured no words, in case of inconvenient ears passing too close.

'Come!' said Cadfael, springing to life. 'We must report this. Bring the bucket,' he added with authority. 'It's the details that make the tale ring true.'

He led the way at a run, the wine flask still gripped in his hand, and the scullion galloping after, splashing water overboard from his bucket at every step. At the hall door Cadfael rushed almost into the arms of one of Bohun's knights, and puffed out his news breathlessly.

'The lord marshall – is he within? I must speak to him. We're just come from FitzRobert's chamber. He's not there. The bed's empty, and the man's gone.'

Before the marshall, the steward and half a dozen earls and barons in the great hall it made an impressive story,

242

and engendered a satisfying uproar of fury, exasperation and suspicion; satisfying because it was also helpless. Cadfael was voluble and dismayed, and the scullion had wit enough to present a picture of idiot consternation throughout.

'My lords, I left him before noon to go out and help the chaplain with the dead. I am here only by chance, having begged some nights' lodging, but I have some skills, and I was willing to nurse and medicine him as well as I could. When I left him he was still deep out of his senses, as he has been most of the time since he was hurt. I thought it safe to leave him. Well, my lord, you saw him yourself this morning . . . But when I went back to him . . .' He shook a disbelieving head. 'But how could it happen? He was fathoms deep. I went to get wine from the buttery, and hot water to bathe him, and asked this lad to come and give me a hand to raise him. And he's gone! Impossible he should even lift himself upright, I swear. But he's gone! This man will tell you.'

The scullion nodded his head so long and so vigorously that his shaggy hair shook wildly over his face. 'God's truth, sirs! The bed's empty, the room's empty. He's clean gone.'

'Send and see for yourself, my lord,' said Cadfael. 'There's no mistake.'

'Gone!' exploded the marshall. 'How can he be gone? Was not the door locked upon him when you left him? Or someone set to keep watch?'

'My lord, I knew no reason,' said Cadfael, injured. 'I tell you, he could not stir a hand or foot. And I am no servant in the household, and had no orders, my part was voluntary, and meant for healing.'

'No one doubts it, brother,' said the marshall shortly, 'but there was surely something lacking in your care if he was left some hours alone. And with your skill as a physician, if you took so active a soul for mortally ill and unable to move.'

'You may ask the chaplain,' said Cadfael. 'He will tell you the same. The man was out of his senses and likely to die.'

'And you believe in miracles, no doubt,' said Bohun scornfully.

'That I will not deny. And have had good cause. Your lordships might consider on that,' agreed Cadfael helpfully.

'Go question the guard on the gate,' the marshall ordered, rounding abruptly on some of his officers, 'if any man resembling FitzRobert passed out among the wounded.'

'None did,' said Bohun with crisp certainty, but nevertheless waved out three of his men to confirm the strictness of the watch.

'And you, brother, come with me. Let's view this miracle.' And he went striding out across the ward with a comet's tail of anxious subordinates at his heels, and after them Cadfael and the scullion, with his bucket now virtually empty.

The door stood wide open as they had left it, and the room was so sparse and plain that it was scarcely necessary to step over the threshold to know that there was no one within. The heap of discarded coverings disguised the fact that the straw pallet had been removed, and no one troubled to disturb the tumbled rugs, since plainly whatever lay beneath, it was not a man's body.

'He cannot be far,' said the marshall, whirling about as fiercely as he had flown to the proof. 'He must be still within, no one can have passed the guards. We'll have every rat out of every corner of this castle, but we'll find him.' And in a very few minutes he had all those gathered about him dispersed in all directions. Cadfael and the scullion exchanged a glance which had its own eloquence, but did not venture on speech. The scullion, wooden-faced outwardly but gratified inwardly, departed without haste to the kitchen, and Cadfael, released from tension into the languor of relief, remembered Vespers, and refuged in the chapel.

The search for Philip was pursued with all the vigour and thoroughness the marshall had threatened, and yet at the end of it all Cadfael could not fail to wonder whether FitzGilbert was not somewhat relieved himself by the prisoner's disappearance. Not out of sympathy for Philip, perhaps not even from disapproval of such a ferocious revenge, but because he had sense enough to realize that the act contemplated would have redoubled and prolonged the killing, and made the empress's cause anathema even to those who had served her best. The marshall went through the motions with energy, even with apparent conviction: and after the search ended in failure, an unexpected mercy, he would have to convey the news to his imperial lady this same evening, before ever she made her ceremonial entry into La Musarderie. The worst of her venom would be spent, on those even she dared not utterly humiliate and destroy, before she came among vulnerable poor souls expendable and at her mercy.

Philip's tired chaplain stumbled his way through Vespers, and Cadfael did his best to concentrate his mind on worship. Somewhere between here and Cirencester, perhaps by now even safe in the Augustinian abbey there, Olivier nursed and guarded his captor turned prisoner, friend turned enemy – call that relationship what you would, it remained ever more fixed and inviolable the more it turned about. As long as they remained in touch, each of them would be keeping the other's back against the world, even when they utterly failed to understand each other.

245

Neither do I understand, thought Cadfael, but there is no need that I should. I trust, I respect and I love. Yet I have abandoned and left behind me what most I trust, respect and love, and whether I can ever get back to it again is more than I know. The assay is all. My son is free, whole, in the hand of God, I have delivered him, and he has delivered his friend, and what remains broken between them must mend. They have no need of me. And I have needs, oh, God, how dear, and my years are dwindling to a few, and my debt is grown from a hillock to a mountain, and my heart leans to home.

'May our fasts be acceptable to you, Lord, we entreat: and by expiating our sins make us worthy of your grace . . .'

Yes, amen! After all, the long journey here has been blessed. If the long journey home proves wearisome, and ends in rejection, shall I cavil at the price?

The empress entered La Musarderie the next day in sombre state and a vile temper, though by then she had herself in hand. Her blackly knotted brows even lightened a little as she surveyed the prize she had won, and reconciled herself grudgingly to writing off what was lost.

Cadfael watched her ride in, and conceded perforce that, mounted or afoot, she was a regal figure. Even in displeasure she had an enduring beauty, tall and commanding. When she chose to charm, she could be irresistible, as she had been to many a lad like Yves, until he felt the lash of her steel.

She came nobly mounted and magnificently attired, and with a company at her back, outriders on either side of herself and her women. Cadfael remembered the two gentlewomen who had attended her at Coventry, and had remained in attendance in Gloucester. The elder must be sixty, and long widowed, a tall, slender person with the remains of a youthful grace that had lasted well beyond its prime, but was now growing a little angular and lean, as her hair was silvering almost into white. The girl Isabeau, her niece, in spite of the many years between them, bore a strong likeness to her aunt, so strong that she probably presented a close picture of what Jovetta de Montors had been in her girlhood. And a vital and attractive picture it was. A number of personable young men had admired it at Coventry.

The women halted in the courtyard, and FitzGilbert and half a dozen of his finest vied to help them down from the saddle and escort them to the apartments prepared for them. La Musarderie had a new chatelaine in place of its castellan.

And where was that castellan now, and how faring? If Philip had lived through the journey, surely he would live. And Olivier? While there was doubt, Olivier would not leave him.

Meantime, here was Yves lighting down and leading away his horse into the stables, and as soon as he was free he would be looking for Cadfael. There was news to be shared, and Yves must be hungry for it.

They sat together on the narrow bed in Cadfael's cell, as once before, sharing between them everything that had happened since they had parted beside the crabbed branches of the vine, with the guard pacing not twenty yards away.

'I heard yesterday, of course,' said Yves, flushed with wonder and excitement, 'that Philip was gone, vanished away like mist. But how, how was it possible? If he was so gravely hurt, and could not stand . . .? She is saved from breaking with the earl, and . . . and worse . . . So much has been saved. But *how*?' He was somewhat incoherent in his gratitude for such mercies, but grave indeed the moment he came to speak of Olivier. 'And, Cadfael, what has happened to Olivier? I thought to see him among the others in hall. I asked Bohun's steward after any prisoners, and he said what prisoners, there were none found here. So where can he be? Philip *told* us he was here.'

'And Philip does not lie,' said Cadfael, repeating what was evidently an article of faith with those who knew Philip, even among his enemies. 'No, true enough, he does not lie. He told us truth. Olivier was here, deep under one of the towers. As for where he is now, if all has gone well, as why should it not? – he has friends in these parts! – he should be now in Cirencester, at the abbey of the Augustinians.'

'You helped him to break free, even before the surrender? But then, why go? Why should he leave when FitzGilbert and the empress were here at the gates? His own people?'

'I did not rescue him,' said Cadfael patiently. 'When he was wounded and knew he might die, Philip took thought for his garrison, and ordered Camville to get the best terms he could for them, at the least life and liberty, and surrender the castle.'

'Knowing there would be no mercy for himself?' said Yves,

'Knowing what she had in mind for him, as you instructed me,' said Cadfael, 'and knowing she would let all others go, to get her hands on him. Yes. Moreover, he took thought also for Olivier. He gave me the keys, and sent me to set him free. And so I did, and together with Olivier I have, I trust, despatched Philip FitzRobert safely to the monks of Cirencester, where by God's grace I hope he may recover from his wounds.'

'But how? How did you get him out of the gates, with her troops already on guard there? And he? Would he even consent?'

'He had no choice,' said Cadfael. 'He was in his right senses only long enough to dispose of his own life in a bargain for his men's lives. He was sunk deep out of them when I shrouded him, and carried him out among the dead. Oh, not Olivier, not then. It was one of the marshall's own men helped me carry him. Olivier had slipped out by night when the besiegers drew off, and gone to get a cart from the mill, and under the noses of the guards he and the miller from Winstone came to claim the body of a kinsman, and were given leave to take it freely.'

'I wish I had been with you,' said Yves reverently.

'Child, I was glad you were not. You had done your part, I thanked God there was one of you safe out of all this perilous play. No matter now, it's well done, and if I have sent Olivier away, I have you for this day, at least. The worst has been prevented. In this life that is often the best that can be said, and we must accept it as enough.' He was suddenly very weary, even in this moment of release and content.

'Olivier will come back,' said Yves, warm and eager against his shoulder, 'and there is Ermina in Gloucester, waiting for him and for you. By now she will be near her time. There may be another godson for you.' He did not know, not yet, that the child would be even closer than that, kin in the blood as well as the soul. 'You have come so far already, you should come home with us, stay with us, where you are dearly valued. A few days borrowed — what sin is there in that?'

But Cadfael shook his head, reluctantly but resolutely.

'No, that I must not do. When I left Coventry on this quest I betrayed my vow of obedience to my abbot, who had already granted me generous grace. Now I have done what I discarded my vocation to accomplish, barring perhaps one small duty remaining, and if I delay longer still I am untrue to myself as I am already untrue to my Order, my abbot and my brothers. Some day, surely, we shall all meet again. But I have a reparation to make, and a penance to embrace. Tomorrow, Yves, whether the gates at Shrewsbury will open to me again or no, I am going home.'

Chapter Fifteen

N THE light of early morning Cadfael put his few possessions together, and went to present himself before the marshall. In a military establishment lately in dispute, it was well to give due notice of his departure, and to be able to quote the castellan's authority in case any should question.

'My lord, now that the way is open, I am bound to set off back to my abbey. I have here a horse, the grooms will bear witness to my right in him, though he belongs to the stables of Shrewsbury castle. Have I your leave to depart?'

'Freely,' said the marshall. 'And Godspeed along the way.'

Armed with that permission, Cadfael paid his last visit to the chapel of La Musarderie. He had come a long way from the place where he longed to be, and there was no certainty he would live to enter there again, since no man can know the day or the hour when his life shall be required of him. And even if he reached it within his life, he might not be received. The thread of belonging, once stretched to breaking point, may not be easily joined again. Cadfael made his petition in humility, if not quite in resignation, and remained on his knees a while with closed eyes, remembering things done well and things done less well, but remembering with the greatest gratitude and content the image of his son in the guise of a rustic youth, as once before, nursing his enemy in his lap in the miller's cart. Blessed paradox, for they were not enemies. They had done their worst to become so, and could not maintain it. Better not to question the unquestionable.

He was rising from his knees, a little stiffly from the chill of the air and the hardness of the flagstones, when a light step sounded on the threshold, and the door was pushed a little wider open. The presence of women in the castle had already made some changes in the furnishings of the chapel, by the provision of an embroidered altar-cloth, and the addition of a green-cushioned prie-dieu for the empress's use. Now her gentlewoman came in with a heavy silver candlestick in either hand, and was crossing to the altar to install them when she saw Cadfael. She gave him a gentle inclination of her head, and smiled. Her hair was covered with a gauze net that cast a shimmer of silver over a coronal already immaculate in its own silver.

'Good morning, brother,' said Jovetta de Montors, and would have passed on, but halted instead, and looked more closely. 'I have seen you before, brother, have I not? You were at the meeting in Coventry.'

'I was, madam,' said Cadfael.

'I remember,' she said, and sighed. 'A pity nothing came of it. Was it some business consequent upon that meeting that has brought you so far from home? For I believe I heard you were of the abbey of Shrewsbury.'

'In a sense,' said Cadfael, 'yes, it was.'

'And have you sped?' She had moved to the altar, and

252

set her candlesticks one at either end, and was stooping to find candles for them in a coffer beside the wall, and a sulphur spill to light them from the small constant lamp that glowed red before the central cross.

'In part,' he said, 'yes, I have sped.'

'Only in part?'

'There was another matter, not solved, no, but of less importance now than we thought it then. You will remember the young man who was accused of murder, there in Coventry?'

He drew nearer to her, and she turned towards him a clear, pale face, and large, direct eyes of a deep blue. 'Yes, I remember. He is cleared of that suspicion now. I talked with him when he came to Gloucester, and he told us that Philip FitzRobert was satisfied he was not the man, and had set him free. I was glad. I thought all was over when the empress brought him off safely, and I never knew until we were in Gloucester that Philip had seized him on the road. Then, days later, he came to raise the alarm over this castle. I knew,' she said, 'that there was no blame in him.'

She set the candles in their sockets, and the candlesticks upon the altar, stepping back a little to match the distances, with her head tilted. The sulphur match sputtered in the little red flame, and burned up steadily, casting a bright light over her thin, veined left hand. Carefully she lit her candles, and stood watching the flames grow tall, with the match still in her hand. On the middle finger she wore a ring, deeply cut in intaglio. Small though the jet stone was, the incised design took the light brilliantly, in fine detail. The little salamander in its nest of stylized flames faced the opposite way, but was unmistakable once its positive complement had been seen.

Cadfael said never a word, but she was suddenly quite still, making no move to put the ring out of the light that burnished and irradiated it in every line. Then she turned to him, and her glance followed his, and again returned to his face.

'I knew,' she said again, 'there was no blame in him. I was in no doubt at all. Neither, I think, were you. But I had cause. What was it made *you* so sure, even then?'

He repeated, rehearsing them now with care, all the reasons why Brien de Soulis must have died at the hands of someone he knew and trusted, someone who could approach him closely without being in any way a suspect, as Yves Hugonin certainly could not, after his open hostility. Someone who could not possibly be a threat to him, a man wholly in his confidence.

'Or a woman,' said Jovetta de Montors.

She said it quite gently and reasonably, as one propounding an obvious possibility, but without pressing it.

And he had never even thought of it. In that almost entirely masculine assembly, with only three women present, and all of them under the empress's canopy of inviolability, it had never entered his mind. True, the young one had certainly been willing to play a risky game with de Soulis, but with no intention of letting it go too far. Cadfael doubted if she would ever have made an assignation; and yet. . . .

'Oh, no,' said Jovetta de Montors, 'not Isabeau. She knows nothing. All she did was half promise him – enough to make it worth his while putting it to the test. She never intended meeting him. But there is not so much difference between an old woman and a young one, in twilight and a hooded cloak. I think,' she said with sympathy, and smiled at him, 'I am not telling you anything you do not know. But I would not have let the young man come to harm.'

'I am learning this,' said Cadfael, 'only now, believe me. Only now, and by this seal of yours. The same seal that was set to the surrender of Faringdon, in the name of Geoffrey FitzClare. Who was already dead. And now de Soulis, who set it there, who killed him to set it there, is also dead, and Geoffrey FitzClare is avenged.' And he thought, why stir the ashes back into life now?

'You do not ask me,' she said, 'what Geoffrey FitzClare was to me?'

Cadfael was silent.

'He was my son,' she said. 'My one sole child, outside a childless marriage, and lost to me as soon as born. It was long ago, after the old king had conquered and settled Normandy, until King Louis came to the French throne, and started the struggle all over again. King Henry spent two years and more over there defending his conquest, and Warrenne's forces were with him. My husband was Warrenne's man. Two years away! Love asks no leave, and I was lonely, and Richard de Clare was kind. When my time came, I was well served and secret, and Richard did well by his own. Aubrey never knew, nor did any other. Richard acknowledged my boy for his, and took him into his own family. But Richard was not living to do right by his son when most he was needed. It was left to me to take his place.'

Her voice was calm, making neither boast nor defence of what she had done. And when she saw Cadfael's gaze still bent on the salamander in its restoring bath of fire, she smiled.

'That was all he ever had of me. It came from my father's forebears, but it had fallen almost into disuse. Few people would know it. I asked Richard to give it to him for his own device, and it was done. He did us both credit. His brother Earl Gilbert always thought well of him. Even though they took opposing sides in this sad dispute, they were good friends. The Clares have buried Geoffrey as one

255

of their own, and valued. They do not know what I know of how he died. What you, I think, also know.'

'Yes,' said Cadfael, and looked her in the eyes, 'I do know.'

'Then there is no need to explain anything or excuse anything,' she said simply, and turned to set one candle straighter in its sconce, and carry away with her tidily the extinguished sulphur match. 'But if ever any man casts up that man's death against the boy, you may speak out.'

'You said,' Cadfael reminded her, 'that no one else ever knew. Not even your son?'

She looked back for one moment on her way out of the chapel, and confronted him with the deep, drowning blue serenity of her eyes, and smiled. 'He knows now,' she said.

In the chapel of La Musarderie those two parted, who would surely never meet again.

Cadfael went out to the stable, and found a somewhat disconsolate Yves already saddling the chestnut roan, and insisting on coming out with his departing friend as far as the ford of the river. No need to fret over Yves, the darkest shadow had withdrawn from him, there remained only the mild disappointment of not being able to take Cadfael home with him, and the shock of disillusionment which would make him wary of the empress's favours for some time, but not divert his fierce loyalty from her cause. Not for this gallant simplicity the bruising complexities that trouble most human creatures. He walked beside the roan down the causeway and into the woodland that screened the ford, and talked of Ermina, and Olivier, and the child that was coming and minute by minute his mood brightened, thinking of the reunion still to come.

'He may be there already, even before I can get leave to go to her. And he really is well? He's come to no harm?'

'You'll find no change in him,' Cadfael promised heartily. 'He is as he always has been, and he'll look for no change in you, either. Between the lot of us,' he said, comforting himself rather than the boy, 'perhaps we have not done so badly, after all.'

But it was a long, long journey home.

At the ford they parted. Yves reached up, inclining a smooth cheek, and Cadfael stooped to kiss him. 'Go back now, and don't watch me go. There'll be another time.'

Cadfael crossed the ford, climbed the green track up through the woods on the other side, and rode eastward through the village of Winstone towards the great highroad. But when he reached it he did not turn left towards Tewkesbury and the roads that led homeward, but right, towards Cirencester. He had one more small duty to perform; or perhaps he was simply clinging by the sleeve of hope to the conviction that out of his apostasy something good might emerge, beyond all reasonable expectation, to offer as justification for default.

All along the great road high on the Cotswold plateau he rode through intermittent showers of sleet, under a low, leaden sky, hardly conducive to cheerful thoughts. The colours of winter, bleached and faded and soiled, were setting in like a wash of grey mist over the landscape. There was small joy in travelling, and few fellow-creatures to greet along the way. Men and sheep alike preferred the shelter of cottage and fold.

It was late afternoon when he reached Cirencester, a town he did not know, except by reputation as a very old city, where the Romans had left their fabled traces, and a very sturdy and astute wool trade had continued independent and prosperous ever since. He had to stop and ask his way to the Augustinian abbey, but there was no mistaking it when he found it, and no doubt of its flourishing condition. The old King Henry had refounded it upon the remnant of an older house of secular canons, very poorly endowed and quietly mouldering, but the Augustinians had made a success of it, and the fine gatehouse, spacious court and splendid church spoke for their zeal and efficiency. This revived house was barely thirty years old, but bade fair to be the foremost of its order in the kingdom.

Cadfael dismounted at the gate and led his horse within, to the porter's lodge. This ordered calm came kindly on his spirit, after the uncontrollable chances of siege and the bleak loneliness of the roads. Here all things were ordained and regulated, here everyone had a purpose and a rule, and was in no doubt of his value, and every hour and every thing had a function, essential to the functioning of the whole. So it was at home, where his heart drew him.

'I am a brother of the Benedictine abbey of Saint Peter and Saint Paul at Shrewsbury,' said Cadfael humbly, 'and have been in these parts by reason of the fighting at Greenhamsted, where I was lodged when the castle fell under siege. May I speak with the infirmarer?'

The porter was a smooth, round elder with a cool, aloof eye, none too ready to welcome a Benedictine on first sight. He asked briskly: 'Are you seeking lodging overnight, brother?'

'No,' said Cadfael. 'My errand here can be short, I am on my way home to my abbey. You need make no provision for me. But I sent here, in the guardianship of another, Philip FitzRobert, badly wounded at Greenhamsted, and in danger of his life. I should be glad of a word with the infirmarer as to how he does. Or,' he said, suddenly shaken, 'whether he still lives. I tended him there, I need to know.'

258

The name of Philip FitzRobert had opened wide the reserved, chill grey eyes that had not warmed at mention of the Benedictine Order or the abbey of Shrewsbury. Whether he was loved here or hated, or simply suffered as an unavoidable complication, his father's hand was over him, and could open closed and guarded doors. Small blame to the house that it kept a steely watch on its boundaries.

'I will call Brother Infirmarer,' said the porter, and went to set about it within.

The infirmarer came bustling, a brisk, amiable man not much past thirty. He looked Cadfael up and down in one rapid glance, and nodded informed approval. 'He said you might come. The young man described you well, brother, I should have known you among many. You are welcome here. He told us of the fate of La Musarderie, and what was threatened against this guest of ours.'

'So they reached here in time,' said Cadfael, and heaved a great sigh.

'In good time. A miller's cart brought them, but no miller drove it the last miles. A working man must see to his business and his family,' said the infirmarer, 'all the more if he has just risked more, perhaps, than was due from him. It seems there were no unseemly alarms. At any rate, the cart was returned, and all was quiet then.'

'I trust it may remain so,' said Cadfael fervently. 'He is a good man.'

'Thanks be to God, brother,' said the infirmarer cheerfully, 'there are still, as there always have been and always will be, more good men than evil in this world, and their cause will prevail.'

'And Philip? He is alive?' He asked it with more constriction about his heart than he had expected, and held his breath.

'Alive and in his senses. Even mending, though that may

259

be a slow recovery. But yes, he will live, he will be a whole man again. Come and see!'

Outside the partly drawn curtain that closed off one side cell from the infirmary ward sat a young canon of the order, very grave and dutiful, reading in a large book which lay open on his lap-desk. A hefty young man of mild countenance but impressive physique, whose head reared and whose eyes turned alertly at the sound of footsteps approaching. Beholding the infirmarer, with a second habited brother beside him, he immediately lowered his gaze again to his reading, his face impassive. Cadfael approved. The Augustinians were prepared to protect both their privileges and their patients.

'A mere precaution,' said the infirmarer tranquilly. 'Perhaps no longer necessary, but better to be certain.'

'I doubt there'll be any pursuit now,' said Cadfael.

'Nevertheless . . .' The infirmarer shrugged, and laid a hand to the curtain to draw it back. 'Safe rather than sorry! Go in, brother. He is fully in his wits, he will know you.'

Cadfael entered the cell, and the folds of the curtain swung closed behind him. The single bed in the narrow room had been raised, to make attendance on the patient in his helplessness easier. Philip lay propped with pillows, turned a little sidewise, sparing his broken ribs as they mended. His face, if paler and more drawn than in health, had a total and admirable serenity, eased of all tensions. Above the bandages that swathed his head wound, the black hair coiled and curved on his pillows as he turned his head to see who had entered. His eyes in their bluish hollows showed no surprise.

'Brother Cadfael!' His voice was quite strong and clear. 'Yes, almost I expected you. But you had a dearer duty.

260

Why are you not some miles on your way home? Was I worth the delay?'

To that Cadfael made no direct reply. He drew near the bed, and looked down with the glow of gratitude and content warming him. 'Now that I see you man alive, I will make for home fast enough. They tell me you will mend as good as new.'

'As good,' agreed Philip with a wry smile. 'No better! Father and son alike, you may have wasted your pains. Oh, never fear, I have no objection to being snatched out of a halter, even against my will. I shall not cry out against you, as he did: "He has cheated me!" Sit by me, brother, now you are here. Some moments only. You see I shall do well enough, and your needs are elsewhere.'

Cadfael sat down on the stool beside the bed. It brought their faces close, eye to eye in intent and searching study. 'I see,' said Cadfael, 'that you know who brought you here.'

'Once, just once and briefly, I opened my eyes on his face. In the cart, on the highroad. I was back in the dark before a word could be said, it may be he never knew. But yes, I know. Like father, like son. Well, you have taken seisin of my life between you. Now tell me what I am to do with it.'

'It is still yours,' said Cadfael. 'Spend it as you see fit. I think you have as firm a grasp of it as most men.'

'Ah, but this is not the life I had formerly. I consented to a death, you remember? What I have now is your gift, whether you like it or not, my friend. I have had time, these last days,' said Philip quite gently, 'to recall all that happened before I died. It was a hopeless cast,' he said with deliberation, 'to believe that turning from one nullity to the other could solve anything. Now that I have fought upon either side to no good end, I acknowledge my error. There is no salvation in either empress or king. So what have you in mind for me now, Brother Cadfael? Or what has Olivier de Bretagne in mind for me?'

'Or God, perhaps,' said Cadfael.

'God, certainly! But he has his messengers among us, no doubt there will be omens for me to read.' His smile was without irony. 'I have exhausted my hopes of either side, here among princes. Where is there now for me to go?' He was not looking for an answer, not yet. Rising from this bed would be like birth to him; it would be time then to discover what to do with the gift. 'Now, since there are other men in the world besides ourselves, tell me how things went, brother, after you had disposed of me.'

And Cadfael composed himself comfortably on his stool, and told him how his garrison had fared, permitted to march out with their honour and their freedom, if not with their arms, and to take their wounded with them. Philip had bought back the lives of most of his men, even if the price, after all, had never been required of him. It had been offered in good faith.

Neither of them heard the flurry of hooves in the great court, or the ringing of harness, or rapid footsteps on the cobbles; the chamber was too deep within the enfolding walls for any forewarning to reach them. Not until the corridor without echoed hollowly to the tread of boots did Cadfael rear erect and break off in mid-sentence, momentarily alarmed. But no, the guardian outside the curtained doorway had not stirred. His view was clear to the end of the passage, and what he saw bearing down upon them gave him no disquiet. He simply rose to his feet and drew aside to give place to those who were approaching.

The curtain was abruptly swept back before the vigorous hand and glowing face of Olivier, Olivier with a shining, heraldic lustre upon him, that burned in silence and halted him on the threshold, his breath held in half elation and half dread at the bold thing he had undertaken. His eyes met Philip's, and clung in a hopeful stare, and a tentative smile curved his long mouth. He stepped aside, not entering the room, and drew the curtain fully back, and Philip looked beyond him.

For a moment it hung in the balance between triumph and repudiation, and then, though Philip lay still and silent, giving no sign, Olivier knew that he had not laboured in vain.

Cadfael rose and stepped back into the corner of the room as Robert, earl of Gloucester, came in. A quiet man always, squarely built, schooled to patience, even at this pass his face was composed and inexpressive as he approached the bed and looked down at his younger son. The capuchon hung in folds on his shoulders, and the dusting of grey in his thick brown hair and the twin streaks of silver in his short beard caught the remaining light in the room with a moist sheen of rain. He loosed the clasp of his cloak and shrugged it off, and drawing the stool closer to the bed, sat down as simply as if he had just come home to his own house, with no tensions or grievances to threaten his welcome.

'Sir,' said Philip, with deliberate formality, his voice thin and distant, 'your son and servant!'

The earl stooped, and kissed his son's cheek; nothing to disturb even the most fragile of calms, the simple kiss due between sire and son on greeting. And Cadfael, slipping silently past, walked out into the corridor and into his own son's exultant arms.

So now everything that had to be done here was completed. No man, nor even the empress, would dare touch what Robert of Gloucester had blessed. They drew each other away, content, into the court, and Cadfael reclaimed his horse from the stable, for in spite of the approaching dusk he felt himself bound to ride back some way before full darkness came, and find a simple lodging somewhere among the sheepfolds for the night hours.

'And I will ride with you,' said Olivier, 'for our ways are the same as far as Gloucester. We'll share the straw together in someone's loft. Or if we reach Winstone the miller will house us.'

'I had thought,' said Cadfael, marvelling, 'that you were already in Gloucester with Ermina, as indeed you should be this moment.'

'Oh, I did go to her – how could I not? I kissed her,' said Olivier, 'and she saw for herself I had come to no harm from any man, so she let me go where I was bound. I rode to find Robert at Hereford. And he came with me, as I knew he would come. Blood is blood, and there is no blood closer than theirs. And now it is done, and I can go home.'

Two days they rode together, and two nights they slept close, rolled in their cloaks, the first night in a shepherd's hut near Bagendon, the second in the hospitable mill at Cowley; and the third day, early, they entered Gloucester. And in Gloucester they parted.

Yves would have reasoned and pleaded the good sense of resting here overnight and spending some precious hours with people who loved him. Olivier only looked at him, and awaited his judgement with resignation.

'No,' said Cadfael, shaking his head ruefully, 'for you home is here, yes, but not for me. I am already grossly in default. I dare not pile worse on bad. Do not ask me.'

And Olivier did not ask. Instead, he rode with Cadfael to the northern edge of the city, where the road set off north-west for distant Leominster. There was a good half of the day left, and a placid grey sky with hardly a breath of wind. There could be a few miles gained before night.

'God forbid I should stand between you and what you need for your heart's comfort,' said Olivier, 'even if it tears mine to refrain. Only go safely, and fear nothing for me, ever. There will be a time. If you do not come to me, I shall come to you.'

'If God please!' said Cadfael, and took his son's face between his hands, and kissed him. As how could God not be pleased by such as Olivier? If, indeed, there were any more such to be found in this world.

They had dismounted to take their brief farewells. Olivier held the stirrup for Cadfael to remount, and clung for a moment to the bridle. 'Bless me to God, and go with God!'

Cadfael leaned down and marked a cross on the broad, smooth forehead. 'Send me word,' he said, 'when my grandson is born.'

Chapter Sixteen

HE LONG road home unrolled laborious mile by mile, frustrating hour after hour and day after day. For winter, which had so far withheld its worst, with only a desultory veil of snow, soon melted and lost, began to manifest itself in capricious alternations of blinding snow and torrential rains, and roads flooded and fords ran too full to be passable without peril. It took him three days to reach Leominster, so many obstacles lay in the way and had to be negotiated, and there he felt obliged to stay over two nights at the priory to rest Hugh's horse.

From there things went somewhat more easily, if no more happily, for if the snow and frost withdrew, a fine drizzling rain persisted. Into the lands of Lacy and Mortimer, near Ludlow, he rode on the fourth day, and outlines he knew rose comfortingly before his eyes. But always the thread that drew him homeward tightened and tore painfully at his heart, and still there was no true faith in him that any place waited for him, there where alone he could be at peace.

I have sinned, he told himself every night before he slept. I have forsaken the house and the Order to which I swore stability. I have repudiated the ordinance of the abbot to whom I swore obedience. I have gone after my own desires, and no matter if those desires were devoted all to the deliverance of my son, it was sin to prefer them before the duty I had freely and gladly assumed as mine. And if it was all to do again, would I do otherwise than I have done? No, I would do the same. A thousand times over, I would do the same. And it would still be sin.

In our various degrees, we are all sinners. To acknowledge and accept that load is good. Perhaps even to acknowledge and accept it and not entertain either shame or regret may also be required of us. If we find we must still say: Yes, I would do the same again, we are making a judgement others may condemn. But how do we know that God will condemn it? His judgements are inscrutable. What will be said in the last day of Jovetta de Montors, who also made her judgement when she killed to avenge her son, for want of a father living to lift that load from her? She, also, set the heart's passion for its children before the law of the land or the commandments of the Church. And would she, too, say: I would do it again? Yes, surely she would. If the sin is one which, with all our will to do right, we cannot regret, can it truly be a sin?

It was too deep for him. He wrestled with it night after night until from very weariness sleep came. In the end there is nothing to be done but to state clearly what has been done, without shame or regret, and say: Here I am, and this is what I am. Now deal with me as you see fit. That is your right. Mine is to stand by the act, and pay the price.

You do what you must do, and pay for it. So in the end all things are simple.

On the fifth day of his penitential journey he came into country familiar and dear, among the long hill ranges in the south and west of the shire, and perhaps should have made one more stay for rest, but he could not bear to halt when he was drawing so near, and pushed on even into the darkness. When he reached Saint Giles it was well past midnight, but by then his eyes were fully accustomed to the darkness, and the familiar shapes of hospital and church showed clear against the spacious field of the sky, free of clouds, hesitant on the edge of frost. He had no way of knowing the precise hour, but the immense silence belonged only to dead of night. With the cold of the small hours closing down, even the furtive creatures of the night had abandoned their nocturnal business to lie snug at home. He had the whole length of the Foregate to himself, and every step of it he saluted reverently as he passed.

Now, whether he himself had any rights remaining here or not, for very charity they must take in Hugh's tired horse, and allow him the shelter of the stables until he could be returned to the castle wards. If the broad doors opening from the horse fair into the burial ground had been unbarred, Cadfael would have entered the precinct that way, to reach the stables without having to ride round to the gatehouse, but he knew they would be fast closed. No matter, he had the length of the enclave wall to tell over pace by pace like beads, in gratitude, from the corner of the horse fair to the gates, with the beloved bulk of the church like a warmth in the winter night on his left hand within the pale, a benediction all the way.

The interior was silent, the choir darkened, or he would have been able to detect the reflected glow from upper windows. So Matins and Lauds were past, and only the altar lamps left burning. The brothers must be all back in their beds, to sleep until they rose for Prime with the dawn. As well! He had time to prepare himself.

The silence and darkness of the gatehouse daunted him strangely, as if there would be no one within, and no means of entering, as though not only the gates, but the church, the Order, the embattled household within had been closed against him. It cost him an effort to pull the bell and shatter the cloistered quiet. He had to wait some minutes for the porter to rouse, but the first faint shuffle of sandalled feet within and the rattle of the bolt in its socket were welcome music to him.

The wicket opened wide, and Brother Porter leaned into the opening, peering to see what manner of traveller came ringing at this hour, his hair around the tonsure rumpled and erected from the pillow, his right cheek creased from its folds and his eyes dulled with sleep. Familiar, ordinary and benign, an earnest of the warmth of brotherhood within, if only the truant could earn re-entry here.

'You're late abroad, friend,' said the porter, looking from the shadow of a man to the shadow of a horse, breathing faint mist into the cold air.

'Or early,' said Cadfael. 'Do you not know me, brother?'

Whether it was the voice that was known, or the shape and the habit as vision cleared, the porter named him on the instant. 'Cadfael? Is it truly you? We thought we had lost you. Well, and now so suddenly here on the doorsill again! You were not expected.'

'I know it,' said Cadfael ruefully. 'We'll wait the lord abbot's word on what's to become of me. But let me in at least to see to this poor beast I've overridden. He belongs at the castle by rights, but if I may stable and tend him here for the night, he can go gently home tomorrow, whatever is decreed for me. Never trouble beyond that, I need no bed. Open the door and let me bring him in, and you go back to yours.'

'I'd no thought of shutting you out,' said the porter roundly, 'but it takes me a while to wake at this hour.' He was fumbling his key into the lock of the main gates, and hauling the half of the barrier open. 'You're welcome to a brychan within here, if you will, when you're done with the horse.'

The tired chestnut roan trod in delicately on the cobbles with small, frosty, ringing sounds. The heavy gate closed again behind them, and the key turned in the lock.

'Go and sleep,' said Cadfael. 'I'll be a while with him. Leave all else until morning. I have a word or so to say to God and Saint Winifred that will keep me occupied in the church the rest of the night.' And he added, half against his will: 'Had they scored me out as a bad debt?'

'No!' said the porter strenuously. 'No such thing!'

But they had not expected him back. From the time that Hugh had returned from Coventry without him they must have said their goodbyes to him, those who were his friends, and shrugged him out of their lives, those who were less close, or even no friends to him. Brother Winfrid must have felt himself abandoned and betrayed in the herb garden.

'Then that was kind,' said Cadfael with a sigh, and led the weary horse away over the chiming cobbles to the stables.

In the strawy warmth of the stall he made no haste. It was pleasant to be there with the eased and cossetted beast, and to be aware of the stirring of his contented neighbours in the other stalls. One creature at least returned here to a welcome. Cadfael went on grooming and polishing longer than there was any need, leaning his head against a burnished shoulder. Almost he fell asleep here, but sleep he could not afford yet. He left the living warmth of the horse's body reluctantly, and went out again into the cold, and crossed the court to the cloisters and the south door of the church.

If it was the sharp, clear cold of frost outside, it was the heavy, solemn cold of stone within the nave, near darkness, and utter silence. The similitude of death, but for the red-gold gleam of the constant lamp on the parish altar. Beyond, in the choir, two altar candles burned low. He stood in the solitude of the nave and gazed within. In the night offices he had always felt himself mysteriously enlarged to fill every corner, every crevice of the lofty vault where the lights could not reach, as if the soul shed the confines of the body, this shell of an ageing, no, an old man, subject to all the ills humanity inherits. Now he had no true right to mount the one shallow step that would take him into the monastic paradise. His lower place was here, among the laity, but he had no quarrel with that; he had known, among the humblest, spirits excelling archbishops, and as absolute in honour as earls. Only the need for this particular communal peace and service ached in him like a death-wound.

He lay down on his face, close, close, his overlong hair brushing the shallow step up into the choir, his brow against the chill of the tiles, the absurd bristles of his unshaven tonsure prickly as thorns. His arms he spread wide, clasping the uneven edges of the patterned paving as drowning men hold fast to drifting weed. He prayed without coherent words, for all those caught between right and expedient, between duty and conscience, between the affections of earth and the abnegations of heaven: for Jovetta de Montors, for her son, murdered quite practically and coldly to clear the way for a coup, for Robert Bossu and all those labouring for peace through repeated waves of disillusion and despair, for the young who had no clear guidance where

271

to go, and the old, who had tried and discarded everything: for Olivier and Yves and their like, who in their scornful and ruthless purity despised the manipulations of subtler souls: for Cadfael, once a brother of the Benedictine house of Saint Peter and Saint Paul, at Shrewsbury, who had done what he had to do, and now waited to pay for it.

He did not sleep; but something short of a dream came into his alert and wakeful mind some while before dawn, as though the sun was rising before its hour, a warmth like a May morning full of blown hawthorn blossoms, and a girl, primrose-fair and unshorn, walking barefoot through the meadow grass, and smiling. He could not, or would not, go to her in her own altar within the choir, unabsolved as he was, but for a moment he had the lovely illusion that she had risen and was coming to him. Her white foot was on the very step beside his head, and she was stooping to touch him with her white hand, when the little bell in the dortoir rang to rouse the brothers for Prime.

Abbot Radulfus, rising earlier than usual, was before his household in entering the church. A cold but blood-red sun had just hoisted its rim above the horizon to eastward, while westward the sharp pricking of stars still lingered in a sky shading from dove-grey below to blue-black in the zenith. He entered by the south door, and found a habited monk lying motionless like a cross before the threshold of the choir.

The abbot checked and stood at gaze for a long moment, and then advanced to stand above the prone man and look down at him with a still and sombre face. The brown hair round the tonsure had grown longer than was quite seemly. There might even, he thought, be more grey in it than when last he had looked upon the face now so resolutely hidden from him.

'You,' he said, not exclaiming, simply acknowledging the recognition, without implications of either acceptance or rejection. And after a moment: 'You come late. News has been before you. The world is still changing.'

Cadfael turned his head, his cheek against the stone, and said only: 'Father!' asking nothing, promising nothing, repenting nothing.

'Some who rode a day or so before you,' said Radulfus reflectively, 'must have had better weather, and changes of horses at will along the way. Such word as comes to the castle Hugh brings also to me. The Earl of Gloucester and his younger son are reconciled. There have been fighting men at risk who have been spared. If we cannot yet have peace, at least every such mercy is an earnest of grace.' His voice was low, measured and thoughtful. Cadfael had not looked up, to see his face. 'Philip FitzRobert on his sickbed,' said Radulfus, 'has abjured the quarrels of kings and empresses, and taken the cross.'

Cadfael drew breath and remembered. A way to go, when he despaired of princes. Though he would still find the princes of this world handling and mishandling the cause of Christendom as they mishandled the cause of England. All the more to be desired was this order and tranquillity within the pale, where the battle of heaven and hell was fought without bloodshed, with the weapons of the mind and the soul.

'It is enough!' said Abbot Radulfus. 'Get up now, and come with your brothers into the choir.'

THE CADFAEL COMPANION
Robin Whiteman

Introduction by Ellis Peters

Since the publication of *A Morbid Taste for Bones* in 1977, millions of readers throughout the world have been captivated and enthralled by the exploits and adventures of Brother Cadfael. Set in England and Wales during the turbulent reign of King Stephen, the novels are a rich blend of historical fact and derived fiction: people and places, real and imagined, are woven with such skill and confidence into the fabric of the whole that without access to the author's mind or knowledge of her references it becomes almost impossible to disentangle. But Cadfael fans, like the good monk himself, are endlessly curious ...

While writing and researching *Cadfael Country*, Robin Whiteman discovered a wealth of fascinating material relating to Cadfael and his colourful world. Indexing the mysteries produced a list of over one thousand characters and locations, factual and fictional - some appearing in only one story, others recurring again and again. An encyclopaedic guide to these, and to Cadfael's plants and herbs, plus a glossary of mediaeval terms, form *The Cadfael Companion*. First published in 1990, the book delighted Cadfael enthusiasts everywhere. It has now been fully revised and updated to include commentary on the most recent titles in the series.

SHREWSBURY ABBEY
The "home" of Brother Cadfael.

The Abbey Church has remained in use beyond the dissolution of the monastery as a Parish Church.
It is open every day to welcome visitors.
Gifts to the Abbey Restoration Project are most welcome.
Enquiries to:
The Abbey, Abbey Foregate, Shrewsbury SY2 6BS
Tel: 01743 232723

The complete **Brother Cadfael** series by Ellis Peters

The prices shown above are correct at time of going to press. However, the publishers reserve the right to increase prices on covers from those previously advertised without prior notice.

WARNER BOOKS

WARNER BOOKS
P.O. Box 121, Kettering, Northants NN14 4ZQ
Tel: 01832 737525, Fax: 01832 733076
Email: aspenhouse@FSBDial.co.uk

POST AND PACKING:
Payments can be made as follows: cheque, postal order (payable to Warner Books)
or by credit cards. Do not send cash or currency.

All U.K. Orders	**FREE OF CHARGE**
E.E.C. & Overseas	25% of order value

Name (Block Letters) _____

Address _____

_____

Post/zip code: _____

☐ Please keep me in touch with future Warner publications

☐ I enclose my remittance £_____

☐ I wish to pay by Visa/Access/Mastercard/Eurocard

Card Expiry Date
